On the Border

For all my family.

In memory of James McCartan, Brian Murphy and Mickey Cunnane.

On the Border

A Novel of South Armagh 1921–22

MARIE McCARTAN

First published in 2020 by Marie McCartan
County Armagh
Northern Ireland

Amazon paperback	ISBN: 978 1 78846 150 4
Paperback	ISBN: 978 1 78846 147 4
eBook – mobi format	ISBN: 978 1 78846 148 1
eBook – ePub format	ISBN: 978 1 78846 149 8

Produced by Kazoo Independent Publishing Services
222 Beech Park, Lucan, Co. Dublin
www.kazoopublishing.com

Kazoo Independent Publishing Services is not the publisher of this work. All rights and responsibilities pertaining to this work remain with Marie McCartan.

Cover design by Andrew Brown

Printed in the EU

Author's Note

On The Border is a novel set on the Armagh–Louth border during 1921–22. The characters are fictional, but the historical figures and events are real. The book is loosely based on stories my mother, Brigid Murphy (née Grant), told about her family life during the Troubles and about the men who fought on the border at Dungooley. At that time people's lives were a mixture of religion and superstition, and though there were many religious holidays, customs from pagan times were also observed. Their dialect was Scots-Irish.

Daily newspapers from the time were an important source, as they covered what was happening in the courts and in the locality, as well as advertising clothing and the price of goods and livestock – details that help to create a clearer picture of everyday life during the period. Crossmaglen Fair was brought to life for me by photographs from a collection of old glass negatives. Accounts given by members of the Fourth Northern to the Bureau of Military History provided a picture of how the conflict was fought and how it affected the men and women involved.

Marie McCartan (née Murphy)

Chapter 1

On Cashel Mountain Bryan Grant shovelled clay into meal bags. He would scatter it later where it would leave no trace. When the entrance to the dump was closed over with whin bushes he stepped back and viewed it with a critical eye. To him it seemed very obvious, but he concluded that if you didn't know it was there, you wouldn't know it was there. When the arms and ammunition were buried and the finishing touches added the military would have difficulty finding it. It was autumn, the bracken was plentiful and when it was piled up among the whins no one would know that the mountain had ever been disturbed. Bryan leaned on the shovel and watched small birds eating blackberries and haws as they prepared for the coming winter. On his farm at the foot of the mountain, the harvest had been saved and gathered in, the thatch secured on the roof and the turf dried out. They were almost ready for the winter's cold and storms, but they didn't know what else the close of the year would bring. The political situation was very uncertain.

The War of Independence, bitterly fought against the British since January 1919, had ended in a truce on 11 July 1921. "A cessation of hostilities" had been agreed between Lloyd George, the British prime minister, and Éamon de Valera, the leader of Sinn Féin. A settlement was currently being negotiated in London between the Irish representatives and the British government. The British had centuries of experience in the art of manipulation and double-talk and the Irish were novices. Two thousand people had been killed since 1919 and the people were war-weary, anxious for an end to the fighting and a good outcome to the talks.

The townland of Cashel, which Bryan surveyed now from the mountain, was in South Armagh in the North of Ireland. The Northern population was mainly Protestant and loyal to Britain. To maintain the union the Protestants had been granted a statelet of six Northern counties, which would soon be partitioned from the mostly Catholic South. Armagh was one of the six counties. No one knew what would happen, but the Northern Catholics hoped the proposed partition deal would be reversed. Bryan knew that a partition was a dividing wall, but he didn't know what form a government partition would take. Locals thought it might be a wall or a fence, and people reacted in different ways. The more optimistic and religious thought that if you said your prayers then with the help of God it would be all right. The cynics expected the opposite. Others sat on the fence so that they could say they knew all along what would happen. Many were fatalistic, almost indifferent – the authorities would decide, and their hopes, fears or opinions wouldn't count. That's the way it had always been.

The history of Ireland was littered with failed rebellions, the pike put away till the call came to rise again. This time they had come further than ever before and Bryan hoped there would be a peaceful settlement, but he knew that as of old they would be wise to keep the pike ready. The IRA was using the truce to stock up with more modern weapons in readiness for the return to war.

Bryan was a farmer. He wasn't part of the IRA but he did what he could. His son, Hughie, who had been helping him to dig the hole under the rock earlier, was a volunteer with the 4th Northern Division. He had gone down to the farm to harness the jinnet to the slipe that would haul the arms up to the rock when the lorry came. Hughie was twenty-five years old, thin, but wiry, around five foot ten in height, with dark brown hair, blue eyes and freckles. A bit wild, people said, and always up to some kind of divilment, but a dacent lad for all that. Like many of his comrades he no longer slept at home because it was too dangerous for him and for his family. The Special Constabulary and military constantly staged encircling round-ups in the area. They conducted drives and sweeps akin to grouse shoots except they were trying to beat out rebels instead of game birds. Those they caught were assaulted and hauled away to an uncertain fate, and their families were subjected to intimidation and harassment from then on. Hughie's unit was highly mobile and had a safe house at the back of the mountain where they could come and go, for the moment, without their activities being observed or reported.

In the South, the Black and Tans and the Auxiliaries, notoriously brutal British police regiments that had rampaged through the countryside killing and terrorising the residents, were confined to barracks for the duration of the truce. In the North the military were confined to barracks, but the Special Constabulary were not subject to the same rules. Drawn mainly from the Protestant community and the UVF, an illegal paramilitary organisation, the Special Constabulary had A and B sections. The A Specials carried out normal police duties while the B Specials, or B men, patrolled their own home areas at night and in emergency situations. Charging through the countryside in armoured Crossley tenders, the former Black and Tan lorries, the Specials continued to terrorise the community. They knew the roads and the people and seemed to appear out of nowhere. The 4th Northern Division saw them as a very dangerous enemy. The people didn't differentiate between the military, paramilitaries or Specials and they referred to all of them as Tans or the Black and Tans.

A lorry coming to Bryan Grant's or any house in the area was a rare event and would cause talk, so the weapons had to be unloaded and hidden and the lorry gone as fast as possible. People were extremely poor and there were those who informed the authorities about anything unusual. If they were discovered by the IRA the penalty was death, but it was a reliable source of much needed income for anyone willing to take the risk.

When he had the jinnet and slipe ready, Hughie looked into the barn and saw his little sister, Mary, spring a rat from a trap then wrap it in her cardigan and scramble out of the mound of loose corn. She didn't brush the corn from her clothes or shake it out of her boots as she seldom felt discomfort. She was eleven and didn't go to school because she had epilepsy; also known as the 'blessed sickness' because it was sent by God. She was regarded as a special child, and as few restrictions were imposed on her, she had become somewhat precocious. When she realised Hughie had caught her freeing one of the rats that her father was trying to exterminate, she adopted a defensive stance that reminded him of a bantie rooster.

"You skittery, wee rodney," she declared crossly, "snakin' up on me like that. You could a scared me into hurtin' meself."

He had to laugh because she knew no fear. She was skilful at springing the trap and had never been injured, but he wondered why the rats didn't bite her.

"I know them and they know me," she answered enigmatically.

It was acknowledged within the family that she "knew" animals and could communicate with them. She was taking the rat to an old cottage called the Spelig to mark him so that God would know him. When Hughie said that God wouldn't want to know an aul rat she told him that a rat was one of God's creatures too and they would all sit down together one day under their own elm tree.

"Where did you hear that aul crack?" he asked, laughing.

But she hurried past him and out through the gate. Her little dog, Jocko, had appeared and was pulling at the cardigan trying to get at the rat. Catherine, their mother, a small, plump, middle-aged woman, was at the door transferring newly boiled garments from a steaming black pot to a basin. She tucked a stray lock of fading sandy hair back into her hair net and explained that the Holy Rollers had come by the previous summer and spoken to Mary about sitting under her own elm tree. The Holy Rollers was a sect of travelling preachers who rolled on the ground when overcome by the ecstasy of prayer. Catherine reminded Hughie that Mary had a long memory but hadn't the wit to hold her tongue and he would need to be careful about what he said or did in front of her. This lorry was coming soon and she should be kept closed in the house while it was there because she might well say the wrong thing at the wrong time.

Hughie shrugged the warning off. "Have a titter of wit, Ma," he said, grinning. "She's away now to put a mark on a rat. What harm could Mary do?"

He emptied the heavy pot for her in the trinket at the foot of the street, then as he joined Mary at the ditch across the road, Sarah Cullen came round the corner carrying a willow basket. She was a tall, pretty young woman in her early twenties with brown eyes and dark curls. She came from Newtownhamilton, some miles away, but stayed for long periods with her grandmother, Addy Murray, further on up the Cashel Road.

Ah Jaysus, thought Hughie, another one that can't hold her tongue. If she's anywhere near here when the lorry comes, the lads will do for her.

He and Sarah had once been very close. He loved her and hoped to marry her someday, but discovered too late that not only was she promised to another man but that the man was a B Special. She was consorting with the enemy. Most of the 4th Northern Division saw Sarah as a security risk and some of them wanted her shot. They wouldn't hesitate if she was there when they arrived with the arms.

Sarah looked up, smiling, then stopped abruptly when she saw Hughie and nervously twisted her gloves together. She seemed grateful when Mary asked if she wanted to see the rat that she was marking for God. She said it was a nice rat and thought God would be happy, but she had to run on because her granny was waiting for the groceries. Hughie leaned on the ditch silently tossing pebbles onto the road, then finally spoke out.

"Watch yourself, Sarah, people are talking about you," he warned her, "dangerous people. Be very careful."

She looked as if she might cry and then edged quickly past him, catching his knee with the corner of her willow basket.

"Be more than careful," he murmured as he ruefully rubbed his knee, but she didn't look back.

He was shaken from his reverie as a cloud blocked the autumn sun and Mary shivered, hugging her cardigan and the rat closer. She jumped down from the ditch, raising a pungent smell from a clump of wild garlic stalks, and went towards the Spelig.

The old cottage in the Spelig was built on an outcrop of stone. It was surrounded by beech trees and screened from the road by a fuchsia hedge. In the ruins Bryan had fashioned rough cages and hutches for Mary's collection of injured wild creatures. She used a puffball, archangel tar and thick cobweb to stop bleeding, moss for padding and scraps of material and wool that provided colourful bandages. Since her father had told her about a rat that had lost a leg then gnawed a spool down to make a wooden leg, she always kept a wooden spool. In the old garden a drake and a flock of ducks swam on a pond that had once been a spring well. As Hughie stepped through the hedge into the garden, the sunlight filtered through the trees and shimmered above the water. There was a moment of absolute stillness like in the split second before an ambush or a gun battle. He quickly pulled Mary down behind him then with his revolver at the ready surveyed the area, but the ducks were undisturbed and the dog sniffing busily round the door of the cottage would have sensed an intruder. A sudden shiver crept up his spine. A goose just walked on my grave, he thought, as he replaced the gun in his shoulder holster. He shook himself, feeling a bit foolish, then turned around to help Mary up and dust her down. He smiled at her puzzled expression.

"I thought the big black drake was going to go for you," he said solemnly.

Mary glanced at the drake foraging above and below the waterline, then looked up at Hughie and giggled. He was just playing with her. He smiled and ruffled her hair as they made their way over to the cottage. He was her favourite out of all the family and he loved her too. He knew she followed him when he left the house and that she listened to and repeated conversations, but he didn't see any harm in it.

In one of the cages a half-grown fox cub snarled at them then cowed away into a corner. Mary said it was ready to be let go and asked Hughie would he come up the mountain with her, but suddenly he heard the sound of a lorry coming. The noise of the engine seemed very loud, and if the Specials were about they couldn't miss but hear it. He urged Mary to hurry up, but patiently held the rat while she painted a cross on its back and put tar on the skinned area on its leg. He then ordered her back to the house, but she refused to go. She promised not to tell anyone about the lorry coming and he made his way back to the road.

But Mary had never seen a lorry before and was curious. She slowly sidled up from the Spelig, and Hughie's friend Gerard Molloy, long and lanky, laid down his rifle then leaned over the ditch and swung her out onto the road. Gerard was cross-eyed and she was never quite sure where he was looking.

The mountain road was narrow, not much better than a cart track, and the lorry was the full width of the road. There was little room left for the men working feverishly to get it unloaded. The nearer guards were alert and watchful, with hands resting lightly on the revolvers holstered inside their long coats. Others held rifles at the ready and scanned the countryside through field glasses. They all wore caps or hats pulled low over their eyebrows. Tarpaulin-wrapped packages were swiftly unloaded, positioned on the slipe and dragged up the mountain, with Hughie driving the patient jinnet. A wooden box slid down from the tailboard of the lorry and hit the road with a bell-like jingling noise. The officer in charge berated the young fella responsible, then turned on Gerard and ordered him to get that friggin' child away to Hell out of there. What in the name of Jaysus was he thinking when they could be fired on at any minute? Gerard led Mary across the road then shouted for Catherine, who ran outside and took her in. Mary wasn't used to anyone speaking harshly to her and was a little upset. Catherine gave her bread and a drink of buttermilk, then helped her into bed for an afternoon nap. The dog lay down beside the bed.

Because of her affliction Mary was seen as not right in the head. Dr Horgan, the only doctor for miles, was based in Newtownhamilton. He didn't know much about epilepsy and said she'd either grow out of the fits or she'd die in one. He said to use a padded spoon to stop her tongue choking her while she was in a fit, and he left a bottle of medicine – an improvement on the original treatment, which was a powder made from a ground-up otter's testicle or mouse's liver. Catherine put her trust in God. The doctor was overworked and could only do so much. He was paid with a dozen eggs and a live chicken with trussed up legs that he threw almost contemptuously into the back of the trap, along with the cabbages, turnips and other produce he got in lieu of payment. In recent years he'd got a motorbike, and as he traversed the countryside with brimming panniers, one local wit remarked that he looked like an ass with bardughs on him.

As Mary got older, the fits were less frequent, but her front teeth were broken from repeated insertions of the padded spoon. She was a delicate-looking child, with golden hair, freckled skin and large, pale-blue eyes that seemed to fill her sharp face. White eyelashes and eyebrows made her appear fragile and otherworldly, but she was also stubborn and wilful. "God's child," the neighbours murmured because the belief was that she had been touched by God and the spasms were due to her having seen the face of God. Some thought she brought luck but others feared her. The more superstitious thought she was a changeling, a child left by the fairies. They made the sign of the cross when they met her and didn't look directly at her for fear she might put a spell on them. People pitied poor Catherine because she had a cross to bear. Mary was simple. She would never grow up like the others and would always have to be minded, but it was God's will. Other special needs children in the community with different ailments or more profound disabilities than Mary were regarded as not quite human and referred to as "it" rather than he or she.

Mary wandered around the small mountain community with her terrier dog Jocko. He lay on the mat beside the settle bed where she slept with her sisters at night and would raise the alarm if anything happened to her. The family had learnt to trust his instincts. Mary knew what was happening at all the houses along the mountain and would repeat details out of the blue, startling those who thought that she was too mentally retarded to notice anything.

With Mary dozing in the bed, Catherine's attention was once more drawn to the lorry outside. It was taking much longer than she had anticipated. Yet when she looked at the clock again, it hadn't been there that long. She was nervous and more than a little scared. She prayed as she kneaded the coarse salt into the newly churned butter and welcomed the pain as the salt seeped into the hacks on her hands, offering it up for the suffering souls in Purgatory to keep everyone safe from harm.

"Dear Jesus," she begged, "let them get done and the lorry away to Hell out of here, God pardon me safe soul for cursing, before the Tans or some of them other bastards show up."

Prayer was her only recourse. If the arms were found on their wee bit of ground the consequences would be severe, but she had no control over what they were doing outside and they wouldn't give a woman any heed. But, if being caught with 'seditious literature' such as a Sinn Féin newspaper could get you six months in jail, then what could you expect for having a lorry-load of arms?

The 4th Northern Brigade led by Camlough man Frank Aiken was on active service all the time in the area, but Catherine knew little about their activities until the deeds were over and done. The previous December they had attacked the RIC barracks in Camlough, a village about eight miles from Cashel, but the garrison held them off. Military reinforcements arriving from Newry and Bessbrook were attacked with bombs and gunfire from the top of a railway bridge known as the Egyptian Arch, but they retaliated using a machine gun. One volunteer was killed, one arrested at the scene and others were captured by a search patrol. Later the military and Specials burnt down half the village of Camlough, with premises belonging to known Sinn Féin supporters being targeted. Early the next morning Frank Aiken's hay and hayshed were totally destroyed by fire, and the following Thursday his house was burnt to the ground, as was the residence of another prominent republican. In January three Specials from Camlough barracks were ambushed and wounded near the burnt-out ruins of Frank Aiken's house. Following that incident three other properties belonging to Frank Aiken were burnt out and an attempt was made to burn a fourth. A few days later John Doran, said to be a Sinn Féiner, was taken out of his house by masked raiders and shot dead. His father and brother escaped into the countryside and stayed there until the next day. At Silverbridge, over the road from Cashel, two young men were "shot while trying to escape", murdered in cold blood by the military. One lad's mother begged for his life. She showed the soldiers a photograph of her older son who'd fought in the war and was wearing the British army uniform, but they laughed at her, broke the photograph and shot the young fellow dead in front of her.

McGeeney's pub in Cullyhanna, another village not too far away, was wrecked by Specials and military. A Special was wounded in an ambush near Camlough and an RIC barracks was burnt out in Rostrevor, further away in County Down. When two Specials were shot in Belfast, a man was murdered in Armagh in retaliation, then a Special was killed in a bomb attack in Warrenpoint. In March, six IRA members were executed by the British in Cork and four more were hanged in Mountjoy Jail in Dublin.

Locally the mail was continuously raided, with all official letters and the postmen's bicycles being taken by the IRA. On one occasion the pay for the Specials stationed at Jonesborough barracks was also apprehended. Four Specials cycling to a service in Creggan church near Crossmaglen were ambushed, one was killed and the other three were seriously injured. On 23 April Camlough barracks was fired on again and on the twenty-fourth a big military round-up took place in Mullaghbane and all over the South Armagh area. Johnny McCoy, a friend and neighbour of the Grants, was badly wounded. He was taken to Newry General Hospital then to the Military Hospital in Belfast. Three other Volunteers, Mick McCann, Paddy Kelly and Barney Murphy, were also arrested. Frank Aiken escaped capture on that occasion.

Farmers were shot at in the fields and a man was shot dead near Belleeks. When the Specials came under attack in Newry, the town was put under curfew, with only essential personnel being allowed permits; anyone who disregarded the curfew would be shot. The IRA removed and burnt Belfast goods from the trains and sometimes the trains were also burnt. Bread men selling Belfast bread had their goods taken and on occasion their carts were destroyed. The rectory near Mullaghbane, a former Church of Ireland building, was situated in a prominent position with a panoramic view of the valley. The 4th

Northern received word that it was to be occupied by military and Specials, and as it overlooked their divisional headquarters, it was felt something would have to be done about it. In the nick of time they got orders to burn it. Forty to fifty men got flax tow from a nearby mill, spread it throughout the building, sprinkled it with paraffin oil and lit it. It burned fiercely and when the military convoy arrived the next morning from Armagh, all that was left was a smouldering ruin. Fortunately there was no other building in the area big enough to house them and they had to return the way they came.

Four of the men arrested following the ambush at the Egyptian Arch were sentenced to fifteen years' penal servitude each. In June two men were found murdered near Camlough, with labels attached to their bodies stating that they were police spies. Some said they had been shot by the IRA, but others believed it was the Specials who'd killed them and put the placards on them. It was a cycle of killing and reprisal. When a Special was killed and another wounded in an ambush near Newry, a Camlough farmer was shot dead in retaliation. James McGuill, a Sinn Féin councillor from Dromintee, narrowly escaped being murdered when his public house was raided by masked men said to be military.

In June, the Ulster parliament had its first sitting and the king and queen came over from England for the official opening. The troop train bringing horses and cavalry back to the Curragh after the ceremony was derailed at Adavoyle near Jonesborough. Shortly before the truce came into effect, four young Catholic men were taken out of their homes and murdered along the roadside near Altnaveigh. A Protestant railway worker was killed in retaliation. Cardinal Logue, the Archbishop of Armagh, was held up by the Specials in what was seen by Catholics as a total lack of respect for their church ministers, but the Specials had little heed for what anyone thought of them and drove around Camlough and other areas shooting into the air and intimidating people.

Catherine shuddered at the thought of what might happen if they turned up there before the lorry got away, but she doggedly continued shaping the butter before placing it in a butter firkin in the corner. She brushed dust and crumbs from the stone floor into the street for the hens to eat, but didn't look at the lorry or the men working at it. You couldn't tell what you didn't know, but she knew that wouldn't save her if the military came hammering on the door. She dried the table and replaced the enamel basin on the rungs underneath. The big black iron kettle was simmering over the fire, but it was too early to turn the bellows and get the fire going properly. The kitchenware was made from cast iron and was heavy and unwieldy, but despite her size she was strong and had developed a knack of swinging it onto the crane then over the fire. She prepared pots of soup and potatoes for later and set them ready on the hearth.

When all the arms were unloaded and buried, the men made sure that the dump under the big rock was well hidden and finished off the camouflage with intertwined briars. A man might tackle the whins, but he would think twice before rummaging in the briars. Bryan and Hughie obliterated the traces of drag marks with swatches of broom.

The lorry was long gone before Brigid, Susan and Katy arrived home from school and Catherine breathed a lot easier. The girls were weary from the two-mile walk, and even though it had been enlivened by games and skirmishes with neighbouring children, their new winter boots chafed feet that had been bare all summer. Brigid was a thin, serious child of nine years old, with brown hair, grey eyes and a small straight nose. Katy was eight, red-haired and plump and easy to tease, with blue eyes and a round freckled face. Susan was seven, nervous and over-anxious, with the youngest child's constant need for reassurance. She was dark-haired and brown-eyed and glowered at the world from beneath thick, dark eyebrows. A wee black smerry, a throwback, people said when they saw her with the others, not elaborating as to what.

They told Catherine all about their day in the girls' school, the harshness of the teacher who swung the girls round by their plaits if they couldn't answer a question. Sometimes a girl couldn't stop spinning and would hit her head off the wall. They didn't want Catherine to plait their hair, but she said it was either plait it or cut it all off. The teacher constantly picked on a girl who was left-handed, tied her hand behind her back and forced her to write with her right hand. Katy said that she called the girl a skitter, but Catherine thought it was probably a kitter – one who is left-handed.

They had soup then went looking for Mary, who was stretching sleepily in her parents' bed. When she told them about the lorry, Catherine reminded them not to tell anyone about anything that happened or anyone they saw coming or going around the house. Strange men in long coats were going about the countryside asking questions about the IRA. These men were policemen and soldiers and if they came to the farm, the children were to run away up the mountain and hide. But they were used to such warnings and were always subconsciously listening for tenders and looking for escape routes and hiding places.

Catherine then asked for three souple-tailed girls to go out to the haggard and gather the eggs. Collecting eggs restored normality to their existence. Then, armed with a saucepan and two bowls, they set off to look for where the hens were laying out. They were only children, but there was danger everywhere and she hated having to drub it into them all the time, but these days a scared child was safer than a brave child. The military and Specials were ruthless, with no scruples about how they got their information, and even a childish remark could prove costly. Mary regularly repeated adult conversations and people found that very amusing, but those reporting on the IRA might not dismiss what she said as idle prattle.

She leaned on the half door and listened as the girls called to each other. She hoped they'd be careful with the eggs because the egg man wouldn't take a cracked egg. When they came back with the eggs, she would send them to the shop at Redmond's Crossroads to get a tin of paraffin oil for the lamps. The evenings were drawing in and she could see the blue flame of frost in the fire. Catherine buttoned Mary into her coat and warned her to keep up with the others. She was as hardy as a wild duck, but the risk of pneumonia or, God forbid, TB, was always present. In winter the children wore good knitted jumpers and heavy overcoats and were fed fresh milk, vegetables and eggs to keep them healthy. Poorer people did what they could with what they had.

When the girls said their coats were too heavy and the shop was only over the road Catherine gave in and let them go on without them. She gave Mary some rags to stop her tearing strips from her petticoat to put under the birds on the bare branches. Brigid carried the oil can and the money and was warned not to spill the oil on her clothes or forget the change. After securing the arms dump, Bryan had gone to Umericam to get turf and would meet them at the Crossroads. Catherine told them to be careful on the broad road and to say nothing about nothing to nobody, especially Shusie at the shop. There wasn't much happening in the countryside that Shusie didn't know about, but Catherine didn't like the girls being interrogated. They slung their boots over their shoulders and set off barefoot, hoping that a quick paddle in the river would divert Mary from looking for black rabbits. Sometimes they came across birds and animals that were different colours from what was thought normal. An albino blackbird had been seen near the Spelig, and Bryan once saw a white hare on the mountain. Opinion was divided with regard to these sightings. If a person had good fortune after such an encounter then the creature was lucky, but if they had bad luck, future sightings were seen as a sign that something bad would happen.

At Ballinasack Bridge, near the main road, they edged down the bank to look at the river. The water level was low, but later in the year it could become a raging torrent that flooded the road. The riverbed was strewn with large stones washed there over the years by floodwater. They hoiked up their skirts, stepped onto the stones and stood looking into the water. Small fish and spricks darted from under the stones into the shelter of the bank and hid in the shadows. The girls dangled their stone-bruised, blistered feet in the small waterfalls that cascaded over the stones. At first the cold water was soothing, but when it began to cause pain and numbness they waded back to the bank and coaxed dry stockings onto wet feet. Mary didn't get into the water but poked around under the low bridge with a long stick. Jocko wagged his tail, his small body quivering excitedly as he sniffed along the bank. He was happy here in the kingdom of the water rat and always hopeful. He loved sheughs and rivers and muddy flax dams.

"What are you looking for, Mary?" Susan shouted.

Mary quickly shushed her and whispered that she was looking for an otter Hughie said he had seen there, but she was vague about when that had been. Susan scornfully reminded her that Hughie said he'd seen a kingfisher under the bridge and that it was just another of his stories. But Mary said she had seen a kingfisher there one time and he'd said not to talk about the lorry coming, but it had come and she'd seen it too. They pleaded with her not to talk about the lorry when they were at the shop and she agreed that she wouldn't. Jocko got covered in mud and they tried to wipe it off, but he wriggled free and ran up the road. The road to the Crossroads was wide and free from overhanging branches. As there was very little traffic at that time of evening they were free to run and play across it.

In the shop, Shusie, a big-boned, sallow-skinned woman with sharp brown eyes, and greying hair swept back and secured in a bun at the nape of her neck, reigned supreme from a high stool behind the counter. Her brother Jem and a neighbour Dan sat on the hearth stools beside the fire. Shusie's fire never went out, winter or summer, and was referred to locally by those she called "smart people" as the eternal flame. Sometimes it might look dead, especially in the summer when the sun shone directly on it, but a few turns of the bellows soon had it blazing again. Some women thought that the sun put the fire out and closed the curtains when they were cooking and baking.

Shusie was kind hearted and gossipy, with a caustic turn of phrase for those she found wanting, and there were many. She tried to remain impartial in the present political troubles, but the Crossroads was on the main road between the town of Newry and the town of Crossmaglen and was an important place. It was the ideal location for the police to stop and search cars and carts for weapons and also to pick up news and information. The RIC from Camlough barracks patrolled there and called with Shusie at night to chat and have tea. She knew the policemen well and all about their families, but recently the newly formed B Specials had also begun to police the area. She was polite to them, but wary. The RIC were drawn from all over Ireland and many were Catholic, but the Specials were from the other side and were all

Protestant. Tony Hurst, a young Special from Newtownhamilton, was courting Sarah Cullen, who was staying with her grandmother, Addy Murray, up above Bryan Grant's house on Cashel Mountain. Shusie knew Tony's mother's people, but she kept her distance and opinions to herself and tried to be civil, but neutral.

In the shop was a cuckoo clock that she had ordered from a magazine. She often placed orders for items she felt she couldn't do without. Once it was a revolutionary comb that was supposed to put a permanent wave in her hair, but unfortunately the wave was in the S-shaped teeth of the comb and the impression lasted for a fleeting second before fading and leaving Shusie's hair as straight as before. Unfazed by her lack of success with the comb, she ordered a corset that promised to give her an hourglass figure. The corset, or stays, that arrived didn't fit, but she inserted a strip from another set of stays and was quite happy with her new purchase, although she never quite achieved the hourglass figure. Magazines and newspapers provided her with endless items of conversation and advice to share with anyone who came into the shop. One newspaper had an advice section with suggestions for the many ways in which vinegar could be used. Shusie advised customers to set the legs of their beds in tins of vinegar and this would prevent lice getting into the bed. If you already had lice in the bed, a good dab of vinegar would take the sting out of a louse bite or a bee sting. Or if a cat pissed under the bed, a splash of vinegar would remove the smell and stop the cat going there again. Warm vinegar removed nits from hair and a hanky soaked in vinegar was the well-known cure for a headache. Anyone who had a household problem that couldn't be solved came to enquire if vinegar would provide the answer.

At the shop, while Jem went outside to fill the oil can, Shusie quizzed the girls about school and what they were learning. They kept a furtive eye on the dog for fear any of the muck would fall on Shusie's floor, then they paid for the oil without any hard questions being asked. They were heading outside to see if there was any sign of Bryan, when Mary remembered the cuckoo clock. Brigid pulled her by the coat sleeve to try and steer her out through the door, but Mary wasn't for moving.

"I want to hear the cuckoo, Shusie," she said.

"Sure, child dear and darlin' the cuckoo clock doesn't work," Shusie explained. "It was cuckooing there, morning, noon and night and no one could get a wink of sleep and the cuckoo was took out of it and put away and I don't know where it is."

"I want to hear the cuckoo, Shusie," Mary insisted.

She plonked herself down on the floor, looking up to where an ornate green and red clock that looked like a small Swiss house hung over the fireplace. Above the clock face was a door that shot open, and the cuckoo, at one point, popped in and out on the hour. Pendulums resembling bulrushes were suspended on thin brass chains below the clock.

"Come on, Mary," Brigid pleaded. "Mammy said that we were to be home before dark."

But when Mary began to rock back and forth the children became very anxious and Jocko made little yapping noises. The adults also knew that the situation could get out of hand very quickly. It had happened before.

"In the name of God can you not remember what you did with the cuckoo, Jem?" Shusie demanded.

She hoped that if they made the pretence of looking for it and then not finding it, Mary would be satisfied. Jem, in his sixties and two years Shusie's junior, shook himself, adjusted his waistcoats and cardigans and rose stiffly and reluctantly from his perch beside the fire. He tamped his pipe down and put it in his waistcoat pocket then footered and fumbled around the fireplace and groped along the high mantelpiece as if the cuckoo might suddenly appear.

"Begod, Mary, it was there yesterday," he said. "I saw it meself, someone must have moved it. Did you see it, Dan?"

"It's mebbe in the hearth stool," Dan offered.

Jem awkwardly prised the seat from the hearth stool. He wasn't the most agile of men and was well known for being clumsy. Recently he had sat astride the wrong end of a branch he was cutting and fell into a blackthorn hedge. Shusie was reported to have spent a fortnight picking thorns out of his arse and withered the neighbour who asked, "Was the vinegar any help?" Fortunately he hadn't been seriously injured, but it had left him slower than usual, with people asking if it was possible that he could be any slower.

"Where's the cuckoo? I want to see the cuckoo! I want to see the cuckoo!" Mary repeated, rocking faster and faster as she became more agitated.

"Begod, I got it!" Jem said triumphantly.

He fished a small blue object that didn't look anything like a bird from the depths of the hearth stool.

"Well, for God's sake put it on quick and turn the hour hand to one!" Shusie urged.

When Jem attached the cuckoo to the wire and adjusted the clock the cuckoo flew out and cuckooed.

"Do it again," Mary begged.

Jem turned the clock again.

The little blue cuckoo flew out of the clock, cuckooed then fell from the wire into the fire where it burned fiercely and turned to ashes without another cheep.

"Begod!" said Jem in surprise. "It's a sign."

"By Jesus, it's a sign alright," said Shusie, tight-faced. "It's a sign that we'll not have to go through that rigmarole again."

Susan began to cry just as Bryan entered the shop.

"And who should arrive at the heels of the hunt when the divarsion is all over, but bandy Bryan Grant, the man that's descended from the Kings of Scotland!" Shusie observed wryly.

Bryan, though still a handsome man in middle age, was bow-legged. Shusie reminded him of this to make sure he knew his place. Bryan's ancestors had come over to Ireland as soldiers with Edward the Bruce, brother of Robert the Bruce, the King of Scotland. On 14 October 1318 Edward the Bruce was killed fighting the English a few miles south of Cashel Mountain at the Battle of Faughart in County Louth and was buried there.

"Be cripes, I'm sorry to hear that, I'll pay you for it," sighed Bryan when Shusie related the sad tale of the cuckoo.

She laughed wryly as she brushed aside his offer of payment. What in the name of God would she charge him for a wooden cuckoo that had had its day? Sure it would have been lying in the hearth stool for the next twenty years if Mary hadn't asked for it. It didn't matter.

"Everything quiet above?" Jem asked.

Bryan nodded. He knew that Jem wasn't as slow as he walked aisy. He observed what was happening and who was coming and going at the Crossroads and passed the information on to Bryan. He knew that the lorry-load of arms had been expected at Grants' that day.

"It was quiet here the day too," he remarked, meaning that the military hadn't been around.

"Sarah Cullen went up by earlier," said Shusie. "You'd want to watch her."

Bryan frowned and nodded.

"Come on, yis puffers," he said to the girls. "The jinnet and cart are at the door and we'll be home in two shakes of a lamb's tail."

Mary had lost interest in anything to do with the cuckoo clock and had become vague and detached. Bryan scooped her up and carried her out to the cart. The girls said goodbye to Shusie and the two men as they hurried out of the shop.

"God help them people. They have a cross to bear and no one knows it better than themselves," Shusie observed.

The men nodded in agreement and sat for a while looking at the cuckoo's ashes.

"It come a long way to end its days in a fire at the Crossroads," said Shusie.

"Where did it come from?" Dan asked.

"Away out foreign," said Shusie. "Switzerland. It's there on the map."

She gestured vaguely in the direction of a map of Europe that was stuck on the wall. It had come in a newspaper during the war. It was meant to help people plot the advances and retreats made by the British army against the Germans, but news was hard to come by and no one bothered too much. The war was over now and the paper had become yellow and the edges torn, but it hadn't been removed from the wall. Jem knew that if he took it down there would be a clean spot on the sooty wall and that Shusie would harass him to paint it. Shusie already knew this and had decided to leave it there until spring, as Jem wouldn't be able to object or make excuses about painting when everyone else was doing it.

"Begod, mebbe if we got another cuckoo, Mick Callaghan might be able to fix the clock," Jem suggested.

"Mick the sodger?" snorted Shusie. "What would he know about fixin' cuckoo clocks?"

"Sure he was sodgerin' out foreign. He was a bumadeer," Jem explained.

"Bumadeer or not, he was sodgerin' out foreign, not learnin' to fix cuckoo clocks," said Shusie. "There wasn't too many cuckoo clocks in the trenches from what I heard and there was nothing in any of the newspapers about them learnin' sodgers to fix cuckoo clocks."

"You wouldn't know what they learned them in the army," said Jem, undefeated.

"You could be right, Jem," said Dan.

Shusie stared them down and they retreated once more to stare at the ashes.

"Isn't it wonderful too," Dan marvelled, "all the way from Switzerland."

Dan had never travelled further than Newry, which was ten miles away. Jem was about to continue the conversation, but Shusie quelled him with a look. They put in their day with conversations such as this and she could only tolerate so much of it. Just then a pony and trap came rattling round the bend and slowed to a halt. It was one of the many that stopped at the Crossroads on the way back from Newry. The pony waited as people got down from the trap and stood for a while, shouting snippets of information into Shusie before balancing parcels evenly on bicycles they had left there that morning and walking or cycling off home. Jem collected parcels and other items that had been brought out from Newry. These would be kept in the shop until the person who ordered them picked them up. Shusie would demand a full description of what was inside and its purpose before she handed the item over. Newspapers were printed every day in Newry and sent out to the shop once a week. They had news of what was happening all over the world as well as in Ireland and the locality. *News from the Courts* printed the various terms of penal servitude that members of the 4th Northern were receiving, depending on the offence. Inquests were held days after a death and the findings often covered several pages of the broadsheet. Jem and Shusie told those who couldn't read what was in the paper and others could read it for themselves, as it was usually wrapped around a purchase.

The cuckoo clock wasn't mentioned again in the shop, but sometimes when Shusie wasn't there, Jem spun the hour hand round and watched as the wire shot in and out. When Mary came to the shop she always looked up at the clock and murmured, "Poor wee bird."

Chapter 2

The 4th Northern Division set up camps on Camlough Mountain and along the Armagh–Louth border for training in drilling, signalling, bomb-making and the handling of various weapons. The Northern authorities knew about the camps but were reluctant to raid them during the truce.

Hughie found time to come back to help Mary release the fox cub. He looked at the big tar cross she'd painted on its back and said God couldn't miss that and would probably be able to see it from Heaven. The cub would soon shed its coat and the cross would be shed with it, but there was no point telling her that. She tucked its head under her arm and clutched the hind legs close to her chest, then led Hughie up the stony mountain track.

"Look down there, Hughie!" she cried. "The willows are dancing."

The willows dipped and swayed in the breeze as if to a secret tune. Hughie patted her head fondly and put his arm around her shoulders to help her along. The wriggling cub was putting her off balance on the steep slope, but she grimly clung on to it and when they were far enough away from the house Hughie decided that it was safe to let it go. When she set it down, it crouched there looking small and frightened, but when she tried to recapture it, he reminded her that it was a wild creature that would grow into a big fox and kill every hen in the country. He handed her a stick and she charged at it uttering a wild strangulated scream, and as the startled cub plunged into the whins she sent the stick flying after him. At the foot of the mountain she looked back and wiped tears away with her sleeve then asked Hughie about freeing the rat. He said he couldn't go with her, but he would take it with him far away and let it go. He left with the rat in a bag and Mary returned well satisfied to the house where the girls were preparing to go out and gather rosehips.

Autumn was a time of gathering up and gathering in. The days were getting shorter and the setting sun displayed harsher shades of red. Blackberries had to be picked before the Divil threw his coat over them and spoiled them. The children went out enthusiastically and returned exhausted, but with full buckets. As they flopped down like puppets on the settle bed, Catherine removed all the visible thorns with a sewing needle. Deeper, festering thorns would require poultices of raw bacon or bread, hard squeezing, many tears and a dusting of Boracic powder.

Rosehip syrup was next on the list, but they had to be careful because it was also the ranting season, when the wild buck goats came down from the mountain in search of mates. Along the roads they marched, their long, matted coats exuding a malodorous aura and fierce curving horns ready to challenge and defend their rights. If there was no smell it was safe to venture out.

Gathering rosehips was the same as their other expeditions and they got the usual reminders and cautions before they set out. They knew what was edible in the hedgerows and what was sour or poisonous. Berries should be free from mildew and worms, blaeberries were footery and hard to pick, but sometimes they collected enough to make a tart. Crab apples and elderberries were boiled to make jelly. Rosehips looked inviting, but the insides were full of woolly seeds and the flesh tasted woody.

They found some wild rose briars, but the hips were scarce and hard to dislodge. Progress was slow. The briars snagged at the cuffs of their jumpers and the sharp thorns cut into their flesh. They sat dejected on the ditch until Mary announced there were rakes of hips over by Addy's and ran off trailing the milking bucket. They weren't allowed near Addy's, but they had to mind Mary, so they started after her, covering the tins to keep the hips from bouncing out.

Addy was a tall, thin, swarthy, black-haired woman in her mid-fifties. Some said she blackened her hair with boot polish; others said it was soot because she never washed herself. She looked older than her age and it was said that she was worn by life. She was different from other women and indifferent about what they thought of her. She had a daughter called Una, who lived in Newtownhamilton, but she had never had a husband. She didn't talk about it and though not many were brave enough to ask, they speculated as to who Una's father might be. Una's daughter, Sarah Cullen, Hughie's one-time girlfriend, spent her time between Addy's house in Cashel and her mother's house in Newtownhamilton.

Addy had a house and a small piece of ground where she grew potatoes and vegetables. She also read the cups, cards and palms of the young women who paid her to look into the future for them. They wanted to know if they would get married and who they would marry. A rich man would be a bonus, and though rich men were thin on the ground, Addy didn't disappoint them. She told them what they wanted to hear. At the start of a cup reading she'd drain the last drop of tea and say, "You'll pass water before this night is over." They couldn't dispute that prediction. She generally had a positive message for all the girls: "There'll be a man coming across the sea for you soon" or "There's someone in this cup has the best of hearts for you" or "There's someone in the cup that you wouldn't think of, but he has his eye on you" or "There's a fella here. He could be called John." She knew most of the girls and she knew the local gossip, so her readings were usually accurate.

Older people sometimes had their cards read to see if they were going to die from whatever ailed them. They said she was better than any doctor. If the cards held bad news, she'd slowly place them face down and say she'd read no more. She didn't need to, as they now knew that they were done for, doomed, and she'd accept no money for the reading. She had cures for a stye on the eye, erysipelas and shingles. Many people frequently availed of her services, but young men played cards in her house at night and this was frowned upon.

It was said that she used coaxiorum, a potion supposedly made from camomile, that kept men enthralled so that they had no will of their own and deserted their wives to be with her. The men sniggering at the back of the chapel on a Sunday morning, out of earshot of the priest, agreed that when Addy was in her heyday she didn't need a potion to keep men enthralled. It was easier for a deserted woman to believe that her man left because of a mysterious potion than because he was no good or had lost interest. Addy also kept a buck goat and charged people to get their nanny goats mated. She assured the owners that the mating process had been carried out because she had seen it. That was frowned upon too. That was men's work. A woman who thought anything of herself didn't do that sort of thing or talk about it.

She was looked down on because she had no shame and didn't keep her house clean, but she had other services that women secretly availed of and paid for with whatever they could gather up. Fr Carron, the parish priest, stopped short of reading her out on the altar as a sinner because he didn't really know what powers she had. Addy had no magical powers, but she knew a lot of secrets. She was always affable when the priest was forced by some irate female parishioner to call on her to try to make her mend her evil ways.

"Sit your holy arse down there, Father," she'd say as she threw a hen off a chair and wiped it down with a dirty rag. "I'll just make us a drop of tay. Sure, we're all just trying to make a living. You heard I was making a potion in a black saucepan? Not at all, Father dear, the only black saucepan I have is that wee one there that I use for boiling an egg. Would you like a boiled egg? There's no such thing as coaxiorum. It's mebbe something in the water. I heard if the water is took out of a certain well it puts men astray in the head. That could be what them women are talking about. Are you not staying for a cup of tay and the water just fresh from the well? Sure, call anytime, Father, you're always welcome and I'm always here."

The parish priest had been warned not to eat anything in her house because of her bad housekeeping. It seems that a young curate had visited her and after racking his brain to see what he could eat that she couldn't contaminate finally decided on a boiled egg. She duly boiled the egg and set it in an eggcup then took a hairpin from her head, inserted it into the egg, withdrew it and said, "Done to a turn, Father."

Priests were said to have the power to put horns on anyone who was a constant sinner. This mostly applied to those who were too fond of the drink and wouldn't stay out of the public houses. One hardened and unrepentant drinker is reputed to have told the priest, "If you put horns on me, Father, the first place they'll go is up your arse!"

Needless to say they were careful who they threatened. When Fr Carron first came to the parish, he visited Addy to say he'd been told that she had a child that had no father. Addy modestly kept her head down as she listened to him.

You're the parish priest, Father, and you're schooled and book-larned till all is no more, she thought. But you know and I know that there isn't a crater born on this earth that doesn't have a father. I know who Una's father is and he knows who he is; he's a respectable man and a pillar of the church just like yourself, but a pig will always hoke in muck.

"Och, I was young then, Father, and the Divil got the better of me. I told the priest that in Confession and when the child was born I rared her as good as any child in the parish," she told him.

"I pray that God will forgive you," the priest replied. "And that you will not lead any more men astray. If there was no bad women there would be no bad men."

Addy kept her head down and meekly nodded in agreement, but said nothing. She knew that if men wanted to go astray they didn't need much leading, but she didn't want to antagonise him. She didn't know what powers he had either and wanted to go to Heaven at the end of her days.

Women like Addy were in a peculiar position because people, respectable and otherwise, availed of their clandestine services, but if anything went wrong, they were the scapegoats. In some areas such women were often taken to court, accused by their neighbours or local farmers of "putting the blink" on them or "overlooking" their stock. It meant that bad luck had been wished on them by someone who had the power to do it. This might include a cow that suddenly stopped producing milk, a cow that dropped a calf – had a stillborn calf – the butter turning in the churn or the churn failing to produce butter, the hens ceasing to lay, or all of these. In many cases the woman was warned by the judge that if she continued "putting the blink" on people she would go to jail.

Addy, like many women of her ilk, lived cautiously on the fringes, taking advantage where she could while trying not to draw too much attention to herself.

The girls followed Mary towards Addy's, hoping they would find plenty of rosehips and get the bucket filled and be away home before Addy knew they were there. They weren't allowed in Addy's house because not only did she have a dubious reputation, but they would also be quizzed for news.

"I can smell the buck goat," Mary declared loudly.

They shushed her as best they could, but then the smell enveloped them like an unseen mist, stinging their eyes and making it difficult for them to breathe. The buck goat was at his most odorous at this time of year. Some farmers kept a buck goat running with their cattle, as it was thought that the goat ate herbs and other plants that were poisonous to cattle. Addy had reared her goat from when he was a kid, and the girls could see him now grazing in the field behind her house. He was a magnificent creature, with a long, thick, brown and white coat and large curved horns. Magnificent but pungent. They climbed higher up the rocks to where the smell was less potent. Jocko foraged in the undergrowth, disturbing a blackbird that flew away with a startled cry. They paused in their picking to see if Addy would come out to investigate the noise, but when no one appeared they silently resumed their work, with hearts thumping so loudly they thought she might hear them too.

"Addy Murray is a dirty clart," Mary suddenly cried.

"Shut up, Mary!" Brigid whispered fiercely. "She'll hear you and come out and we'll be in trouble."

"No ospectickle woman keeps a buck goat, Catherine," Mary continued in a confiding grown-up tone. "Or charges for it ayther."

She was obviously repeating a conversation she had overheard.

The girls frantically plucked at the abundant hips, but their small hands were unable to hold more than a couple at a time, causing many to slip frustratingly through their fingers and tumble down the rocks. They had almost reached their target when Addy's half door opened and Sarah Cullen came out into the yard. Geese and hens ran cackling and honking towards her, and just as it seemed she might be overwhelmed, she deftly diverted them by scattering a handful of corn in the direction of their feeding trough. As they pecked greedily at the corn, she casually filled the trough for them. Something caused her to look up, and she saw the girls gazing down.

"Hello there," she smiled. "I thought I heard voices. What are you wee girls doing up there on those rocks?"

"We're getting rosehips," Katy explained. "Mammy is going to make rosehip syrup for us. It's very good for you."

"I'm sure it is," Sarah agreed. "Are you going to come down and see us for a wee while?"

As they shook their heads, Addy came out and leaned her bosom on the half door.

"Come on down," she invited. "You'll have a drop of goat's milk."

"We don't like goat's milk," Brigid said.

"Well, aren't you the consaty girls that doesn't like goat's milk and isn't Bryan Grant your father, a gentleman farmer," Addy said, laughing wryly and shaking her head. "Sure, you can take a mug of water and an oatmail biscake. Come on."

"We have to be home before dark," said Brigid in desperation.

"It'll not be dark for an hour yet," Addy countered. "Come down here now and give us a while of your crack."

Brigid knew that unless they made a fast run for home, they were trapped. There was nothing else for it; they had to go down. Jocko ran into the yard scattering geese and outraged hens in all directions, then cowered behind Mary when the geese made a counter-attack. Geese were known to be aggressive and unpredictable, and as the girls waited, Sarah shooed them away with the broom then opened the half door and ushered the girls inside. They sat uneasily around the table on three-legged stools as Addy handed out mugs of well water she'd scooped from a covered bucket. She gave each of them a triangular biscuit that she had made earlier on the griddle. The biscuits, made from coarse oaten meal, were thin and crunchy and stuck to their teeth. Mary rambled about the kitchen, touching pictures and ornaments. She was no stranger to Addy's house or any of the houses along the foot of the mountain.

"How's your Hughie?" Sarah asked her.

"He is very well, thank you," Mary replied politely. "How's yon Special?"

Brigid and the girls stiffened and stopped eating. Sarah cast a quick look at Addy, whose mouth had dropped open in surprise.

"He's well too, thank you, Mary," Sarah replied calmly.

"What about your father?" Addy asked. "Is he away to work in the mines yet?"

"No, he hasn't gone yet," Brigid told her.

Bryan usually travelled to Scotland to work in the coal mines in the autumn after the harvest had been gathered or in the months before the harvest was ready.

"Is he keeping well in himself?" Addy persisted.

Brigid assured her that he was. Many years later, courtesy of a lost insurance agent, the Grants discovered that Addy had taken out a life insurance policy on Bryan and therefore took a great interest in his health and whereabouts. Having an insurance policy on someone who wasn't a relation was not an unusual practice; it was a guaranteed lump sum for a few pence a month provided the contributor didn't die before the insured. Addy knew that the mines were dangerous places and it was an ill wind that blew nobody good. Bryan Grant wouldn't begrudge her a few pounds if the mine fell in on him.

The cottage was warm and the girls began to relax.

"Isn't it terrible times that's in it now," Addy remarked. "You don't know who's walking the roads day or night. It's a danger of your life to go out at all. Strangers coming and going all over the place, it never used to be like that. I heard there was a lorry come by your house one of the days. When did the lorry come?"

"We didn't see a lorry," Brigid answered. "We're at school every day."

“Lorries don’t be often on this road, bar the Tans wracking about. Do yis ever see that Gerard Molloy fella at all?” Addy continued. “It used to be he was never off the road and now I don’t know when I seen him.”

“Gerard Molloy, Gerard Molloy is a skitter,” Mary remarked mildly.

The girls began to get alarmed. If Addy kept on about Gerard Molloy and Mary started talking about the lorry they were in deep trouble. They had to get out of there. Brigid suddenly doubled over clutching her stomach.

“I have to go home,” she gasped. “I have an awful pain in me belly. I have to go outside, I think I’m going to vomit.”

Addy looked at her suspiciously. The worm was wriggling off the hook and there was nothing she could do; a clever blade that Brigid one.

“Mebbe me oatmail biscakes didn’t agree with you, mebbe you better run on home,” she said grudgingly. “Tell your mother I have a goose for her for Christmas.”

She watched as the girls ran up the lane. The light was fading earlier every day.

“What in the name a Jaysus are you at, Sarah?” she demanded, turning sharply from the door. “You’d want to watch yourself, me girl, because if yon poor, wee, afflicted, half-witted child is talking about you and the Special then everyone else in the country is doing it too. There’s bad times coming. I can feel it in me water.”

Sarah shrugged carelessly. “I know all the lads, on both sides, sure they wouldn’t harm me.”

She had been reared in Newtownhamilton but became ill when she was eighteen and was advised to get plenty of country air and if possible live in the country. Shusie at the Crossroads wondered why she couldn’t get country air in Newtownhamilton. Sure the town wasn’t that big that a body couldn’t take a walk outside it.

She was a fine-looking young woman who looked much like Addy when she was younger, and although Addy was surprised by Mary’s question, the whole country did know about Sarah and the B Special.

Following her brief relationship with Hughie she had gone back to Newtownhamilton and Tony Hurst. She often met him when he was on patrol with his unit at the Crossroads. Hughie and his comrades lying out gathering intelligence on the Specials sometimes saw their meetings. Hughie endured the ribald remarks and threats against Sarah with restraint and dignity, but as he watched her laughing up at Tony he always felt a surge of extreme anger that faded to sadness when he remembered how close they had once been.

He first met her one sunny summer evening when he was twelve years old. As he was feeding the hens, something raced through them and scattered them in all directions. He saw that it was a long-limbed girl who was slightly smaller and maybe a year younger than him. Her glossy, dark hair was barely restrained by a blue ribbon and her skin was lightly tanned, with a scattering of freckles. She wore a pretty, flowered dress, and as she assessed him from behind half-closed brown eyes she scuffed the toe of her shiny patent boot in the dust. She said she was Sarah Cullen and she was visiting her granny, Addy Murray.

She spun around the yard, opening doors and peering into the outhouses, then ran into the house where Catherine was idly rocking the cradle with her foot and Bryan was dozing with his hands folded across his stomach. Mary, the long-awaited baby, was sleeping. She was just a few months old.

"What's in there?" Sarah demanded as she glanced into the cradle.

She turned without interest when she saw that it was a baby and ran out again onto the road and pulled the flowers from the hollyhocks and jumped on them. Hughie was upset because his mother was so proud of her flowers and now this strange girl had destroyed them.

"Go home," he shouted. "Go home and don't come back."

She called to him, but he didn't answer and went into the house to have his tea.

"Who was thon will-o'-the-wisp of a young one that spun in and out of here before you could say Jack Robinson?" Bryan asked when he came into the house.

When Hughie said she was Addy's granddaughter, Sarah Cullen, Catherine decided she must be Una's daughter, from Newtownhamilton.

She'd seen a hackney car going up the road earlier on and wondered who was in it. Hughie hoped Sarah wouldn't be staying long, but it turned out she was staying for a week. Hughie's older brothers Peter and Barney were hired on farms near Banbridge in County Down, and he worked with his father in the daytime. But in the evenings he always crossed the mountain to Gerard Molloy's house. He gradually realised that Sarah was following him and dawdled along, thinking that he'd allow her to catch up then run away from her. He knew the shortcuts and she would be hampered by her skirts, but she didn't try to catch up, she just followed doggedly behind him day after day.

"There's your girl after you again, Hughie," Gerard Molloy laughed.

They watched her head bobbing up and down as she sought a way through the bracken and briars, then he climbed higher up and thought no more about her. Much later, as Hughie made his way home, she was sitting by the side of the road threading rowan berries to make a necklace. Her face and arms were scratched and her stockings torn. The braid was hanging down from her dress. Bits of bracken clung to her hair and her patent boots were scuffed and dirty. She seemed momentarily defeated, but when he asked did she want to see some fox cubs, she looked up with such a bright happy smile that he felt ashamed at having left her to her own devices.

"Just this once," he warned.

"Just this once," she agreed as she skipped along beside him.

She followed him for the rest of the week, but he didn't wait for her and didn't speak to her if she caught up to him. He ignored Gerard's up-cast eyes and knowing smile as she tagged along behind them. Then she was gone, back to Newtownhamilton, and they forgot about her.

After that she didn't visit very often, or if she did he didn't meet her. When he was old enough to be hired, he joined his friends and neighbours labouring on the farms of County Down. Peter and Barney went to work in England and from there to Canada. Hughie was home from the hiring and having his tea one evening when Catherine said that Sarah was coming back to stay with Addy. The poor girl hadn't a drop of blood in her at all and only just got hired when something came over her and she had to give it up. The doctor advised her to live in the country and eat spuds and cabbage and buttermilk to see would that get some iron into her.

Hughie was only half-listening as he buttered slices of wheaten bread for his wee sisters. He had four of them now: Mary, Brigid, Katy and Susan, who had been born at regular intervals over the past few years. In the barren years, Catherine had lit a candle each Sunday so that she would be blessed with more children, but when the four little girls came one after the other, she feared she might have lit too many.

Catherine asked Hughie if he remembered Sarah following him and Gerard all over the mountain, but he hadn't seen her or thought about her in years and had little interest in her. He and Gerard had recently been sworn into the Army of the Volunteers and were training all the time to become soldiers with the 4th Northern Division. They had followed the events in Dublin, from the ill-fated Easter Rising in 1916 to the execution of its leaders and the internment of other revolutionaries in prisons in Wales and England. A man from Mullaghbane had cycled to Dublin to take part in the Rising. They couldn't wait to join up, wished they could have gone with him, but they had been too young then and the time was not right. Now they were ready to fight for Ireland and had quit the hiring to become apprentices with a blacksmith in Forkhill, two miles up the road. The blacksmith had always been an invaluable ally in making and providing weapons for Ireland's many rebellions. The lads knew they also needed this skill to make new weapons and repair those they already had. Hughie had no time in his life for women. The call to arms had come and he would not be distracted. Yet when he met Sarah again, his first thoughts were not for Ireland and the Cause.

She was standing at the head of Addy's lonin, gazing out over the valley with her back to him, and turned, startled, as his boot dislodged a small stone that rolled to a halt at her feet. He drew back in surprise because he had been expecting to see the swarthy countenance of Addy. Black-avised was how Catherine described Addy. Yella skinned was how Addy saw herself. Hughie apologised for scaring her and the young woman assured him that she hadn't been frightened. They regarded each other for a moment, but there seemed nothing more to say and Hughie made to move off. But the young woman introduced herself as Sarah Cullen and asked did he remember her. She smiled a quick, bright smile that lit up her face, and as she extended her hand, a memory surfaced of a tattered and forlorn girl threading rowan berries.

"Aye, Sarah," he murmured. "Ma was right, a different Sarah now."

She had grown tall and her skirts now skimmed the dusty road. Her dark hair was confined in a bun at the back of her neck, her lips were pale and her skin was sallow from lack of sunshine and probably the lack of iron that his mother had spoken about. Her deep-brown eyes were the only animated feature she possessed. She said she had been sick for a while but she was on the mend thanks to Addy's cabbage, and Addy had plenty of cabbage. She would be staying there for a couple more weeks and then she'd be going back to Newtownhamilton, where she had an apprenticeship with a dressmaker.

"Well, sure mebbe I'll see you before you go," Hughie said lightly.

And he did see her again. It wasn't by chance that he walked that road home and it wasn't by chance that Sarah was standing smiling at the top of Addy's lonin as he came striding down the hill. Their conversations were general: local gossip, the state of the country, and gradually veered into what they hoped for the future. Then, all too soon, she had to go back to her job in Newtownhamilton. He shook her hand warmly and held it longer than was necessary until she pulled away, lifted her skirts and ran down the lonin to Addy's cottage. She looked back and waved at him before going inside. He thought about her often, waking in the night with the aching memory of her smile, imagining he caught a waft of her perfume as he passed a flowering honeysuckle on a summer's evening, pausing dreamily in the midst of a task to remember how she looked.

"It must be love," said Gerard Molloy. "They say it comes on you like a soot drop."

"I suppose you would know all about it," Hughie remarked.

"As much as the next man," Gerard grinned. "I see girls at the dances, fine girls and they're watching me and waiting on me to ask them to dance, but then they be disappointed when I don't ask, for I have no time for women, yit."

"The girls don't be looking at you at all, that's all in your head," Hughie scoffed. "You'd be hard up for a fruit when you'd tackle an onion."

"You just watch them smiling and winking at me the next dance we're at," Gerard said, smirking.

Hughie tried to divert his thoughts to other matters. He didn't know when he would see Sarah again, but she returned to Cashel within a couple of months. The doctor said that she wasn't ready yet to sit for long days in front of a sewing machine. She was there one evening waiting as Hughie came down the hill. He stopped in surprise when he saw her. She came quickly towards him and stopped directly in front of him, then impulsively extended both her hands to him. He paused to drop his knapsack and took her hands in his.

"I missed you, Hughie," Sarah said shyly. Suddenly she seemed a little embarrassed.

"I missed you too," Hughie assured her.

He led her over to sit down on the ditch where they sat talking as if they had been parted for years. This became the pattern of their lives. They met at every opportunity and sat together on the ditch until Addy came out into the yard and began banging buckets together. Then they would reluctantly move apart and Sarah would go back to the cottage. Hughie wanted Sarah to walk further down the road with him, but Addy sent word that sitting on the ditch at the top of the lonin was far enough. He wasn't happy about it but he knew that a young woman had to protect her reputation. They tentatively began to speak of a future together. Hughie's plans could only be realised once Ireland was free and he had no doubt that it would happen soon. He thought he might go to Canada and join his brothers. It was a new country and there was plenty of work and money to be made. He would send for Sarah and they could stay there until they got enough money together to buy a good farm here at home.

"Would you follow me over there?" Hughie asked.

"I remember a time when you didn't want me following you." Sarah laughed.

They talked and laughed about that childhood time, then Hughie held her close and kissed her and asked her would she promise to wait for him. He told her that at the present time he was in no position to ask her to marry him. Sarah seemed reluctant to make a promise and after some persuasion she finally told him that Addy had forbidden her to make any promises of that nature. That evening they parted on less than loving terms. Hughie, confused and angry, confided in his mother. Catherine was both relieved and annoyed. She hadn't been happy about the romance because of Addy and her daughter, Una's, ambivalence in regard to their reputations and the holy sacrament of matrimony. Sarah would have inherited that bad blood. That wasn't what she wanted for her son, but she was also annoyed to discover that Addy, and the hard neck of the woman, didn't think that Hughie was good enough for her granddaughter. She sympathised with Hughie, but in the privacy of their bedroom she ranted on to Bryan.

"Let the hare sit," Bryan advised. "These things have a way of working themselves out, one way or the other."

Hughie thought that he would be able to get Sarah to make him a promise, but to no avail. A rift developed in their relationship, and though it seemed tiny at first, it soon became a chasm that neither would cross. One evening he arrived at the lonin to meet her, but she wasn't there. He waited undecided and when she didn't appear he went to talk to Addy.

"She's gone beyant to Newtown," Addy informed him. "I don't know what she told you, but she's promised to a young fella from there this long and many a day. He come up to Redmond's Crossroads the day to get her and she's away back with him. It's a pity that she didn't tell you that at the start. I would a told you, but it's only now that I see what way the wind was blowin'. I thought yis were only having a bit a divarsion."

Hughie walked away in disbelief. He felt the breath catch in his throat and forced back a sob. He sat down on their spot on the ditch at the top of the lonin, then, realising where he was, jumped up and aimed a kick at the stones, hurting his foot.

How could she do that to him? When Gerard and the boys wanted him to ask her about the layout of Newtownhamilton barracks and what military was in it, he had refused. Sarah would not be sullied by the Troubles. Well now, by Jaysus, he would find out all he needed to know about Newtownhamilton and the barracks and it wouldn't matter a hate about her. As he walked along reliving their conversations, he realised that he had been the one making all the plans for both of them. Aye, she had listened to him and told him of her dreams, but she had never agreed to anything. And she had snuggled up to him as he kissed and caressed her, but didn't mention she was already promised to another man – yet he knew that she had been fond of him. Och, Jaysus Christ, what was he going to do without her? When he entered the house, Catherine and Bryan exchanged glances at the look of him.

"Sarah's gone," he stated glumly as he sat down at the table.

"I know, son," Catherine said sadly. "I seen her going by with a bag round dinnertime the day."

She put a consoling arm round his shoulders and gave him a quick hug, then she set down two boiled eggs for his tea. He smiled wryly in acknowledgement.

"A man has to ate, no matter what happens," she stated.

Gerard Molloy also felt the pain of Sarah's betrayal. It was as if she had stabbed both of them through the heart. He understood the need for Hughie to plot revenge on Newtownhamilton barracks and it had always been a possible target. With their unit they filtered in to assess it one winter's evening. From a hidden position they watched for several hours, noting the comings and goings. Finally a couple emerged from the barracks. The man was tall and in uniform. The woman clinging to his arm wore a long coat and a hat that shaded her face and covered her hair. It was hard to tell who they were. When they paused close by, it became clear to the watchers that the woman was Sarah. She smiled up at the man as he pulled her close and kissed her. Hughie loosened his grip on his revolver as Gerard leaned a cautioning hand on his arm. He took a deep breath and relaxed slightly. He was surprised by the surge of anger and jealousy that overcame him. For two pins he would have shot her so that he would never have to see that treacherous smile again, especially when it was directed at another man. The couple moved on down the street. The watchers withdrew from the shadows and made their way out of the town.

"It must be a hard thing to watch your woman hanging out of a B man," Gerard remarked sympathetically.

But there was nothing that Hughie could say. He found out later that the young Special was Tony Hurst, who came from well-to-do farming people. If Sarah was promised to a man like that, it wasn't surprising that Addy didn't want him upsetting the applecart. After that he avoided Addy's. Although he knew Sarah was there from time to time, he didn't want to meet her, but once he met her by accident.

"I'm sorry," she said. "I didn't mean to leave like that. Granny made me."

"You were promised to another man," he pointed out. "What took you leading me on?"

"I didn't mean to," Sarah replied. "It just happened and I didn't know what to do. And I had no one to talk to."

Hughie glared at her angrily. She might be all grown up, he thought, but she was still the wee girl that had destroyed his mother's flowers.

"Granny said that all this IRA carry-on and freeing Ireland would never amount to much and that you'd be no good to a girl like me for you'd likely be killed," Sarah continued.

"Yon Special is likely to be killed too," Hughie stated.

Sarah gave a horrified gasp and put her hand to her mouth, and Hughie, realising that he might have said too much, walked quickly away. As time went by, he forgave her a little, and though there was always an ache there in a hidden corner of his soul, he allowed it to stay there as something pure and precious that he could take out occasionally and examine in a time when life was becoming increasingly savage. There was grumbling within the 4th Northern that something would have to be done about Sarah, and though Hughie tried to keep the situation contained, he knew that the day would come when he'd have no control over what happened to her.

Addy was thinking along similar lines.

"What makes you think that the boys wouldn't harm you! Daughter, dear and darlin', have you no wit at all? You could be tarred and feathered or worse. Did you not hear what they did to the telegraph girl out at Newtownhamilton? The IRA hacked off her hair and then threw her and hair and bicycle over the ditch," Addy said sharply.

Tarring and feathering and hacking off women's hair were punishment for fraternising with the enemy. One woman had her hair sheared for walking out with a policeman, a middle-aged woman had her face and breast tarred because her son joined the Specials, and a Kilkeel girl had her hair cut off with a slash hook.

"And stay away from Hughie Grant. You were warned before about that," Addy continued. "I see them boys going about the road with guns. I don't know what they're doing and I don't want to know, but you take bloody good care that you're not caught up at the wrong end of it. Aye, you can shrug your shoulders, but I'm in this world longer than you and I seen before how quick things can turn from bad to worse."

Sarah shrugged again and sat down on the hearth stool. She turned her back to Addy and poked sulkily at the fire.

You couldn't talk to her. The young never have much sense, Addy thought sadly.

Back at the rocks, the girls scrabbled up some of the hips that had fallen down from up above, pulling handfuls of scutch grass in their haste and casting them into the bucket. Then they ran like the hammers of Hell for home, but after an initial burst they slowed down. The rosehips were hopping out of the bucket and they were losing too many. Once they were out of sight of Addy's cottage, they felt safer. They told Catherine that Addy had asked about the lorry and about Gerard Molloy. She was more concerned about the questions Addy had asked than them being there. Brigid explained the sudden pain in her belly and Catherine praised her, but warned them not to go anywhere near Addy's again unless she sent them. It had been foolish to think that a lorry would come there and no one would remark on it. Addy was all right, but she was nosey and a gossip and Sarah was coortin' a Special and that would be no good for her in the long run.

That night in the settle bed, Brigid thought about Sarah, who was kind and friendly with shiny hair that smelt of flowers and always had time to talk to them when they met her on the road. She had a scent bottle with a pattern etched into the glass and a wee glass stopper for dabbing the scent on her wrist. She promised Brigid she could have the bottle when it was empty. Catherine had spoken about Sarah with a mixture of pity and annoyance and Brigid drifted into sleep hoping that nothing bad would happen to her.

Chapter 3

The settle bed was in the kitchen and was used as a seat during the day, but it was pulled out at night to make a bed for the girls. They were asleep now and turned over almost as one, murmuring softly as they adjusted to the shape of each other. Catherine smiled as one of them let out a loud tatterera of a fart. It must have been the turnips, but as Bryan would say, that's your engine working. She threaded a darning needle and positioned the heel of a sock over her knuckle, but the glowing embers of the fire had a mesmerising effect and her thoughts drifted. Bryan wasn't home yet. He was usually there to say the Rosary and she wondered where he could be. Their bedtime was around nine o'clock and he liked to sit and talk for a while before that. The crickets were chirping on the hearth. It was thought that their singing kept the fairies away, but she wasn't thinking about the fairies. Hughie hadn't been home for days and she worried about him constantly, but she had come to the uneasy conclusion that if anything happened to him, someone would let them know. As yet there was no formal border between the six Ulster counties and the rest of Ireland, but the Specials and IRA were fighting along the county boundaries of Louth, Monaghan, Cavan, Leitrim and Donegal, in what was now regarded as the border area. There had been sporadic shooting between the Specials and the 4th Northern at Cullaville, not far from Crossmaglen, but Catherine preferred not to know what Hughie was doing, and Bryan didn't tell her anything about his activities. She liked to think that he was busy enough guarding the safe house at the back of the mountain and worried mostly about his health. He was sleeping out in the open when they were on manoeuvres and living conditions in the safe house were basic, but it didn't do for him to neglect himself. The last time he was home, he had a nagging cough and though he was always slight and wiry, he seemed to be getting thinner. The handkerchief that fell out of his coat pocket was stained with old blood, but he might have cut himself on barbed wire or killed and skinned a rabbit. It was mebbe just a cough, but when it was coupled with the bloodied handkerchief, the spectre of TB rose to haunt her.

TB was a very infectious and deadly disease that affected the lungs. It was incurable and greatly feared by everyone. Families affected were avoided because it was spread by coughing. It was also believed that these families got TB because they had a "wakeness" – a weakness – in them that would be passed down through the generations and they would eventually die out. Pity for the affected families coupled with fear of the disease bred a kind of contempt for them, and the advice to anyone contemplating marrying into such a family was, "Don't do it. The breed of them is riddled with TB."

Catherine hadn't yet told Bryan her worries over Hughie's health because talking about it might bring something on him and the words couldn't be taken back. She couldn't control what happened to him, but she could pray for him and with the help of God he would be all right.

When she heard a noise outside, she knew it was probably Bryan, but she felt her body tense. With the times that were in it you wouldn't know who it could be, but then the dog rose silently from the mat beside the settle bed. He padded over to the door with his hackles raised and his head to one side, but soon his tail began to wag, and when he trotted back and lay down again, she knew that a friend was without. Bryan lifted the latch and entered, bringing cold air and an impression of mist. He removed his cap and scarf, paused a moment to adjust his cravat in the looking glass beside the door, then came over to the fire to warm his back. Catherine set the darning aside, poured him a mug of tea from the delft teapot that was drawing on the hearth and handed it to him.

"Thank you, kindly," said Bryan. "That's getting to be a cowl night."

He added milk and sugar to the tea then sat down opposite to her, warming his hands on the mug. She gazed at him fondly, happy to have him home safely.

Bryan was five foot ten with a spare frame. His cheeks were rosy now from the cold, but generally his skin was tanned brown from being out in all weathers. The cravat he wore was his only vanity, a habit he had acquired in Scotland. To cheer himself up after working in the dust and dirt of the coal mines, he took to wearing a colourful cravat. When they first met at a farewell dance for his cousin Jimmy, who was emigrating to America, Bryan's hair had been very dark, almost black, but by the time he was thirty it was almost grey. That night, when the musicians launched into their first tune, he came over and stood in front of Catherine.

"Would you fit the flure?" he invited.

She looked up at his smiling face and quizzical blue-grey eyes and she knew she had met her match. She took the hand he offered and after a few missteps they soon adjusted to the tempo of the dance. With a bit of practice she thought he might do.

He was a kind, easy-going man. If called on to discipline the children he did it in such a way that the child was truly remorseful at having caused so much sorrow to such a good man. If he caught them in the act of doing something wrong, he gave them a gentle skelp on the bottom with his cap.

When they were first married, Catherine accompanied him to Scotland where he worked in the coal mines. She was not happy with his choice of occupation, as his brother George had been killed in an explosion in the mines. With their young sons, Peter and Barney, they found accommodation in a grim tenement building that was full of poor people like themselves. The Scots people were friendly, but it was a grindingly hard life; groceries, coal and water had to be trailed up dirty, dark stairways and chamber pots emptied out at the back of the building on a common midden. At first Catherine had been shocked by the seeming hordes of gaunt, half-starved, rat-faced children who followed her, demanding a "piece". She had no idea what a piece was until a neighbour woman informed her that a piece was a slice of bread.

"Give them nothing," the woman advised, "or you'll never be rid of them, and mind your own weans for they'll take it off them."

Catherine felt sorry for these youngsters as many had scabby faces, sore eyes, runny noses and rickety bones, but she soon saw the wisdom of her neighbour's advice. Even though it seemed heartless, it was better to chase them away in the beginning than to be mobbed every time she went outside. The noise in the building was unrelenting. By day, doors slammed continually. Children cried and shouted and bullied and stole food from each other. Women loudly scolded them and screamed at their neighbours. They fought endlessly over whose turn it was to keep the stairway and landing clean. At night the men came home drunk, either singing or fighting, and regularly beat their wives and children. The women supported each other when a child was born or died, both frequent occurrences. They sympathised over a black eye or a broken nose, and even though their territory was mean and miserable, they insisted that it was respected. A particularly savage row was fought between two of Catherine's neighbours, Eileen and Jemima, both seasoned street fighters. Jemima spent all morning cleaning the stairs and when some child went to the toilet on it, she blamed wee Jimmy, Eileen's son. But Eileen said it was Jemima's own son, wee Alex, who was the guilty party. Both children were about three years old. Eileen watched and waited until she finally caught wee Alex repeating the dirty deed. She gave him a couple of sharp smacks then marched him triumphantly up the stairs to Jemima's door. Jemima opened the door, looked from Eileen's smug face to her bare-arsed screaming son, then punched Eileen in the mouth. Eileen retaliated in kind and the row spilt out onto the landing, with all the other women leaning against their doorjambs watching, but not taking sides. The women punched, kicked, scrabbed, nipped, bit, ripped clothing and pulled each other's hair out in handfuls until finally they backed off panting and exhausted. There was no winner, but they were both satisfied. It relieved the tension and tedium of tenement living for a short while. Eileen stopped at Catherine's door and wiped the blood from her nose with the back of her hand. She explained that Jemima's son, wee Alex, "was runnin' roon with nae troosers on him an he was shittin' all o'er the place". She knew to look at it that the shit "wasnae her wee Jimmy's. Everyone kens their ane dirt."

Catherine listened but said nothing. She knew that she daren't take sides because she was an outsider and therefore very vulnerable. She stored Eileen's observation in the back of her mind for future use, as she realised the truth of it: "Everyone kens their ane dirt."

When there was a slow-down at the pits and Bryan decided to take the family back home to Cashel and the small mountain farm, Catherine wasn't sorry. The tenement was a hard place to rear children. On the mountain there were still moments of peace and quiet, but recently it was sometimes hard to find peace of mind.

Bryan was taking a long time to get warmed-up and relaxed after coming in from the chilly night air, but she knew he would tell her in his own good time why he was home late.

"You can't bate a good hot mug of tay," he remarked. "I called with me mother after I finished counting the sheep and was coming straight home from Umericam when I met Jem Redmond at the Crossroads. He asked me to come in for a bit of a crack and that's what kept me late. I had two half ones of whiskey."

Two half ones with Jem was a rare event and Catherine asked had something happened at the Crossroads.

"Well nothing much different than usual," Bryan replied, "except that Rosie Redmond was out and about again the night before."

Rosie Redmond was Jem and Shusie's aunt. She claimed to be a descendant of Redmond O'Hanlon, the sixteenth-century rapparee who operated on the Chancellor's Road near Newry, robbing the rich as they travelled to Dublin in their carriages. Redmond is said to have been betrayed and killed by his half-brother, Art, for a reward offered by the Redcoats. When Art left the body where it had fallen and went to summon the Redcoats, another cousin came along and cut off Redmond's head so that he couldn't be identified. Some say that

Redmond O'Hanlon was secretly buried in Killeavy Old Churchyard, but others say that he faked his own death and went off to Canada where he had a clatter of children and lived to a ripe old age. Regardless of what the truth might be, it is said that when a member of the O'Hanlon clan is dying, the headless ghost of Redmond, driving a death coach drawn by four black horses, comes back to escort him or her to the next world.

Rosie Redmond was now ready to board the death coach and join her ancestors. She lived upstairs at the Crossroads from where, until recently, she had ruled the roost. When she rapped with her stick on the floor to get attention, Shusie usually said to either Dan or Jem, "Gop the stairs. Spanny Doe want you," or sometimes it was, "Go and see what Fanny Dooglas is looking this time." She seldom gave Rosie her proper name. Recently, incredible though it seemed, there were rumours that Rosie, who was bedridden and dying, had been seen several times by reliable people out roaming the countryside.

"She can't be out and about," Catherine decided. "She's been laid up for years. I doubt them ones down there at the Crossroads are pulling our legs."

"Everyone's talking about it and they don't know how she manages to do it," Bryan informed her. "She's been seen out and about, but she doesn't leave the bed. Two young lads seen her walking in the trees at the foot of the garden the other night and thought Rosie was doting and rambled off and they ran in and told Shusie, but when Shusie went up to the room, there she was lying in the bed. An aul crippled woman wouldn't have got from the garden to the room that quick. And no matter what way she came in or went out she'd have to pass Shusie, and she didn't. Rosie isn't doting and she's not denying that she is out and about. She's waiting on the Coachman and she'll not go till he comes for her. And young Patsy Conlon came round the corner at the Crossroads in the dark the other night with no lights on the bicycle. He saw two sets of legs standing out on the road that looked like Jem and Dan talking, so he rode the bicycle in between them to give them a fright, but sure it wasn't them at all; it was Jem's aul mare and he rode smack into her belly, buckled the wheel on the bicycle and hit his head off the road. He's not feeling too smart at the minute."

Bryan stared into the fire for a moment or two before he spoke again.

"Sergeant Ennis was at the Crossroads the night too," he said finally. "He sent Jem out to cap me and bring me in. He walked with me as far as Ballinasack Bridge. He says that the Specials in Camlough barracks have the names of all the 4th Northern men round here and Hughie's name is on it along with all the other lads. They know where they live and all about them and they're likely to come looking for them. They're stationed at Ballymoyer House out be Whitecross, and the Crossroads is a good spot for them to watch the roads and get information. The RIC are getting done away with and the Specials are taking over. Ennis has to retire. He comes from Limerick but he can't take the family back there because the RIC men in the South are getting killed every day. It's a danger to their lives to be going about at all and their families are getting dog's abuse. He'll go to Scotland. His sister is married to a Donegal man and they have a pub in Glasgow. Isn't it a tarra the way things change? He was the man in charge, cock of the walk, and now he's the same as the rest of us. He doesn't like the Specials and they haven't much time for him ayther seeing as he's a Catholic. He warned me to be very careful and to trust nobody outside the family. He said the people giving information would surprise me, but he wouldn't tell me more than that."

Catherine felt her heart stop. She realised how dangerous the situation had become. Maybe the sergeant had told him who the informers were, but he wouldn't tell her.

"Well, he's a dacent man for an RIC man. He didn't have to tell you that," she said. "Hughie needs to be very careful. Sarah Cullen is up and down this road like a lintie. She's a rattling sort of girl forbye what she did to him and he still has a notion of her, but barring that she's Addy's granddaughter, what do we know about her? There's nothing for the likes of her round here, so what takes her coming back? Could it be her that's informing?"

"I don't know, but if she is, she's playing a very dangerous game and she'll come to a bad end. Addy has boys droppin' in after dark to play cards and sup a drop of drink and there would be plenty of talk about what's going on and who's doing it and she would have no bother getting any information. The right or wrong of it won't matter to the B men. But Addy would see the danger where the young one wouldn't, and she must think she's safe enough coming here," Bryan commented.

"Well, suppose you're right," Catherine agreed. "But she's always down at the Crossroads and that doesn't go unnoticed, and then she comes back on her own. The Special doesn't walk her home."

"No, it's a droll way of coortin," Bryan grinned. "He'd be the foolish man to go there his lone."

"Och, I'm weary in me bones the night, Bryan," Catherine said with a yawn. "I hope there's nothing coming on me. I'll say the Rosary in the bed. Sometimes life makes you tired."

"When you're tired of life sit down on a stone," Bryan advised unhelpfully.

She went off to bed, leaving him by the dying fire. He didn't hear the muted, contented chirping of the crickets because he was wondering about Sarah and what her role might be. Her loyalty lay with the Special and that made her dangerous to the IRA and to the family. The sergeant's warning was disturbing, and though he hadn't named Sarah outright, he had hinted that care was needed. A rumour was also spreading about the possible excommunication of the IRA. Bryan was reluctant to tell Catherine, because if Hughie was excommunicated and killed he wouldn't receive the last rites and would never get to Heaven and her prayers would be no good to him.

And he was about to add another burden to Catherine's life, but he didn't know how to broach it. His mother Ellen was no longer fit to live alone in Umericam and would have to move in with them. She was crabbed and crotchety, and though Catherine said little about her, good or bad, he knew they were wary of each other. He would convert the old milk house at the back of the kitchen into a bedroom for her and it would all have to be done before Christmas. But the pratas had to be gathered first. Hughie and Gerard wouldn't be helping this year, which left him short of hands. His intention was to get the pratas gathered as quickly as possible because the harvest field had become a dangerous place. The Tans shot farmers dead for sport like they were rabbits or pheasants, and the Specials were no better, but a body had to keep going; there was no help for it. He gathered himself wearily and went to bed. Sometimes a good night's sleep made things look a bit better in the morning.

The day of the prata picking was grey and cold with a steady mizzling rain, but barrin' two fut of snow they weren't dependent on the weather. Bryan had planted a few acres of pratas, along with turnips to feed the sheep and other vegetables that had to be harvested before the frost set in.

Oiney and Mickle Grant, Bryan's cousins, bachelor brothers from further up the mountain, came every year to help him gather the pratas. They were middle-aged and weather-beaten, strong and sturdy of frame, with beetling eyebrows shading eyes that crinkled and narrowed as light and conversation dictated. Oiney was the taller of the two, with fading brown hair, while Mickle was grizzly fair.

They gathered Bryan's pratas first, then Oiney and Mickle's, and so on until everybody in the neighbourhood had their crop picked and in. The girls were also expected to help, but Susan and Katy protested bitterly, while Brigid set to work and Mary and Jocko haunted the hedgerows in search of wildlife. As the patient jinnet pulled the plough through the sticky clay, Oiney scattered the pratas in a wide arc across the back of the drill with a graip. Full buckets were emptied into pits dug out at intervals around the field. The pits were long and low and resembled little earthen houses with triangular ends. When a pit was full, the pratas were covered over with straw and a thick layer of earth to keep the frost and snow out. Throughout the winter they were extracted as quickly as possible and the pit carefully resealed.

The children's hands soon became frozen, their fingertips swollen and painful. When Susan's hands turned cold and white, Bryan sent her home. Then Katy began to cry and he sent her home too. Brigid worked steadily. Heavy clay clung to her boots, slowing her down and sapping her energy. She tucked her cold hands into her armpits to try and warm them up, while Mary held her hands under the jinnet's nose.

Catherine brought bottles of tea and warm scones.

The men sat under the hawthorn hedge with their backs cushioned by the tufts of long grass on the ditch. The girls tried to reach the few haws that were left, but raindrops fell from the branches and ran down inside their upturned sleeves. More rain was expected and the tea break had to be short because the ground would get too muddy for the jinnet. Mickle and Oiney removed their caps to greet Catherine, then shyly scratched their heads and put them back on again. They discussed the latest news. The mail car had been stopped again near Forkhill and the mailbags removed by the IRA. Catherine worried that she wouldn't get letters from the lads in Canada. Oiney said that the mail had to be sent out; it was the law and sure if the IRA found a letter from the boys in Canada wouldn't they give it to Hughie to give to her. Catherine looked at him in surprise. That hadn't occurred to her. It had seemed a far more distant event.

"Mebbe you're right, Oiney," she said. "But it wouldn't look too good if I was getting me post from the IRA."

They speculated about the talks being held now in London. Collins wouldn't let them off with anything. He'd hill them off in Dublin till they had to give in to him. Things in the North didn't look good. There was trouble with the Specials all the time. Locally the sightings of Rosie Redmond were the main topic. Oiney thought it was a story put out by Shusie to get more people to go to the shop, while Mickle thought a thing like that would keep people away from the shop.

"Did you see her, Mary?" Mickle asked.

Mary nodded and everybody laughed.

"Ah God, Mary, you're a character!" Oiney grinned. "Where did you see her?"

She pointed up the hill towards the mountain. The adults smiled indulgently, while the other girls listened, boggle-eyed. The souls of the dead were said to come back if they couldn't settle in the other world, but Rosie wasn't even dead yet. What would they do if they met her?

"She came down the hill and then she just went down into the ground like this," she said.

She sank down slowly, curling into a ball as if the earth was absorbing her, then got up and ran off unconcerned. Well, that was Mary. The men threw the dregs of their tea into the hedge and the girls collected the mugs and tea bottles.

"You'd wonder what the likes of her does see that the rest of us doesn't. Do you mind the day she near drownded above in the flax hole?" Oiney said to Catherine.

The flax hole was by the roadside near to Oiney and Mickle's farm. It was deep and dangerous, the top of it covered with green scum and water lilies and wildflowers growing along the edges. The fence around it hadn't been maintained and had fallen down. Catherine had taken Mary with her on an errand and they met Oiney on the road near the flax hole. As the adults were talking, Mary tried to walk across the top of the flax hole. They heard a loud plop and saw her head about to disappear below the waterline. Catherine quickly groped in the murky water, found a plait and jerked Mary's head above the water, then Oiney waded in and lifted her out. She spluttered a bit, but otherwise seemed unharmed, oblivious to the dirty water dripping onto the road around her feet.

Every time they spoke of it, Oiney was on the point of draining the flax hole and fixing the fence, but he never did it. He knew that God was looking after Mary and she'd come to no harm.

"But what would be the end of her or the end of any of them?" Oiney wondered. "People getting killed all over Ireland and thousands of young lads lost beyant in the muck and the mire in France, sure they'll never be found. What is it all for?"

Catherine had no answer.

Mickle wondered what would happen now that the Unionists had got six counties and their own parliament. They had no need for Tans nor English nor anyone else because the Specials was their army. They would never hand the north of the country back to Dublin. They'd howl on to it till there wasn't a man jack left standin', nayther Protestant nor Catholic. United Ireland me arse. Collins and them would do well not to trust John Bull ayther.

Bryan agreed with that and quoted an aul neighbour Paddy Morgan, who had great hatred for the English over what they did to Napoleon. "Dirty, rotten, corrupted England, look what they did to Napoleon Bonnyparty, the greatest man that ever lived. When they couldn't bate him, they put him away out on an island in the middle of the ocean with a ket! A bloody ket! What would a man like that have to say to a ket or a ket have to say to him? And when they couldn't get the better of him there, they poisoned him."

As they tramped back to where the jinnet was tethered, it occurred to them that the travelling people or tinkers hadn't come by this year to pick pratas on the bigger farms. Something must have held them up. Coming to Cashel was part of their pattern. It would be unusual for them to go elsewhere.

By the time all the pratas were gathered it was almost dark and as Bryan carefully applied salve to the hacks on his hands, he told Catherine that Oiney had met Robert Dunbar and he would soon be coming by. Catherine was pleased. It had been almost a year since they'd seen him.

Robert Dunbar was a travelling man of uncertain origin, but he wasn't a tinker. He was possibly the younger son of a wealthy family who hadn't inherited anything, or maybe a defrocked priest. Perhaps he had fallen on hard times because of gambling debt or killing someone in a duel, or maybe it was to do with a woman. Women were always causing trouble for good men, but nobody really knew why he roamed about the country. He was an educated man in his late fifties, tall and striking in appearance, with greying hair, a long grey beard, bushy eyebrows and shrewd light-blue eyes. His coats were worn in layers, the outer one long and heavy and trailing the road. He carried a stout blackthorn stick and a green canvas sack. He called at all the houses in an area, imparting news and gossip, and always stayed the night at Bryan Grant's, where he got food to eat and to take away, hot water to wash himself, his hair or beard trimmed, and cobbling was available if his boots needed mending.

He was a welcome visitor in an area that was starved of information from the outside world. He could converse with everyone. He knew everything, from how well a new baby was thriving to the price of eggs. He could talk about politics and matters of law and if he didn't know the answer to a question, he would find it out and send word back. In one pocket he carried a whetstone to sharpen a small knife and in another he had onions, which he sliced into his tea. A visit from Robert was well worth waiting for.

The last time he had called, Biddy Kane had come to Bryan's to see him. She lived half a mile away on the same road as Oiney and Mickle. She was a solid, plain-faced woman in her sixties who tended to act nervous and fluttery. She had never married, never been axed, she said, and she had doggedly refused to be matched. Her first cousin had been married off at eighteen to a man three times her age and was sent to bed at nine o'clock every night. Biddy said she'd have none of that carry-on. She'd go to bed when she pleased. She wore bright, rainbow coloured shawls that she crocheted from different remnants of wool, and also had a trunk full of fancy hats, clothes and footwear that had been shipped to her by her relatives in America.

She had come traipsing over before dark to see if Bryan would help her to fix a stone wall that had collapsed. The wall was an excuse for the visit as she already knew that Robert was expected and didn't want to miss him.

Bryan invited her in and after some initial protestations she agreed to have a cup of tea. She stayed on past ten o'clock enjoying the crack and then, because it was a very dark night, Bryan offered to walk her home, but she refused, saying that it was only a hen's race up the road. He offered to lend her the hurricane lamp, but she said she was well used to tramping home in the dark after being out on her ceilidh. Sure what could befall her?

She fluttered off, wrapped in her colourful shawl, and Catherine washed the delft while Bryan and Robert lit up their pipes from the embers of the fire. It was past eleven o'clock when they heard a timid rapping. Who could it be? Robert stood up supportively as Bryan pulled the door open. Biddy fell in onto the floor. She was dishevelled and bedraggled with her hair hanging down round her face. Her shawl was matted with leaves and grass and the scalloped edges were beginning to unravel. Livid scratches covered her hands and arms and her face was streaked with blood. They were shocked by her appearance. Luckily the children were fast asleep.

"Good God, Biddy," Catherine cried, "what happened to you?" She rushed forward and helped Biddy from the floor to a chair by the fire, then wrung the dishcloth out and began to clean up the scratches.

Biddy took the dishcloth and flapped it in front of her face as if to create more air. Bryan swiftly poured her a mug of tea with a good measure of whiskey added.

Robert stroked his beard and watched Biddy with a very concerned expression. They all waited anxiously as she gulped down the tea, and when she had regained her composure, she related her incredible story.

"I went out the gate and up the road with not a bit a bother on me," she began. "Och, it was dark when I came out and I couldn't see a styme, but I could see rightly after a few minutes and I trudged along till I came to the Fairy Crossing."

Here she paused and looked around at her audience, who were still and attentive. They were well aware that nobody knew the boundaries between the human and fairy territories as precisely as Biddy.

"If I'd given heed to your advice and took the lamp with me, Bryan, I would a knowed not to stop there," she continued. "But stop I did to get me bearings and sure I must have stopped on their side of the crossing. I wasn't standin' more than a minute, but the king of the fairies was waiting and he lit on me like a divil. Then, though I seen or heard no signal, the rest of them lit on me too. They had swords with them that were like, like big hat pins, and they stuck them into me and pulled at me shawl trying to drag me and drive me across the line. I hit out at them as best I could, but it was like trying to bate off a swarm of wasps. Then I managed to pull meself back across the line where they couldn't touch me. What they wanted with an aul woman like me I don't know, but you can bet your life it was for nothing good. When I gathered meself together they had spun me round and I was facing for your house again, Bryan, and I took that as a sign that I was better to go back the way I come and start again, so I blessed meself and came on back down."

"Blessing yourself takes the bad luck out of turning back," Catherine murmured.

"I think you made the right decision, Biddy. You seem to have fought a fierce fight and I don't know how you managed to escape, but you're a very brave woman," Robert said solemnly.

Bryan handed her another cup of tea, Catherine shook her head as he began to add whiskey to the tea. Biddy had taken a wee drop earlier and more was maybe not a good idea. Then she gave an involuntary shudder.

"I know it'll sound like the ravings of a mad woman," she tried to joke. "But I think there might be one of them still on me back. I wouldn't like to think that I was bringing them into the house."

"I'll throw some holy water on you and then I'll have a look," Catherine volunteered. "The holy water should get rid of them."

With all the precautions taken, she lifted the bottom of Biddy's shawl and peeled it slowly up over her head. Bryan stood by with the tongs. They found no fairies on Biddy's back, and when she had settled sufficiently, Bryan walked her home. He grasped her firmly by the arm as they approached the Fairy Crossing, but the fairy king neither lit on her nor looked at her, and Bryan delivered her safely into her house.

When he returned they discussed what might have happened to her but could come to no conclusion. The scratches looked like briars might have caused them.

"Tell me this and tell me no more, did either of you ever see or catch a fairy?" Robert asked seriously. "Because it appeared to me that you had done this before."

"Not at all," Catherine said, laughing. "I wouldn't know a fairy from a moth. I don't know what he was going to do with the tongs."

"Well, you never know," Bryan said. "If it was an aul one with a bad leg, I might have been able to get it."

"We shouldn't make jokes about them," Catherine warned. "They might be listening and you wouldn't want to bring them on you."

The next morning Bryan went up the road to see what might have attacked Biddy. At the Fairy Crossing he saw strands of brightly coloured wool, similar to Biddy's shawl, clinging to the long, thick briars that grew from high up on the ditch down to the edge of the road. He concluded that Biddy had misjudged the bend. She must have turned too soon and walked into the ditch. Then as she struggled to free herself, she became more entangled in the briars. And there alone in the darkness she fought a life-and-death struggle against the fairy swords and hands that were trying to drag her across into their world. Well, I'll take nothing away from her story, thought Bryan as he plucked the wool from the briars. Biddy had very little excitement in her life and the winter months were long and dark. She would be the star of many a ceilidh and wake as she related her adventure. People enjoyed a good fairy story, especially when the intended victim was able to outwit the little bastards. Biddy's story would be told and dissected round turf fires for many years to come.

Twelve months had swiftly passed since Biddy vanquished the fairy king, and Robert Dunbar was due to pass by again. Bryan proposed that they should invite Biddy to come along for the night's crack.

"She'll be over anyway when she hears he's about," Catherine said.

"I'll have to make sure that she gets safe home this time," Bryan grinned. "You don't bate the fairies twice."

They sat up until late in the evening, but there was no sign of Robert Dunbar that night.

The next day was All Hallows Eve and Catherine made a barmbrack and put rings and pennies in it to surprise whoever got those portions. The person who got the ring would soon get married and the coin foretold riches. These predictions weren't taken seriously. Vegetables were prepared to make colcannon and also sliced pratas that would be cooked in lard on the big iron frying pan. Nuts and apples were set out in bowls. The apples were for the ducking games and the nuts were for the matchmaking game. A freshly baked apple tart that also had money and rings inside was set out to cool on the windowsill. It was a busy morning, but if Robert Dunbar arrived in the evening there was the promise of storytelling and neighbours calling. A woman's reputation for hospitality could be made or destroyed by the amount of food she had prepared. Bryan might play a few tunes on the melodeon and there could be dancing. A night like that might lift Catherine's spirits quicker than an afternoon praying for the departed, although it didn't do to neglect them either. As one aul fella once said, "God is good and the Divil's not so bad ayther." It was better to try and keep the humour on them all, Catherine decided.

That morning Bryan told her that his mother was moving up from Umericam before Christmas. Although she'd known for some time that this would eventually happen, she had mixed feelings. Every year she prayed hard for Ellen's continuing good health – "Just give me one more year without her, God" – but now time had run out. Ellen was crabbed and she could thole that, but not if she interfered with the rearing of the children. Bryan promised to discuss this matter with his mother, but would she give him any heed? Catherine was used to having the run of her own hearth and it wouldn't be easy sharing it with another woman, especially her mother-in-law.

"Och, sure she'll be company for you when I'm away in Scotland," Bryan said.

Company, me arse, thought Catherine sourly. I'll have to put up with her sniping at me till you get back. She's not my mother, and that's what makes the difference. Catherine's mother had passed away a few years previously, and on occasions when she disagreed with Ellen she wondered why she was still there and her poor mother gone.

The ceremonies for All Souls' Day were held in the afternoon. It was a cold, grey day as Catherine and the girls set off from home. The hedges were dripping and there was a threat of heavy fog later that night. At Ballinasack Bridge they paused to wait for the neighbouring women and children who were going in the same direction.

Brigid stood under a beech tree near the bridge and looked up curiously as a steady flow of leaves and twigs descended from the branches onto her head. Then Eugene Murphy, a boy her own age, jumped nimbly from the branch to the bridge and then onto the road.

"Is that the boy who only went to school for one day?" Katy demanded in a loud whisper as she tugged at Brigid's arm.

"Yes, that's him, that's Eugene Murphy." Brigid nodded.

Katy and Susan stared at him, fascinated, and suddenly Brigid was proud to be associated with this boy who was quite famous in the locality.

His mother had died in childbirth and he had been reared by his father, John, on a remote farm some miles from Cashel. He and Brigid had started school on the same day, but John decided that life would be too lonely for him without Eugene, and when he came to the school to collect him, he asked what he had learnt. Eugene, not wanting to disappoint him, or perhaps to reassure him that he was as clever as they both believed, read from his reading book: "Rare, brer this house will tear." The words were not in the book, but his father couldn't read either, and even if he could, it wouldn't have made any difference.

"You've got as much larnin' the day as will do you," he declared. "There'll be no need for you to be coming back to this school."

He threw the book into the ditch and with that Eugene became a legend amongst the other children. He was only a small boy, but he was very confident and articulate and had big brown eyes like Jocko. He deigned to walk along with the girls while his father tied their ass to a bush near the bridge and walked with Catherine and the other women.

"Are you the one that's afflicted?" Eugene demanded of Mary, who was walking backwards in front of him.

"I don't know." Mary shrugged. "What's afflicted?"

"I don't know." He shrugged as well. "Me Da said one of youse was afflicted and never went out. I seen Brigid and them two before but I never seen you. You must be the one that's afflicted."

Mary screwed up her face and regarded him for a long moment then ran off.

When Susan shyly asked him would he ever go back to school, he said he didn't have to because his da said he had all the larnin' he needed. When Brigid said she was learning geography, he didn't know what it was, but when she explained that it was about maps and to know where places are so you wouldn't get lost, Eugene replied that he always knew where he was.

Susan and Katy looked at him admiringly because he must know everything. Brigid didn't believe that he knew everything, but she envied him because he didn't have to wait in terror for his hair to be yanked out if he couldn't answer a question. In the boys' school they got a clatter across the ear with anything that was handy for the master – a ruler, a book or the globe of the world, and he didn't hesitate to kick them hard up the arse if they moved too slowly. Eugene was a very lucky boy.

At the chapel the girls followed their mother, mimicking what she did. The All Souls' ceremonies were tedious for children, but they had been warned to behave. Mary followed them around, shouting loudly as she prayed in a continuous litany of "Hail Mary, holy Mary." Then she would pause and jump forward in a giant rabbit hop. The old women who whispered like rustling leaves as they said their beads drew their shawls tighter and stepped back to give her room.

"God has a special place for her and she's great at the praying, Catherine, God bless her," they murmured.

Catherine ignored the desperate pleas from the girls to "do something about Mary" and determinedly prayed for the happy repose of the souls of her relatives. When they sat down in the chapel for the service, Mary rambled up and down, swinging from the edge of the seats out into the centre of the aisle. On the road for home the sky was already lowering into dark. Eugene and his father walked along with them.

"Can you say this quick, Brigid?" Eugene piped. "Three grey geese in a green field grazing, grey were the geese and green was the grazing."

Brigid managed to say it successfully, but Katy and Susan got all mixed up and almost collapsed on the grass verge from too much giggling.

"And can you say this one quick?" he asked slyly. "Two asses drawing ashes from Carrer's ash hole."

Brigid knew this was a trap and if she got mixed up she'd say "Carrer's asshole" but she rose to the challenge. She managed to say it once without difficulty, but when Eugene challenged her to say it ten times, she got mixed up after five while he triumphantly completed ten. He asked them could they whistle and chew oaten meal, but as they had no oaten meal with them they couldn't try it. Then he made them try to rub their bellies and pat their heads at the same time. This caused great amusement and when they reached Ballinasack Bridge they were in high spirits. When the adults had finished off their crack Eugene clambered onto the ass's back, and sitting straight and proud like the picture of Jesus in the girls' catechism, he was led by his father into the twilight. Brigid suddenly felt a bit sad. He might be the smartest boy in the world and never have to go to school, but he had no mammy. He wouldn't get barmbrack or fried pratas, play games or listen to ghost stories tonight, and there were no children living nearby that could play with him.

Chapter 4

Catherine swung the frying pan over the fire and cooked the sliced-up pratas accompanied by hissing and sudden small flashes of smoke and flame as the hot lard spat out onto the embers of the turf. The colcannon was heated up and the table set. Bryan lit and adjusted the wicks on the oil lights. When everything was ready, Catherine served the food, which looked delicious and smelt appetising. The long walk to and from the chapel had sharpened their appetites and they ate with relish. Then the barmbrack was sliced and buttered and served with cups of tea. When Susan found the ring, Bryan observed that she'd make a fresh young bride and it would be a lucky man that would get her. But Susan wasn't impressed. She'd wanted the penny, but Brigid had got it and a penny would buy her many items. The possibilities were endless.

Then the girls ducked for apples in a half basin of water set on a chair. Mary didn't like getting her face wet and her teeth weren't sharp enough to sink into an apple. Jocko danced on his hind legs in the middle of the melee, with his front paws raised as if guiding a partner. Then Katy and Susan knocked the basin over and the water rippled across the stone floor and lapped round the boots of Robert Dunbar, who had just entered. He looked about him with amusement then thumped his blackthorn stick three times on the floor.

"God bless all here!" he proclaimed in a deep voice. "'Pon me sowl, Bryan, there's great frivolity in this house."

The children were startled by the sudden appearance of a big man with a loud voice and scuttled off to hide behind the settle bed but re-emerged when they realised it was Robert.

Bryan invited him up to the fire and then went out to get some mailbags to dry the floor, while Catherine dished up a plate of food and set it on the table.

"Get that under your ribs Robert and it'll warm you up," she advised. "There's barmbrack and apple tart when you're ready."

Bryan brushed the water out and dried the floor with the sacks, and when the girls pulled their stools up to the fire for the matchmaking game, he sat down with Robert at the table.

"Are you the afflicted one?" Mary asked Robert as she peered closely at him.

He studied her, straight-faced, for a moment before answering. "I suppose I am. We're all afflicted in one way or another, Mary," he said with a smile.

Catherine allocated the girls three hazelnuts each and placed them close to the fire. The nuts had to be given the name of a boy. Susan, Katy and Brigid named boys that they met on the way to school, but Mary chose Hughie, Jocko and her father. The others objected and in the ensuing argument the fun was gone and they lost interest in the game. It was time for Bryan to tell them a Halloween story. He squeezed in between the girls and related thrilling encounters he'd had with ghosts and fairies, and as the story ascended beyond the bounds of possibility, Catherine took a large pair of woollen socks from her darning basket and gave them to Robert.

"You're a good woman," he said gratefully. "And in the nick of time too, my stockings are down to the last thread. I may have a blister on my heel."

But he said he would attend to all that in the morning. His feet could do with a good soaking and an application of methylated spirits. A travelling man had to have good feet. When Catherine told him to hang his greatcoat on the back of the door, he said he would hang it outside for fear the lice would get on the children. She was unperturbed by this statement; lice of all sorts were a fact of life and were dealt with as they appeared. He asked about Biddy Kane, and Catherine said the children went over to tell her he was expected, but she said she couldn't leave the house of a Hallow's Eve night, which wasn't like her.

"Then I'll call with her in the morning before I leave," Robert said.

Bryan finished his story and walked out with Robert to hang his greatcoat in the barn. Catherine got the girls ready for bed and tucked them in, then sprinkled them with holy water from the corked bottle she kept on the dresser. When the men came back from the barn, they arranged themselves comfortably in front of the fire and Bryan asked Robert what was new on his travels. Catherine knew they had already discussed matters too serious to be shared with women, but that was the way of it.

Robert said that he was on his way round the mountain when a young whippersnapper jumped out from behind a ditch and stuck a gun in his back. He dropped his bag and put his hands in the air and all he could hear was laughter. When he turned around, his captors were Hughie and Gerard Molloy. They asked him up to their camp, but the path was too steep for him, although he could see a squad of them sitting outside. They said the truce was still on, and anyway they could see the Specials coming from miles away. When Robert mentioned partition, Hughie said that there was no border yet and there never would be if they could stop it. They would never agree to the country being split and a border put through it. Catherine asked Robert if Hughie still had a cough. Robert said they were all coughing and scratching. It was scabies, but they called it the republican itch or the grass itch. He'd got it himself in kip shops where people all shared the same blankets. It was a bugger when you warmed up and itched away like billyo. No amount of scratching would ease it and the skin could get torn and infected. Bryan said he'd also got it in working men's lodgings. The only cure was a bottle from the chemist shop that you had to plaster on all over you, and by right all your clothes and bedclothes should be burnt as well, but no man could afford to do that. Robert revealed the cure that aul men that walked the roads used to ease the itch. It was urine, but he didn't say that in front of Catherine.

Robert told them that Belfast was reported to be like a slaughterhouse, with gangs of Protestants roaming the streets murdering Catholics every night of the week. The city was drowning in a sea of blood and carnage and no end was in sight.

Mary stirred in the settle bed. She was awake and listening, but was cool to the touch and seemed to be all right.

"It's atrocity and reprisal followed by atrocity and reprisal. How long more it can go on, nobody knows. It's not safe for a man to walk the roads," he concluded.

"How come you can walk the roads, Robert, and neither the authorities nor the rebels give you any bother?" Catherine asked.

The men exchanged a look before Robert replied.

"I'm a tramp, Catherine," he said simply. "And I have had rough treatment from the Specials, but I get well out of the way when I hear the tenders coming. They took pot shots at me too, but their aim wasn't very good. Those in authority think of me as a vagrant and not worth bothering about."

Catherine suspected that he carried information between different divisions of the IRA. Bryan trusted him and the lads wouldn't have invited him to their camp if they suspected him of spying.

Partition and what form it might take was the next topic of conversation.

"Nobody knows what they'll do," Robert told them. "Some say that they'll blow up the roads that lead into the South and make a border that way. The roads over by Fermanagh are mined already, but they might put a fence or a wall around whatever counties the Unionists get to keep."

"And what will happen to the people that do all their business in Dundalk?" Catherine asked. The local people went there to do their banking, shopping and trading, and the post for the area was dispatched from the town.

"It will cause great disruption because everything to do with the partitioned counties will be administered by the Northern government in Belfast," Robert told her. "Look no more to Dublin for your authority. Unless there's a big turnaround from the English government, the Unionists will rule in the North for many a day to come, because once they have the institutions in place, it will be hard to shift them."

"What about farmers that have ground in Louth as well as in Armagh? What will happen to them?" Catherine wondered.

"We'll have to wait and see, Catherine. I have no idea what might be in the minds of the governments," Robert said.

"There's no sign of things settling here ayther, Robert," Bryan told him. "The big Protestant houses were broke into and guns took out of them. Brookes' Mill in Forkhill and the Rectory at Mullaghbane was burnt and the Methodist church at Crossmaglen was ruined, but we know who's doing that. But it's them burning stacks of hay all over the country with no thought for the poor animals that will be left starved and roaring with the hunger in the wintertime and nothing there to feed them. That's what I don't understand."

"The whole point, Bryan, is to lay the land to waste. The Protestants have the big farms and the good land and the IRA want to make it impossible for them to live here. But the Protestants have their own parliament now and with the backing of the Specials and the British army they will beat the Catholics back into submission again. Many old grudges will be settled by both sides and between neighbours. But in Belfast they're killing Catholics on a large scale, and I don't think that's happening round here."

"It would be aisy to find them in Belfast, Robert, for they all live in their own areas," Bryan told him. "The killing here is mebbe not on the same scale yet, but it might come to that. People are being shot as informers and they say it's the IRA that's doing it, and when the Specials are out on patrol and get shot, they shoot innocent Catholic men in retaliation. They went to a house in Newry looking for a man and when they didn't get him they took an unfortunate fella from another house, threw him into a lorry and took him away. He was found dead in a shed the next day. He was dragged along the road behind the lorry and lumps were tore off him. Then they shot him and cut his heart out and left it sitting on the top of his body. He had nothing to do with the IRA or anybody else."

"And they run over a wee child at Dernaroy with a car," Catherine told him. "Wee John McNally, his mother Brigid has the cure of the whooping cough. He was her first child and the poor wee lad must have toddled out in front of them. They say they were that drunk they didn't even know they done it. They thought they hit a bump on the road. Brigid's brother went to the barracks and kicked and hammered at the door to get at them, but the neighbours pulled him away for fear they'd kill him too. And I'm sure you heard about the trainload of soldiers and horses that went off the tracks at Adavoyle in June when His Majesty come over to open the new parliament below in Belfast."

"Yes, I heard about it at the time, but I was down the country," said Robert. "Was there a bomb on the line?"

"No, it wasn't a bomb. There was three trainloads of soldiers going back to the camp at the Curragh and the 4th Northern lifted part of the track. They intended to get them all, but the first two trains got through and the last one came off the rails and fell down the bank," Bryan said.

"A lot of the soldiers were injured and a train guard was killed. The horses were in the car at the back of the train and them that wasn't killed outright had to be destroyed. People that seen it said it was like a slaughterhouse."

"A young lad from over that way was out pulling thistles in a field near the track and the soldiers shot him dead because he was wearing gloves. They thought it was him put a bomb on the line. Sure if he put the bomb on the line he was hardly going to stand there with his two arms as long as each other waiting for it to go off," Catherine pointed out. "Och, they were going to shoot the first one they seen no matter if he did it or not. We didn't know what way to turn after it. I was afraid of me life and I didn't know whether to let the children out or keep them in. We were waiting day and night for the Tans and the army to burn and destroy the whole countryside, but they were no worse than ever they were. They don't even have to leave the barracks to keep comither on us."

The soldiers rounded up a party of local men and boys and ordered them to dig a deep pit to bury the dead horses. They stood over them with guns at the ready until it was finished. But shortly after that, Kelly, the horse slaughterer from Newry, got leave from the authorities to dig up the horses again and take them away for rendering.

"It's an ill wind, as they say, that doesn't blow somebody good," Robert said. "It's very hard to imagine what that would have been like – people, animals, the train wreckage and carnage all mangled up together. They say that's what it was like over in France during the war, with the soldiers and horses, dead and dying, all tangled up together in the barbed wire."

"Sure it must have been a holy tarra at Adavoyle too. Mary kept saying, 'All the king's horses and all the king's men,' over and over till she near put me astray in the head," Catherine told him.

"It's hard on the children listening to all this talk of carnage and shootings," Robert murmured. "And we can only hope that Collins and the Irish deputation get a good deal in London and that it will be over. But can the English play fair and will the deal suit everyone? It's hard to know."

"Collins is the MP for South Armagh and the people in this part of the country are depending on him. Twenty thousand turned out to see him when he came to Armagh last September," Bryan told Robert. "One end of the city was done up till all was no more with flags and bunting and Hughie and the lads went down to see him and to help with the crowds. People went from Mullaghbane and Camlough, too, and from all over the countryside. They said he spoke well and that he'll be talking for the Northern people, too, when he's beyant. After that he came up along with Aiken and Harry Boland to see the training camp at Killeavy. He's a clever man that wasn't afraid to stand up to them in Dublin, but can he outfox them on their own ground?"

"The weight of the nation is on their shoulders," Robert said. "These negotiations are his only chance and it's a hard task."

"Aye, they have their work cut out in London and good luck to them, for you can't trust the English," Brian said bitterly. "The country is split in two already. The courts are set up in Belfast and we know damn well that's to deal with us Catholics. Six counties, if that's what they settle for, isn't much of a country. Can you have a country that small?"

Before Robert could answer, the door burst open and Hughie and Gerard rushed into the kitchen and stood there white-faced and pinched-looking.

Catherine jumped up in alarm thinking they had been shot, but Hughie reassured her that they were all right and could she make them a drop of tay.

They eased onto the hobs to warm up and there was a clatter as a revolver fell from Gerard's jacket. Hughie quickly retrieved it and shoved it deep into the pocket of his long overcoat. Out of the corner of her eye, Catherine saw what happened, but said nothing.

"Now, get that into you and tell us what has yis in such a state," she commanded as she gave them the tea. "Were yis followed?"

"I hope not," Hughie said fervently.

He looked at Gerard and they both laughed nervously then revealed that they'd just seen the Headless Coachman. They were lying out near the Crossroads waiting for the Specials and heard a strange noise coming nearer and nearer and then they saw the coach with four black horses pulling it, coming down the road. When Bryan wondered had someone been playing a trick on them, Hughie replied that if they were they had a damn good coach and horses. It had definitely been the death coach, but they hadn't been able to see the driver.

The coach was rattling on the road, but the horses' hooves made no sound. Then it went on by and they didn't know where it went. Catherine was a bit disgusted that they'd lit out for the wee hill behind Addy's and didn't know if the coach had stopped at the Crossroads. Bryan would have to take a run over there in the morning to find out if Rosie Redmond was still with them.

"Oh, that reminds me, I must call tomorrow morning with that girl, Biddy Kane," Robert said.

Regardless of her age Biddy would always be referred to as a girl because she had never married and was therefore unknown to man.

"Aye, we had Biddy's drama with the fairies the last time you were here." Catherine laughed. "There's always something happening."

"It's that time of year," Robert said. "Fairies and apparitions don't seem to be about so much in the summer nights."

"The fairies are always about, Robert," Catherine informed him seriously.

Robert inclined his head in acknowledgement of this fact.

Bryan suggested that Hughie and Gerard should stay in the loft overnight and they readily agreed. One brush with eternity was enough for that night, and guns were no protection against the supernatural. Catherine gave them blankets and also set a couple aside for Robert.

"Bless yourselves before you go out," she advised them. "You wouldn't know what else is abroad this night and you are as well to be ready for anything."

They shrugged agreeably, draped the blankets over their shoulders, blessed themselves at the holy water font beside the door and went out to the loft. The back door of the loft opened onto the mountain, providing an escape route if the Specials did a sweep. Bryan stoked up the fire and Robert swaddled himself in a blanket and settled in for the night.

Before dawn a rap on the window informed them that Hughie and Gerard were leaving. They wished them good luck then turned over to sleep for another hour or so.

Later that morning Robert chatted with the girls before they went to Mass on All Saints' Day. When Katy asked would he be there for Christmas dinner, Robert said his relations in Monaghan would give him a bed, for which he was grateful, as he didn't often sleep in a bed. The girls nodded and wondered what that would be like. He sat on the wall and cut his toenails, pared his corns, applied methylated spirits to the soles of his feet and then put his new stockings on. He wrapped the package of food Catherine gave him in a large, coloured handkerchief and placed it inside his coat.

Mary lifted Robert's blackthorn stick and thumped it three times on the floor.

"God bless all here," she cried and everyone laughed. Encouraged by this she began walking around in a tight circle thumping the stick off the floor.

"Atrocity and reprisal," she chanted as she circled faster and faster. "Atrocity and reprisal."

Catherine took the stick away and spun her towards the bedroom, giving Bryan the nod to go on with Robert and the girls.

At the fork in the road the girls turned right towards the chapel, while Robert and Bryan went up the hill to Biddy Kane's house.

Biddy was already up and struggling to get the fire going. She was a bit caught out by having two handsome men call on her at such an early hour, but even with her hair straggling out of the red Spanish comb and a black streak of soot across her forehead, she managed to appear coquettish. She would relate this story in another house. Robert wouldn't leave the country without calling to see her and the early hour made no difference at all – she was always up early, with the smoke rising before the scrake of dawn. But she was having some difficulty walking, and when the kettle was on the boil, she sat down abruptly as if something in her had given way. Then they noticed that she was wearing a man's boot on one foot and a woman's on the other.

"I'm sure youse are wondering why I'm sprockling about in me father's aul boot," she trilled nervously.

"Not at all, my dear lady," Robert said gallantly. "You may do what you choose in the privacy of your own house. If you hadn't drawn my attention to it, I wouldn't have noticed it at all."

"Aye, what befell you, Biddy?" Bryan asked.

"Och, it's a simple enough complaint, Bryan. When I took the goat in to milk her I went over on me ankle on a stone and the blooming thing went up like a bap. Och, I can thole it well enough, but when it gets the better of me I have to sit down. Early to bed and early to rise makes a woman's feet twice their size," Biddy explained with a laugh. "If I hadn't me father's aul boot on I wouldn't be able to get about at all."

"Did you hear the death coach last night?" Bryan asked.

"I didn't and I wouldn't be the one to go looking for it," Biddy declared. "But if Rosie Redmond doesn't go with him soon, she'll be left sitting there."

"Well, if he came last night, she might be away with him already," Bryan laughed. "We're going down to the Crossroads now to find out if she's still there."

"She'll be there. I get no feeling that she's gone beyant, though she's getting pulled in that direction. Now answer me this, Robert, if you can at all," Biddy said. "Some people say that the new border will be dug out like a big sheugh and we'll have to lep across it, and others say it's to be a wall and that they'll cover the top of it with the barbed wire they took home from the war. And they say that once the border is put there we won't be let out of the North of Ireland ever again and them that's on the other side won't be let into it. I've cousins over in Cavan that I might never see again. Did you hear anything about that at all?"

"My dear lady, I have heard many things, but I don't know if any of them are true," Robert replied. "However, as soon as I acquire the correct information, I'll let you know."

"They say that people are dying with typhoid fever in Dundalk, and a potato was dug up that was near four pound weight and new wee baby lambs were born at the end of September, and me mother's clock stopped the other day for the first time ever that I recall. Were any of them things in Colmcille's prophesies? Is the end of the world coming, Robert?" Biddy asked anxiously.

"I don't know, Biddy," Robert answered, bemused. "It will always be the end of the world for some people."

Biddy clasped both hands to her breast and inclined her head in acknowledgement.

"Thank you, Robert. We can always count on you for telling us the right way of things. Bryan, would you ask Catherine would she come over with a poultice for me ankle?" Biddy asked. "I'm crippled with this fut and she has the cure. It's ayther nettles with the white of an egg or chickweed and mebbe you boil them, but I don't know for me head's demented. Someone was rapping on the window last night, but I didn't open the door. Whoever it was didn't spake or make himself known to me."

"You did the right thing, and don't open it for anyone after dark unless you know who it is," Bryan said. "We'll head on down the road now and trouble you no more. I'll ask Catherine to come over and have a look at you and rest that fut if you can. Here, put it up there on that aul milking stool. They say it helps to take the swelling down."

"I'm afraid I feel quite useless when it comes to injuries," Robert admitted. "But don't worry about the rapping, Biddy. Those that arose last night will have gone back into the next world by today."

"It's doubtful that they came from the next world," Biddy said wisely. "But it's enough for me that a gentleman such as yourself takes time out of his travelling to call on me. God bless you and take care of you on the roads of Ireland."

They took their leave of Biddy and started for the Crossroads, but she came hobbling out behind them.

"Oh, Robert," she cried, "I can't let you go without asking you about the magic lantern show. It only came into me head this minute. I heard there was a magic lantern show in Dundalk every week except in the holy season of Lent. Could that be right?"

"Yes, there is a place in Park Street in Dundalk," Robert told her. "It's called a picture palace now and the magic lantern show is a picture show. I've heard it's a marvel and well worth seeing."

"Well, a picture palace, imagine that! But we might never see it," Biddy said sadly. "This new border will stop us going many a place and you daren't go out anyway with the times that's in it, and I hear Dundalk is as bad as the next place."

She went back into the house and closed the door. The men stood there uncertainly for a minute before continuing their journey.

"She's always in some sort of a pickle." Bryan smiled. "She acts like a young girl but she's shrewd enough. I wonder who was rapping on her window of a Halloween night? They don't mean any harm, but they forget that she's there on her own."

"Yes, sometimes the Halloween tricks can get out of hand." Robert sighed. "An old couple I knew were nearly smothered when the door was tied and cayenne pepper was put down the chimney."

"It happens round here too," said Bryan. "A man fell asleep in front of the fire after a few bottles of porter and they put a slate on his chimney. He was lucky that the fire was near out. And at one house they put an ass into the kitchen. Hughie and the lads rap Biddy up at all hours and she makes them a feed, but we know it wasn't them last night. I told her it was dangerous them coming there, but she says it's company for her and she goes all over the place on her ceilidh and finds out things for them. She might act soft, but it suits her purpose."

"Yes, I can see that there's more to Biddy than meets the eye," Robert murmured.

They emerged out onto the broad road and soon they had a clear view of the shop at the Crossroads.

"Not much stir down yonder," Bryan observed. "No wait, I think I see smoke rising, or is that mist? No, it's smoke. If she's up and has the fire lit we should be safe enough."

A few forlorn, red-nosed town-goers huddled against the wall, shivering as they waited for a lift in a passing trap or a car. Either Shusie wasn't out of bed or she was in no mood for early-morning gossip. It wasn't reassuring, but Bryan braced himself and rapped the door. They heard a sharp rasp of bolts, then the door opened a little and she appeared, pulling a long coat over her nightwear.

"Oh, it's yourself, Bryan Grant," she said neutrally, "and Robert Dunbar. For God's sake come on in quick and don't let the hate out. You're early afoot. I'm only after twirling the bellows and putting the kettle on the crook this minute. I'll be the talk of the country."

"If you have the name of early rising you can sleep till dinner time," Bryan observed.

Shusie eyed him for a long moment.

"You would know all about that," she said sourly. "Now tell me what's wrong? Sit down! Sit down, for Heaven's sake. Sure you're here now. Why are men always in the way, hanging about like wet overcoats and taking up room? Did something happen to Mary?"

The two men looked at each other bemused, and then Robert indicated that Bryan should relate the tale.

"No, we called early because we thought that you had trouble," Bryan explained. "Hughie and Gerard said they saw the death coach and the Headless Coachman last night and that he was on his way to the Crossroads. We thought that mebbe he took Rosie."

Shusie laughed a short bitter laugh. "She's not away yet," she said grimly. "We were sitting up with her and Jem went to make cocoa and I thought she had passed beyant, but she sat up straight in the bed and when I looked out the window, he lifted the whip and away he went horses and all."

"Pardon my ignorance, but if the Coachman has no head, how does she talk to him?" Robert asked, puzzled.

"My dear man," said Shusie with great patience. "The Spirits need neither head nor body, but he's not going to keep coming back for ever."

"Why wouldn't he?" Bryan smiled. "You'd think a man like that would have nothing but time."

"Aye, laugh, you crater you, laugh!" Shusie said crossly. "If he doesn't take her, I'll be stuck with her rambling round here and her dead. It's tough enough putting up with her when she's living."

Robert suddenly smacked the palm of his hand against his forehead. "I've got it," he said with satisfaction. "She's a wraith!"

"She's a what?" said Shusie.

"She's a wraith," Robert said. "A spirit that is able to leave a body and return to it while the person is still living."

"She's a bloody nuisance," Jem said grimly as he came through the door and into the room. The sleep was still in his eyes as he vaguely scratched his chest with one hand and adjusted his cap with the other. "I'll make us all some tay if you want to get clothes on you, Shusie," he offered. "Half the time we don't know if she's living or dead, but she'll not go till she's ready. A fadge of bread?"

As he positioned a large bannock of soda bread under his arm and began slicing it upwards with sawing motions, they feared for his throat and chin.

"Ask him about yon tay," Shusie shouted.

"Aye, Robert, would you read that for me?" Jem asked.

"Mazawattee Tea," Robert read. "Tea for the connoisseur."

"What does that mane?" Jem asked.

"Mazawattee? I think that could be a place in India where the tea is grown, but I'm not sure," Robert informed him.

"No, not the Mattiewatsy, Robert, that other word, what does that mane?" Jem persisted.

"A connoisseur? That would be a person who knows what good tea is," Robert explained. "It's a French word."

"Tell Shusie how you say it," Jem said.

Shusie came to the door and listened to him as he pronounced the word again, then she shook her head. "Right," she said decisively, "there'll be no poster put up for Mattsiewatty tay. Quinn's the Milestone tay is all the name it'll get in this shop, no matter what it says on the tay chest." She closed the door behind her, leaving the men faintly puzzled.

"It's that connis hoor thing," Jem explained. "The salesman said that's what it was, but smart boys would be asking what did it mane and how did you say it and then women would get insulted and the priest would be sent for. Do you see what I mane? Shusie doesn't like anyone trying to make an eejit of her. It makes her crabby."

He glanced nervously towards the door, which remained closed, but then there came a rap on the wall.

"I heard that, Jem," came a disembodied voice.

Jem leapt backwards in surprise, then cast his eyes heavenward. "It's getting that you don't know if it's the living or the dead that's talking to you."

"Well, I'll leave you to it," Bryan said. "Give us a shout if anything happens with Rosie and tell Shusie I'm away. Good luck, Robert, and take care of yourself on the roads."

They shook hands and Bryan strode off for the mountain again. Robert smiled at his hasty retreat. In normal circumstances Shusie was difficult, but tired and worn out, she could indeed be very crabby.

"Tell us this, Robert," Jem began as he stroked the stubble on his chin. "Did you hear tell of that new book that's come out, *Tarzan of the Apes*?"

"Yes, I heard about it, but I haven't read it," Robert replied.

"They say that in the jungle a lad was found be monkeys and they rared him from a baby up till he was a man," Jem told him. "Shusie says that monkeys couldn't rare a cumin bean and that the people shouldn't be let read them books at all."

"A cumin bean? Oh yes, I see, a human being." Robert smiled. "I'm becoming a bit slow in my old age."

"Damn the slow," Shusie snorted as she sailed in to perch on her stool behind the counter. "Could a monkey rare a child from it was a baby or not?"

"I don't know." Robert shrugged. "These are stories, they might be true or they might not. We don't know what happens out in the jungle."

"Hmp! Well, I don't think Jem Redmond needs to know about monkeys rarin' childer," Shusie said dismissively as she picked up the newspaper. "Although there's plenty round here might have more gumption if a monkey had rared them. Ladies' fleeced knickers four and elevenpence," she read. "That's four shillings and elevenpence to keep your arse warm in the wintertime. That's robbery. And wait till you hear this! A hundred and thirty-eight tramps arrested drunk and mad after drinking methylated spirits in Dundalk. And the magistrate ordered that they should get a cold bath. The sergeant, a man that seems to have a bit more sense about him, said it would take a regiment of soldiers to bath them. Sure the bath hasn't been made that would hold a hundred and thirty-eight of them. They should be putting them through a mangle and wringing the methylated spirits out of them. Sure if they let it go on like that there won't be a drop of methylated spirits left in the country, and then what will we do?"

As this required no answer, Jem kept his eyes fixed firmly on the fire, while Robert wished he had left the same time as Bryan. He had been hoping for a lift to Crossmaglen, but maybe he should start walking.

When Bryan got home, he and Catherine laughed about the poster for the tea and the trials that Rosie was causing Shusie and Jem. Then he remembered about the poultice for Biddy's ankle. There was very little chickweed at that time of year, but he'd seen some at the back of the milk house and went to fetch it.

"Right, I'll run on up to her now. Keep an eye on Mary till I get back. I'll be as quick as I can," Catherine said as she departed for Biddy's with her sprain remedy.

Bryan checked to make sure that Mary wasn't in any danger and then sat down and lit his pipe. A visit from Robert usually meant that there was plenty of information to be mulled over.

Chapter 5

At the beginning of December, Ellen, with all her worldly goods and her cat, moved from Umericam to Cashel. The milk house had been converted into a bedroom for her. In the beginning she was tearful and lamenting and huddled by the fire, swaddled in shawls and blankets, while Catherine and the girls ran in and out with soup, hot stone jars and turf for the fire. When her cat disappeared, she accused Jocko of killing it and scolded Mary for defending her dog. Childer should be seen and not heard, at least that's the way it was in her day. Bryan searched in vain for the cat until Biddy Kane, calling in to bid Ellen welcome, reminded him that it was a common thing for a cat to go back to where it came from, and it was probably in Umericam. Bryan thought she could be right. He finished briaring the ditches and set off with the girls to look for the cat and bring the sheep up closer to the house for the winter. At the Crossroads Jem hurried out, said a few quiet words to Bryan and gave him a newspaper. After that, Bryan was distracted and walked quietly along, swishing at dockens with his blackthorn stick. At Ellen's old farm, when they had the sheep rounded up and out on the road, Brigid found the cat, hungry and lonely on the doorstep of Ellen's old house. She tucked it halfway up under her jumper then ran ahead to scout for any open gaps and gates on the way home. One time before an aul yoe had run into a woman's kitchen. It had been very embarrassing, but this time they got them home and into the field. Then Brigid gladly handed the cat over to her grandmother. It had been hard to hold when she was walking and clawed at her belly when she had to run. Bryan sat down at the table where Catherine was making bread and opened the newspaper he'd got from Jem.

"The War for Independence is over," he announced grimly. "And God knows what will happen to us here in the North now. Michael Collins and the men that went over with him signed a treaty with the British government in London on the sixth of December. It's all there in black and white in the *Dundalk Democrat*."

Catherine stopped kneading the dough and wiped a floury hand across her forehead. "They signed a treaty with the English? What does that mean? Did they not free Ireland?" she asked.

Bryan said that the treaty granted the Irish people a free state within the British Empire. It would be the same as Canada and Australia. Irish citizens would be required to take an oath of allegiance to the reigning British monarch and the Irish ports would have to be available to the British armed forces.

"It's not much of a bargain," Catherine said bitterly. "They'll get a free state in the South, but they'll still have to bow down to the king, and the British will have charge of the ports. Sure that's nothing different. The British will still be ruling them. Is there any word about what will happen to us here in the North?"

"It doesn't look good," Bryan said. "Collins wanted Churchill to give the Unionists four counties. Then it wouldn't be worth their while having a government, and they have a month to make their minds up about joining the new Free State. They don't need a month. You heard what Craig said at the elections: loyalty to the Crown and the Empire. The parliament is set up in Belfast and they've no notion of Dublin ruling them. They'll get the six counties and we'll be living under them."

"We'll never see a free Ireland," Catherine cried. "I prayed to God that it would be over this time and what did we get? The two ends of nothing. It was all for nothing. What ... ah sure what's the point lamenting? We were here before many a time down through the years. The English couldn't be straight, they just couldn't be straight, it isn't in them. They had to break it up. Look at all the lives that was lost and all that will be lost, for it's not over yet!"

"Steady yourself, me aul girl. A commission is to be set up and we'll all be asked about the drawing out of the new border and mebbe they'll put us on the Irish side of it," Bryan said hopefully as he got up and patted her shoulder.

"I can't see the 4th Northern going along with this," Catherine said. "And there'll be many a Southerner won't be happy about it ayther."

"Well, we'll see. The county councils in the border areas are pledging their support to the new government in the Dáil and that might help us, but the Orange lodges in the same areas are supporting the government in Belfast. It's a tough one and I think you're right, Catherine, there will be more ructions before it's settled."

Catherine could see nothing positive in the treaty and prayed God's curse on the British government, then called Bryan back to ask him to speak to his mother about her cat.

"It can't get out of the room and it pisses in the corner," she told him. "And the smell in there is damnable. I can't use Jeyes Fluid in a room where there's an aul woman. It would be the finish of her. And she won't let me open the window, for that would be the finish of her too. I don't know what to do."

Bryan smiled at the irony; one of the most momentous decisions in the history of Ireland had been made and he had to talk to his mother about cat's piss. He muttered that he would soon need a team of negotiators in his own house, then went into the room to tell his mother that a treaty had been signed.

At eighty-five she was philosophical about it. "It's no more than I expected of them," she said. "The war might be over in the South, but it'll not be over here in my day, nor yours, nor the children's, ayther. There'll be a lot more blood shed for Ireland."

Bryan agreed with her, and they discussed what the decision might mean for them before he brought up the subject of the cat. When he suggested it would be happier in the loft, Ellen agreed. She had never wanted it in the room. It soon settled in the loft, but then, to everyone's surprise, Jocko moved in with Ellen. At first they each tried to hog the fire, but gradually she recognised his value as a foot warmer. He sneaked in at every opportunity and had to be retrieved at night to keep guard by the settle bed. A warm fire in wintertime would test any dog's loyalties.

As Christmas approached, Catherine prepared for a shopping trip to Dundalk. Throughout the year, like all the other local women, she had been 'gathering up' treacle, syrup and dried fruit to make the Christmas cake and pudding. In Dundalk she would trade eggs and butter for groceries and small presents for the children's Christmas boxes. She was travelling with Oiney in the pony and trap and would be away all day. The girls were a bit anxious about her going, but Daddy being in charge promised to be a novelty. He kept them busy, running with fresh bedding for the cow and pigs, and kept watch for fear Mary would try and catch a bird on the dung heap. She wanted one with a wee curk or feather sticking up on the top of its head.

At midday, when he announced that he was going to cook the dinner, there was some groaning as well as great hilarity. He said he was going to cook horse coreen poodeen, a dish he learnt to cook when he was in the Scottish army. When they questioned him about that, he said he was with a regiment called the High Go Shites. They sit on their arse and fight with pot sticks. Ellen asked him to mind his language in front of the childer, but the girls were laughing.

"High Go Shites, High Go Shites," sang Mary as she danced round the room.

But as Ellen commanded Bryan to make her stop for fear she'd go into a fit, Sarah Cullen appeared at the door with a heavy meal bag slung over her shoulder. She carefully lowered it onto the ground, and when Bryan asked her was she carrying stones, she informed him that there was a goose in the bag. As the bag began moving across the doorstep, Ellen told her it was far too early to be laving off a goose and them not wantin' it till Christmas Day. Addy was supposed to pluck it and have it dressed and ready for cooking, and Sarah agreed this was so, but Una, her mother, had taken ill and her and Addy had to go to Newtownhamilton right away to see about her.

When Bryan lifted the bag and said it seemed to be a good weight,

Sarah laughed. She'd carried it the whole way over and she was sweating, but the goose wouldn't fly away because its wings were clipped. She asked the girls about Christmas and then how Hughie was doing. Was he at home? Bryan thought that she probably knew that Hughie was at the safe house and took the girls with him to put the goose in the barn to prevent further questions.

When Ellen asked what was wrong with Una, Sarah said that the doctor thought she might have the jandies, and if her eyes turned yella she was to go straight into the General Hospital. Ellen hoped that wouldn't happen because if the jandies didn't kill you, the General Hospital would. Sarah grimaced, closed the half door quietly behind her then ran lightly through the gate and up the road.

In the barn, Bryan shook the goose from the bag, waited till it righted itself and then returned to cooking the horse corn pudding. Ellen remarked that Addy was a clever blade. She had the goose delivered too early so she wouldn't have the bother of it, and now she was away to Newtownhamilton to fly her kite over Christmas. Jandies me arse!

She'd want to be careful because mocking was catching and she could bring something on herself. That Addy one could hurd mice at the Crossroads. Bryan carried the pot from the fire to the table then dished the poodeen into bowls and poured milk over it.

Brigid said that it was lovely, but the currants were for the Christmas cake. When Bryan looked despondent, they assured him that they would tell their mother that they ate the currants, so he wouldn't get the blame.

"We did ate them," Mary said pragmatically. "They were here in the porridge."

Ellen and Bryan began to laugh.

"Ah, Mary, we can always depend on you to call a spade a spade," Ellen said, wiping her eyes. "Yella male porridge is yella male porridge no matter what fancy name you call it or what fancy ingrediments you put in it."

When Catherine came home exhausted from her day's shopping, she was more annoyed at Addy for sending the goose over too soon than she was at the loss of the syrup and currants. She agreed with Ellen that it may have been a smart move on Addy's behalf, but she'd give her the benefit of the doubt. She also knew that Bryan wasn't a great poultry executioner and that she would have to dispatch the goose. She watched uneasily as it adopted Mary and the girls as its missing flock.

There was a fall of snow before Christmas and two early newborn lambs had to be brought in and warmed by the fire.

"I knew there'd be snow," Ellen told the girls. "I heerd the wind round the house last night and it was blowing straight from Barrawully."

"Where's Barrawully, Granny?" Susan asked.

"Beyond the beyonds," Ellen replied. "You can go no further."

"Is Canada beyond the beyonds, Granny?" Brigid wondered.

"It's not," Ellen conceded. "But it's near it."

The girls happily crunched down the road to school, vying to make the first footprints in the virgin snow and mantled in the euphoria that the first snow of the winter brings. Later that afternoon Hughie and Gerard trekked across the mountain from the safe house. When Hughie complained that it was warmer outside the aul house than inside, Catherine suggested that Bryan take them over some fuel before they starved to death with the cold. She asked had he still got the cough, and he protested loudly when she steered him into the bedroom to put camphorated oil on his chest. Gerard Molloy laughed and called him a mammy's boy as she persuaded him to put on the warm jumper and socks she'd knitted him for Christmas. When he managed to escape outside again he made a snowball and pucked it across the yard with a stick, missing it more often than he hit it. The girls, just home from school, ran after him, laughing and trying to do the same, with the goose honking and sliding amongst them.

"What are you doing with that stick, boyo?" Mary suddenly shouted in a southern accent. "I wouldn't like to see you with a gun!"

They all stopped and looked at her in amazement.

Catherine halted on her way to throw potato skins to the pigs. "Where on earth did you hear that, Mary?"

Mary scuffed the toe of her shoe in the snow and stared intently at the patch of ground that she had cleared. "Over at Annie's," Mary said. "We went over for apples."

Annie McGuinness was a member of the local Cumann na mBan unit, and when Mary went over she saw strange men pucking apples about the orchard with sticks. Hughie confirmed that it was true. Southern boys had been sent down earlier in the autumn on a very secret mission to scout the lay of the land for Michael Collins himself, but the Specials had got wind of them and they had to be pulled out of there very quickly. An unlikely saviour had been a neighbour of Annie's with no affiliation to the IRA. He had seen one of the plainclothes spies stationed with the Specials snooping about near Annie's house and went there after dark to let them know.

Hughie was surprised that Mary got close enough to see what the boys were doing, as the place was well guarded and the Cumann na mBan were coming and going all the time. They should all have been watching. When Catherine asked what the Cumann na mBan did, Gerard laughed and said they made the tay. Hughie warned him he could aisy get shot in the arse for making remarks like that. The women were soldiers the same as them and they were crack-shots. He had trained some of them himself. They carried dispatches and weapons between the camps. It was a very dangerous job, but they could go places and get past people when the men couldn't. They did first aid and looked after the wounded, brought medicine and food and fired shots over the graves at the military funerals. Some of them were in Belfast training to be nurses so that they could keep an eye on the wounded lads in the Military Hospital. The men couldn't do without them.

"I was only joking about the tay, Mrs Grant," Gerard assured her. "No, the women are well fit for anyone. But Hughie learning them to be crack-shots? He couldn't hit a barn door with a baking board."

When Bryan said he would bring firewood up to the old house, they said to leave it till after the snow melted because the cart would leave tracks in the snow and there was always some nosey bastard that might follow them and report them to the Specials. They didn't stay at the old house all the time. When they were on manoeuvres they stayed in different houses and also in outhouses. If an area was safe, a white sheet was hung out on the line or spread over a bush, the doors were left on the latch and there was always soup or stirabout and a bite to ate in the morning before they left. When they were on active service they often slept outside. They were going to Gerard's house now, and Bryan warned them to stay close to the hedges, as they would be a good target on an evening like that with the moon coming up and the snow on the ground. He saw them on their way and then helped the girls complete a scraggy snowman.

Ellen turned away from the window then came and sat down by the fire. She seemed to have something on her mind. "I'm worried about Mary," she began. "She'll come out with something in front of the wrong people and hang the whole lot of us. And that Sarah Cullen one is a dangerous blade and her walking out with a polis man. She's ayther telling him all the tittle-tattle of the countryside or he's asking her to find it out. 'Where's Hughie?' says she the day she took the goose over. Mary's not safe going away across the fields on her own with the times that's in it, and you know that, Catherine. In my day the likes of her would be closed up in a room or tied in a chair be the fire!"

Catherine said, "We're lucky that Mary is as good as what she is and the day will come when she won't be able to run about the country, but from this on you and I will be sharing the one hearth and you'll not tell me how to rare me children."

Ellen looked at her for a long moment then tightened her lips, wrapped her shawl round her shoulders and moved towards her room. "You're making a rod for your own back," she remarked. "But I'll try not to interfere. It won't be aisy for if I see something wrong happening forninst me I have to say it."

Catherine said a swift prayer that God would keep Mary out of harm's way and mebbe keep this aul woman off her back while he was at it.

The snow melted away almost as quickly as it had come, leaving small deposits on the hilltops. It was waiting for more, Ellen predicted. Catherine felt a bit sad now and again when she saw Mary playing with the goose, but they couldn't afford to spare it. When the day of execution came and Bryan said he'd have little heart in killing it when the child had made such a pet of it, Catherine felt a surge of annoyance.

"Well, the sooner it's done, the sooner it's over and may all bad luck go with it," she muttered.

"Good woman, you have a better knack of doing it," Bryan said, patting her shoulder. "I'll take the girls with me and we'll get some wood and take it up to the aul house. I'll tell them the goose flew away to Africa. Flocks are going over all the time." And off he went with a jaunty step.

"Aye, it's aisy for you," Catherine said loudly to his departing back.

"His father was the same with a heart in him like a wet dishcloth," Ellen remarked from the bedroom door. "He used to try and kill the chickens by closing their heads in a door. Many's the time I felt like hopping a skillet off the back of his head and many's a time I did, but little the difference it made to him."

In spite of herself Catherine laughed. She lured the goose into the shed and wedged it against the wall with her leg then took a firm grasp of its neck with both hands and twisted it with a strong, swift movement till she felt the break. She tied its feet together and hung it upside-down from a nail on the shed wall. The head and neck dangled tonelessly at an odd angle while the body twitched and jerked every now and then. She slipped a meal bag loosely up over the body and secured it with a length of cord. She would let it hang there for a few days before plucking and dressing it. She almost wished bad luck on Addy Murray for delivering it too early, but then let it go.

It was nearly dark before Bryan returned with the girls. He had found cigarette butts and boot prints at the edge of the timber stand. Someone had been there and it was a bit disturbing, but maybe it was Hughie and them. They were all watching each other and it was hard to know who it might have been.

With the girls settled and Ellen retired to her room Catherine sat down with the darning and Bryan turned up the flame of the oil lamp to read the newspaper. He said that a flock of geese had flown over when they were getting the firewood. He had made the children listen and told them it was geese, so if they asked what happened to the goose …

"If they ask? Sure you know damn well they'll ask," Catherine said crossly.

Bryan usually removed the heavy bar from the back of the door in the mornings and Catherine had to make sure Mary didn't ramble outside after him. She wouldn't think of putting on boots and stockings and it was well known that wet feet and legs could lead to Bright's disease of the kidneys. She ran outside shouting for the goose, listening for the honking and flapping, but there was only silence. The other girls joined her and they searched everywhere. They found footprints frozen in muck and rotten eggs under the haystacks in the haggard, but no goose. When they went into the field, the sheep all ran to the far corner, but the tip put his head down and charged at them and they knew he would have chased the goose out too. When Bryan came back, he decided that if they had found a spot where the footprints ended then the goose must have lifted off the ground and flown away to Africa with the wild geese. The girls were disappointed. They had hoped for a better outcome.

To distract them from the goose Brian took them up the mountain to look for a white goat they'd seen earlier in the year. They were doubtful that the goose had flown away, but maybe a fox had taken it. As they walked along singing "A fox went out on a starry night", they became convinced that this was what had happened. They didn't find the white goat either.

"It wouldn't be the same anyway, would it, Daddy?" Brigid said sadly.

Bryan shrugged in resignation. He had run out of answers.

Chapter 6

On colder days Ellen stayed in her room, and although she had some difficulty with mobility, her voice and lungs were robust and she made her requirements known.

"Is there nobody out there fit to bring me something to put on this wee excuse for a fire?" she would shout. "I'm here sittin' shivering like a dog in a wet sack, huddered over a fire that wouldn't warm a fairy!"

If the kindling was slow to catch, she was ready with a caustic observation: "'It'll be a fire when it lights,' as the fox said when he pissed on the snow."

She passed her day saying the Rosary and reading her many prayer books. Novels were scarce, but they had some works by Charles Dickens and popular writers. Occasionally she would glance through a book, and if it didn't suit her she would cast it aside with disgust. "Sure that sort of thing would never happen," she'd say scornfully. "What kind of gobberloos do they take us for?"

One of her main concerns was her health, and anyone with a cough or a sniffle wasn't allowed in her room. She was devoid of sympathy when her well-being was threatened. She accused Bryan of wanting to be the finish of her when he took a fit of coughing while he was visiting her. She was conserving her strength to sit down like a Christian and ate her dinner at the table of a Christmas Day. When Catherine and the girls brought holly inside to hang above the pictures, she warned them that she would have no truck with that sort of pagan thing.

Catherine absorbed the warning then said that Bryan had told the girls that the goose had flown to Africa. When Ellen pursed her lips and shook her head in disapproval, the wattles of skin on her neck flapped independently. Her skin doesn't fit her body any more, Catherine thought with detachment. Ellen said that he should have told them the truth at the start. They knew the goose had been got for the dinner, but they'd get over it and think no more about it. Catherine hoped so and continued with the Christmas preparations.

On Christmas Eve, when Catherine made the pudding, the girls were allowed to stir it and make a wish. Then it was steamed over the fire for four or five hours. Delicious aromas of fruit and spices permeated the house and the windows fogged up every time the pot lid was lifted to top up the water. A savoury stuffing was made for the goose, which now hung upside-down at the back of the kitchen door. Catherine said it was a rooster she'd got from the fowl man in exchange for a couple of old hens. The fowl men called round a couple of times a year. They bought old hens and sold pullets. A hen past the lay was only good for the soup pot, but the fowl men would chance selling it as a pullet. The country people knew their hens and made sure they weren't cheated because it suited them to sell their fowl at the gate. Taking poultry to the market in one of the nearby towns was expensive and time consuming.

Before they went to bed, the girls hung their stockings on the mantelpiece for Santy Claus. Their hair was brushed and plaited as they would be starting out early for Christmas Mass. Bryan and the neighbouring men always walked to midnight Mass on Christmas Eve.

"The lads are in the loft," he whispered to Catherine as he slipped into bed around two o'clock on Christmas morning.

Catherine smiled to herself, half pleased, half exasperated. It was a worry to have them around, but surely to God the Specials would be at home with their own people at Christmas and wouldn't be looking for them.

On Christmas morning the girls each found a red apple in their stocking along with a small Christmas box. Brigid got an old nature book about tropical frogs, with colourful drawings of exotic creatures and faraway places. Catherine had bought it in a second-hand shop for a farthing. Susan got a peg doll and a ball of wool to knit a scarf and mittens, and Katy got a tiny baby doll sleeping in a walnut-shell cradle. Mary got a monkey that swung round on a frame when two lengths of elastic were stretched out and then let go. She was delighted with it and the girls laughed heartily as she made it perform.

Soon it was time to set off for the chapel. Brigid and Katy were fasting for Holy Communion. Susan hadn't made her Communion yet, and Mary had an affliction and wasn't considered eligible to receive the Sacraments. Katy was always worried that the priest might drop the sacred host and it would bleed profusely and he would have to get soap and water to scrub the altar clean. Nobody had ever witnessed this phenomenon, but the warning was passed down to each generation.

Brigid was singing in the choir and dared not be late. The choir was conducted by a master from the boys' school. The other master was renowned for beginning the history lesson about the Battle of the Boyne with the statement "Seamus a caca shit his pants!" James the Second of Scotland ran away during the Battle of the Boyne against William, Prince of Orange in 1690, and was henceforth seen as a coward. It was one historical fact that all the boys remembered. The master who trained the choir had little tolerance for anyone and crucified latecomers. The choir, which was mostly schoolchildren, sang the Christmas hymns school-fashion, with each word pronounced precisely and in an exaggerated fashion.

"Stop, stop! You crowd of amadáns!" The master would shout during choir practice. "The word is NOT appy arse! The word is APPEARS! 'See the tender lamb appee-ars … appears!'"

Dressed in jodhpurs and riding boots, he was a bizarre choirmaster and was swift and vicious with the cane. His pupils and the choir treated him warily but mocked him behind his back.

When they reached the chapel, Brigid went up to the gallery, where a few children and adults were stamping their feet and blowing on their hands to try and keep warm. The chapel wasn't heated, and they could see the crystal sheen of frost glistening on the candlelit walls.

Children who had received Christmas boxes whispered to each other, while those who hadn't pretended not to hear. Catherine and the girls sat in the women's aisle, while the men and boys were in a separate aisle. Men and women didn't mix unless a local woman married an Englishman and brought him home on holiday. Englishmen sat in the women's aisle with their wives and children because they didn't know any better. It was laughed about by the men after Mass. An old Church law decreed that women and girls should keep their hair covered in the chapel as it was thought to attract angels and demons, but men removed their hats.

There was a respectful low murmur of conversation as the congregation waited for the priest to come out onto the altar. Susan was pulling ferocious gargoyle faces at a boy in the row behind her. "Mammy, she's mawkin' me," he whined as he tried unsuccessfully to squeeze in behind his mother, who was a sizeable woman. Catherine warned Susan that God would leave her like that and took her by the ear and turned her to face the altar. Katy had her eyes squinted almost shut so that she could make the candles form a line. Mary rambled around the chapel looking at and talking to the various statues. She had been warned not to remove any of the animals or the baby from the crib.

A loud cough signalled that the priest had appeared. As the congregation rose, there was the sound of hustling and shuffling, benches scraping on the stone floor and kneelers creaking in protest as the weight descended on them. Generally the men only knelt on one knee using their caps to cushion the hard kneeling board and shifting to the other knee when they got tired. The women found that if a skirt was positioned right it could give some comfort, as the boards were often covered in a fine grit. A child could raise his knee and wipe the grit off, but women couldn't expose much flesh, not even to a doctor.

The better off, such as shopkeepers, doctors and teachers, were sarcastically known as the Quality and were at a disadvantage in the chapel because they wore hats instead of caps. They couldn't kneel on their hats, but some would ostentatiously spread out sparkling white handkerchiefs before kneeling down on them, which usually prompted ribald remarks from the poorer members of the congregation: "I mind that bastard when he hadn't a blade of grass to wipe his arse" or "He lifted yon white hankercher out of the priest's pocket before he came into the chapel."

There were always pointed comments and muffled laughter before they settled down. The priest mumbled quickly through the Latin Mass with his back to the congregation. They tried to follow what he said but quickly got lost and muttered the Latin as they thought it sounded. Older people completely ignored the priest and prayed on their Rosary beads. The practice of adapting the Latin as English became the basis of a story that was told in many parishes. On Ash Wednesday, as the priest is putting the ash on the people's foreheads, he gets an urgent sick call and asks the sexton to continue till he comes back. The sexton obliges and confidently walks along the line of people making the sign of the cross on their foreheads, saying, "You were born an eejit and you'll die an eejit. You were born an eejit and you'll die an eejit." As no one knew Latin, they couldn't correct him because he may have been right.

Mary had found her way into a seat behind Catherine and as usual prayed loudly along with the older women. They smiled toothlessly and patted her arm. Then Catherine noticed that the noise level behind her had fallen and she anxiously looked around. She knew that Mary might still take one of the wooden lambs out of the crib, then there would be ructions when they tried to take it from her.

"She's with your Hughie and our Gerard at the back of the chapel," Sadie Molloy, Gerard's mother, murmured in her ear. "They came from your house to our house at six o' clock this morning. Before he went off to free Ireland, Gerard wouldn't get out of the bed. Now he's never in the bed. God help Ireland!"

Catherine had to smother a fit of laughing. She caught sight of Mary's head near the back of the chapel, and Hughie gave her the thumbs-up sign. She would be all right till Mass was over. When Fr Carron stepped into the pulpit to deliver the Christmas sermon, he spoke of the stable at Bethlehem, the birth of Jesus – a symbol of peace and joy and new beginnings – and he wished the people a happy

Christmas. He hoped that the treaty that had been recently negotiated in London would be accepted by the people and the politicians, because if it wasn't, what would come after might be worse, and the Volunteers would continue to draw the wrath of the authorities down on the people. He seemed set to continue in this vein, but the coughing began in the men's aisle and spread in a rising crescendo that engulfed the chapel and drowned out the priest. He knew when he was defeated.

"I would advise you all to wrap up warmly as I can see there are a lot of you afflicted with bronchitis, if not worse," he finished dryly. "Happy Christmas, and I hope you all make it through to the New Year."

The people cast their eyes up to Heaven and smiled wryly at each other. Priests and politics didn't mix, and they didn't need to listen to that of a Christmas Day. The conflict would be resolved one way or the other. The IRA in other parts of the country was already challenging the Church. The priests should stand by the people, because it was the people that kept them where they were.

The congregation waited until the choir finished the final hymn and then Brigid came down from the gallery and joined the rest of the family as they visited the crib. The women extracted stalks of straw from the edge of the crib, as it was said to be a cure for the shingles. Good wishes for the season were exchanged and then people filtered out into the graveyard to say a Christmas prayer for the dead. Catherine was shocked when she saw how Hughie looked in daylight. His face was gaunt and his shoulders under the overcoat looked as narrow as a coat hanger. My God, she thought, he's away to scrapings, there isn't pickings on him. When she quizzed him about his health and eating habits, he answered her patiently, saying that the Specials wouldn't ask that many questions. He then produced wood carvings, which only bore a fleeting resemblance to the creatures they were supposed to be, but the girls were delighted with them. The walk home from Mass with the neighbours was full of crack and laughter. The children dancing, skipping and playing games, the adults chatting together, temporarily setting aside worries about what would happen to them and their children when the country was divided.

When Hughie hung back during a bout of coughing, Sadie Molloy raised a questioning and concerned eyebrow. "The camphorated oil and brown paper on his chest is the boy for that," she suggested. "Yes, I know what men are like. You'd think you were going to poison them if you try to give them the cure for anything."

Catherine nodded in agreement. He had a bad cough, that was all, but she knew deep in her heart that the niggling worry, like the cough, wasn't going to go away.

Bryan had the stirabout plumping on the grate and a pot of tea drawing on the hob when they got home. He had toasted slices of soda bread and advised Hughie to sit down and ate something that would stick some flesh to his ribs.

"I'm ating well enough, Da." Hughie grinned. "I'll just throw me coat out in the wee shed. I'll be back in a minnit."

Catherine could see that the pockets of the coat were bulging with items best not mentioned, but the wee shed should be safe enough. After breakfast she stuffed and prepared the goose, placed it in a large pot with some lard and then swung it over the fire to roast. In some houses the goose was hung from the crane without a pot and the melting fat helped with the roasting. Catherine preferred to use the pot so that she could collect the goose fat to make a rub called "goose ame". She added linseed oil and turpentine to increase the volume and give the mixture some heat and sometimes used it on animals with the cruppy, a weakness in the back legs that affected pigs and dogs. A couple of good rubs soon had the afflicted animal not just fit to walk, but to fly. Bryan said it burnt the arse off the poor craters and they had to get up and run about to cool it down.

While the goose was cooking, Catherine helped Ellen onto the commode, a grand, wooden toilet chair with a hinged seat and a flower-decorated chamber pot. When it wasn't in use, cushions were placed on it to make it look more like an armchair. It was an ideal throne when the girls were playing games and also a quiet spot to sit and read. Before Ellen left the bed, she gave Catherine a small object that was wrapped in a lace handkerchief.

"George got it for me not long before he was killed in the mines, but I never had the heart to wear it," she said.

It was a small, leaf-shaped silver brooch tarnished green with age.

"Put it on your Sunday coat," Ellen ordered. "It's no good lying in a handkercher under me pillow and it isn't going to bring George back. Rub it with a drop of methylated spirits and some fine ashes and mebbe that'll brighten it up a bit."

Catherine thanked her and slipped the brooch into her overall pocket. She wondered how she could ever wear it when it reminded Ellen of her dead son. It was sad to think of her forever mourning her dead boy, and Catherine prayed that she would never know what it was like. God forbid that anything should happen to Hughie, and what about the lads in Canada? She knew they existed out there, but couldn't hear them, see them, nor touch them and didn't know if her prayers got through to them. It was as if they were in Limbo where the souls waited before they could enter Heaven.

With Ellen settled comfortably in the armchair in front of the fire and whispering Hail Marys, Catherine returned to manoeuvring the pot so that the goose would be evenly cooked. Every so often the voice from the room reminded her to keep turning the bird to the hate. Eventually, she took a deep breath and said with great patience, "Ellen, dear, please don't spake again till the dinner's ready for I wouldn't like to give you a sudden answer of a Christmas Day!"

Ellen, with great forbearance, said nothing more.

Catherine prepared and cooked the vegetables while Hughie and Bryan foddered the animals and the girls went to look through the gate at the new lambs. Mary still gazed hopefully skywards in search of the goose. In the evening some of the local men were expected to call in for a "trate" that was either whiskey or poteen and a slice of pudding. Bachelors living alone were welcome in everyone's house, as nobody begrudged them a Christmas dinner. One ate in as many as four houses and declared after each meal, "That's the best dinner I had the day!" But Christmas only came once a year, and what they had they shared and even became a bit reckless: "To Hell with poverty, throw another lump of turf on the fire!"

The table was set with the good linen tablecloth, the best delft and the matching cutlery. When Ellen appeared in her black bombazine dress and crocheted white lace shawl, Bryan escorted her to the top of the table where she could sit with her back to the fire. The carved goose was served with roast potatoes and vegetables. Mary's broken teeth made chewing difficult and she ate very slowly. They had almost finished dinner and the pudding was plumping aromatically in a pot when Susan glanced outside and announced that it was snowing again. Suspiciously large snowflakes were floating gently about in all directions, and when Hughie opened the door a guilty-looking, feather-covered Jocko sidled in.

"There's your goose-feather pillow for you, now. Which of youse left the shed door open after you?" Ellen demanded.

Bryan looked at Hughie, who shrugged his shoulders and said that he'd just pulled the door over behind him. He hadn't seen any feathers. The girls turned shocked eyes to the stripped carcass on the serving dish on the dresser, and Mary stopped eating. Her eyes filled with tears and her nose began to run. Shreds of the goose meat mixed with saliva dribbled from her mouth onto her plate.

"Catherine, this child is slabbering all over her dinner. Give me that fork," Ellen snapped impatiently. She slapped the fork from Mary's hand and lifted the plate.

Mary got up and walked slowly to the settle bed and picked up Brigid's frog book. Then she flew at Ellen and beat her about the head and shoulders with the book flittering apart as the blows landed on the old woman.

Hughie, who knew nothing about the goose going to Africa, quickly dragged her into the bedroom where he gently scolded her for attacking her granny.

Although the blows hadn't been very hard, Ellen was shocked by the attack. Bryan made her drink hot punch and as the colour came back to her face she said that she felt a bit more like herself.

With Mary settled, Hughie went to brush the feathers up. He patted Ellen's shoulder consolingly as he passed and made a funny face at the girls.

"She isn't like another. She doesn't know what she's doing," Ellen conceded. "I shouldn't have slapped her, for the likes of her shouldn't be provoked." Then she turned to watch Hughie sweeping up the feathers. "Look at yon fella brushing feathers with a twig and them flying up about worse than the way the dog left them," she scolded. "Pour some boiling water on them, Bryan, or he'll be brushing there till kingdom come." Then Bryan and Hughie challenged the girls to a race down to the bridge and back. They returned in good spirits and set about mending the frog book with a flour paste.

Later in the evening Gerard Molloy and his father, Larry, walked across the mountain to make their ceilidh. Larry was limping and leaning heavily on a blackthorn stick.

"What befell you?" Ellen demanded. "You're hirplin about worse nor meself."

"Sure, I hurted me hinch pullin' out a big stone over be the fairy fort," Larry explained as he stood warming his back at the fire. "I can get aise to nayther sit nor lie."

"I'm sorry to hear that, but you shoulda knowed not to touch nothing that belongs to the fairies, Larry," Ellen said. "It's them that owns the ground and the stones, not you."

"Och, aye, it's too well I know that now, but I thought one big stone from there would save me the hauling two or three out of someplace else," Larry sighed. "Och, I shoulda knew not to bring them on me."

Bryan handed him a glass of whiskey to wet his whistle and ease his pain and then wished him good health.

Whiskey and poteen were kept for both medicinal and social purposes. Hot punch might not cure an ailment but it made the sufferer feel a lot better about his condition. A cotton wool plug soaked with whiskey warmed up a sore ear and eased a toothache. A teaspoon of whiskey was thought to bring the measles rash out more quickly and shorten the illness, while a wee dram, for its own sake, warmed the stomach and induced a sense of confidence and well-being. On festive occasions and hot harvest days, a quart of ale was provided for the men who didn't drink whiskey.

As the older people chatted by the fireside, Hughie taught the girls how to play Old Maid with a pack of cards. Mary emerged from the bedroom and sat shyly on the arm of Bryan's chair. Then Ellen appealed to Catherine to put a stop to the card game. Cards were the Devil's postcards and could lead to gambling and bad living, but Catherine didn't see any harm in it and let the game continue as she read out the last letter that came from the boys in Canada. They had jobs and good lodgings and were doing all right, but it was very cold and they had never seen so much snow. They would go further north in the springtime when it melted.

"They'll never be back," said Ellen, voicing what everyone was thinking.

"We're raring them for the boat, Ellen," Larry agreed. "That's all we're doing, raring them for the boat."

They all stared into the fire, until Bryan remembered a local man made good who came back and bought a farm of land and the mood lightened. It wasn't a one-way journey; the boys would come back. Catherine sent Hughie and Gerard to collect Biddy Kane as she wasn't walking too well yet on her sprained ankle, and the lads readily agreed.

"Did you hear any word of Addy's daughter, Una, being took bad?" Ellen asked Larry.

"Una, the one that was rared in a pot?" Larry said.

"Aye, the Una one, and she wasn't rared in a pot, for there's no shame in Addy. She's took awful bad with something that's mebbe the jandies," Ellen told him. "Addy's away to Newtown to sit with her over Christmas and if there's no betterment on her soon, she'll have to go to the General Hospital to be opened up."

"No, I heard nothing of that," Larry said. "But there was talk that she was keeping open house for the Specials below in Newtownhamilton."

Hughie and Gerard paused on their way out the door and looked over at Larry.

"That young Sarah one was poorly-looking round the time we had the mill. Her belly was sticking to her back," Larry continued. "But I seen her lately and she's got to be a big, sonsy-looking girl. But she'd want to watch herself walking out with yon Special, for she could aisy get tarred and feathered!"

"We'll not talk about that," Catherine advised him softly. "Feathers is the bad word here the day, Larry."

Larry said he should be getting home, but he stretched his leg out to ease his hinch and didn't object when Bryan poured him another dram. He asked Ellen about her sister, Maggie, but Ellen said they seldom spoke. Maggie's family were staunch Hibernians, defenders of the Catholics and enemies of the IRA. There had been bitter clashes between the two parties in Mullaghbane.

"Her grandsons and mine are in two different camps and we arg about it hammer and tongs. She has one of them big horns that you stick in your ear, for she's as deaf as a post, and the roars of her, you would think it was me was deaf. It would wear you trying to have a crack with her, but she's to come to see me this summer, please God, if she's still living."

"Please God she'll make it," Larry said.

A short time later Biddy swept in, exhilarated by the fact that she had just spent fifteen minutes with two of the best-looking young men in the country.

"Ah, Biddy, if I was only twenty years older," Gerard said.

"Och, go on with you," Biddy fluttered, laughing.

Bryan and Catherine laughed along with her, but Ellen sniffed disdainfully. She thought Biddy was a bit light, but she didn't suck the turf stack for that; her mother, God rest her, had been like that too.

Biddy had on her best coat and dress and reeked of mothballs and lavender water. Curled around her neck was a fur tippet that looked like a small dead animal. On closer inspection, it *was* a small dead animal. The head was snuggled under her chin and the paws rested on her shoulder. Opaque glass beads glistened in the eye sockets.

"It come from me aunt in America years ago," Biddy explained as she slid it from her shoulder.

Mary dashed forward to grab the tippet, but Catherine caught her by the arm and spun her away.

"I want the rat," she cried.

"Aye, it does look a bit like a rat, Mary, but they said it was a mink," Biddy laughed. "Och, sure let the poor child have it, Catherine. It's an aul thing that I only wear on high days and holidays."

"She can have it for a wee while before you go home," Catherine conceded. "Chew, dog!" She smacked the jumping dog on the top of the head and hung the tippet on the back of the door.

Mary and Jocko slunk under the table where they could keep an eye on it and be ready to catch it when it tried to escape. Mickle and Oiney Grant arrived with a fiddle, an accordion and a few bottles of stout and soon everyone was in good form and looking forward to a few precious hours of music and crack. The men took turns playing the music, and even Ellen got up for a waltz. She said she would do a bit of lilting only she hadn't the wind for it now; her aul bellows were near done. Biddy couldn't dance with her bad ankle, but she sang "I'll Be Your Sweetheart" in a pleasant but quavery voice, and Bryan sang an old song called "The Dewy Glens of Yarrow". Then it was time for the girls to entertain, and Mary came out from under the table, pushed the others aside and began a little jiggling dance that ended with a hop.

"The burdies' ball, the burdies' ball, the burdies big and the burdies small," she sang tunelessly.

As she relentlessly repeated this refrain, the visitors became embarrassed and the party was in danger of breaking up early, but short of dragging her away, they couldn't persuade her to get off the floor.

"Give her down me aul tippet, Catherine," Biddy suggested.

Catherine wrapped the tippet around Mary's shoulders and settled her into a chair where she sat contentedly talking to it for the rest of the night. The other girls sang their party pieces to much praise and applause. Susan fell asleep at the table, but Katy and Brigid danced on until the party broke up long past ten o'clock. Mickle and Oiney escorted Biddy home. She was almost overwhelmed by so much male attention of a Christmas Day. The men made arrangements to go hunting the next day and then Hughie and Gerard left with Larry to see if there was any further crack or divarsion happening at Molloys' house.

Chapter 7

Bryan was up early on Boxing Day, looking forward to a good day on the mountain and meeting up with the other men who had escaped. Hanging round the house with women was only for invalids and Nancy boys or mammy's boys. He laced up his hobnail boots and tucked his moleskin trousers into the tops of them. Then he pulled on gaiters to protect his trousers as far as his knees. The mountain was covered in briars, concealed rocks and whin bushes, any of which could scrape your leg or worse than that, tear your trousers. Catherine cut him a wedge of stirabout, a thick porridge that had cooled and congealed into a cake, wrapped it in a strip of cloth from a flour bag and put it into the canvas knapsack that he used to carry game. He had given his hunting gun to the IRA as they were always short of weapons, but Oiney and Mickle had shotguns concealed under the hay in their loft. On the hunt everything was discussed and yarns were exchanged – truth or lie, it didn't matter. If it rained they sheltered under trees and if it was fair they sat high up on the rocks, smoking their pipes and observing what was happening in the valley below.

They hunted anything that would go into a pot. Catherine requested a good sized duck, and Bryan said he'd do his best. He wouldn't be back till dark. Later on Hughie and Gerard were to relieve the lads left guarding the safe house, and Catherine decided to send pudding for the lads. Bryan knew the Cumann na mBan had brought them plenty of pudding, but he said nothing. The Cumann na mBan were soldiers and comrades in arms, but older women wouldn't approve of them being unchaperoned in an aul house with a crowd of young men. He would eat the pudding himself and no one need be any the wiser. He strode out for Larry Molloy's, carrying his knapsack and a blackthorn stick. It was cold, but an hour's hard hiking would soon warm them up.

Ellen, stiff and sore from dancing the night before, stayed in bed; it didn't take much to upset her constitution. Catherine settled her comfortably in the bed with a hot water bottle and went to prepare the dinner. The girls were always starving, but that was a good sign when they were growing. They were looking at a picture in an old schoolbook, where a small boy dressed in a sailor suit and hat was bowling a hoop along a pavement. He was followed by two nannies pushing prams and wearing caped uniforms. They questioned Catherine relentlessly about the picture until she had an inspiration. There was a hoop from an aul barrel round the back of the milk house, and if they put on their coats they could bowl it up and down the road. Mary wasn't interested in spinning the hoop, but she seized the opportunity to get outside. Through the window Catherine watched them happily running up and down the road with the hoop, but when she went to feed the hens, she heard the clang of the hoop hitting the road, followed by a scream from Susan and a shout from Katy and Brigid. Mary had pushed Susan and she'd fallen on the hoop. Blood seeped through a hole in the knee of her stocking and dripped onto the road.

As Catherine carried Susan into the house, Mary crawled under the hedge. Something white, possibly bone, was glistening beneath the ragged edges of the wound on Susan's leg. If poison from the bone got into the blood, the child would die. And then there was lockjaw; many a one died from getting a thorn in his finger. When Ellen saw the cut she shook her head sorrowfully.

"The child is done for," she pronounced. "Never in this world will that cut heal. That Mary one will do real harm to someone, mark my words."

"Do you want me to put her in the eejits' ward in the Workhouse?" Catherine demanded angrily. "Do not say one more word! Katy, stop that blerting and help Brigid set the table. I think I hear your father home, thank God."

Ellen glared at her for a long moment and then Bryan entered, stamping his feet and pulling Mary behind him. "I found this poor wee individual shivering down be the sheep trough. Did none of youse know she was out there?" he asked, puzzled.

Then he noticed the tear-stained face of Susan on the settle bed, with her bandaged leg raised up.

"All right," he said, taking in the compressed lips and angry faces of his wife and mother. "Let me get me out of me coat and boots and then mebbe someone could tell me what happened."

He listened calmly and patiently as the accident, the events leading up to the accident and those following the accident were described in great detail. Then he looked over at Catherine. "I took that aul hoop off the barrel because it was rusted and rotten and I threw it round there for fear someone would cut themselves on it," he told her. "Never for one minnit did I think it would be used as a plaything nor put a child's life in danger."

"I didn't think there was any harm in it," Catherine said. "I thought it would keep them warm running up and down the road."

"Well, the harm's done now. Youse women are worse than a crowd of goats. If you aren't going into trouble, you're coming out of it."

Catherine knew that if Susan died she would never forgive herself, and Bryan, easy-going though he was, would never forgive her either. The girls had played with the hoop until dinnertime without injuring themselves, but there was no point in telling him that now. No point at all. Mary had gone into herself and wouldn't speak, respond to questions or eat. Catherine scolded her for what she had done, but she could see from Mary's eyes that she was chasing butterflies in the Spelig. She had no concept of consequences and charged in like a young bull if she wanted something.

As Bryan ate his supper he spoke of the day's hunting. Larry hadn't gone with them. He was like an aul jinnet – he could go up a hill, but had trouble coming down. They had gone to the safe house where Hughie and Gerard took over the guard duty, and the other lads went home. There would be no further word about the treaty or what was happening in Dublin till the New Year.

When Susan was settled, Catherine wondered if she should sit up in case the child got worse, but Bryan said she might be worrying for nothing. Bleeding cleaned a cut. She woke suddenly in the night, but nothing was stirring in the kitchen. Mice and rats scampered across the ceiling boards in the loft above her head. They nested in the thatch and it was difficult to keep them out, especially in the winter, but you got used to what you're reared with, she thought.

Next morning the cut on Susan's leg was jagged and dark red round the edges, but when salve was applied and the bandage put back on she lay back like a queen on a bed of pillows. When Mary, in an effort to divert attention from Susan, showed Bryan her chilblains, he advised her to get the grandmother's fasting spit to cure them, but Ellen wasn't in good fettle and had no spit in her. He gave Mary half an onion to rub on her chilblains and then brought Ellen a mug of tea fortified by poteen. Poteen was a pick-me-up as well as a muscle rub for the elderly and did them as much good from the inside as it did from the outside.

Ellen wondered had the child got hurted because of bad luck due to the holly being put up. But then she'd also heard that it was unlucky to take holly down before Candlemas Day on the second of February.

Candlemas Day is said to be the day Mary went to the temple for purification forty days after the birth of Jesus. Locally candles were blessed on that day. In some parts it was thought that if it was a fine, bright day there was more winter weather to come, but if it was a bad day the winter was over. If a badger came out of its sett and saw snow, it would stay out, but if it saw sun it would go back in again. Snowdrops brought into the house before Candlemas Day was a sign of a death or a parting.

Catherine looked up at the holly and thought of it hanging there collecting dust for another month and said it would be burnt on the sixth of January, the feast of the Epiphany, and that was that. Not to be outdone, Ellen said that there'd be no luck in it if it didn't burn quick.

"Holly always burns quick in a dry house," Catherine said, losing patience. "Now if there's anything else here not to your liking, mebbe we could make you a room out in the byre."

Ellen retired to her room to rethink her tactics. The young ones these days thought they knew it all; it was the way of the world.

The following morning Susan had a high temperature and dark-green pus was bealing through the bandage. The doctor would have to be sent for. Bryan went to inquire if he was in the locality; otherwise he would have to go to Newtownhamilton for him. When Hughie called later that morning, Catherine wondered if she should send for Addy, but he reminded her that Addy used cow dung on cuts and burns, and if the doctor found her there he wouldn't look at Susan. He had threatened before to report her to the polis over her "cures" and she had run him out of the yard with a graip and told him to go to Hell.

Bryan located the doctor not too far away, attending a woman who was "lying in" but was having problems delivering the baby. Shusie said the babies always came arse-ways; it was the breed of them people. The doctor would call as soon as possible but would only take poteen or whiskey in lieu of payment.

He had an awful droot on him. When he rode up on his motorcycle, Hughie came out from the byre and stood awhile, talking about and admiring the motorcycle.

"She's the Unapproachable Big 4 Norton," the doctor said with some pride. "Cost a hundred and twenty pounds, and well worth it, I may add."

He stroked the seat of the motorcycle as if it was the back of a horse.

When Hughie asked if he could have a go on it, the doctor hesitated, then showed him how it worked and warned him not to wreck it or get into any trouble.

Catherine asked the doctor was he out of his mind letting that fella away on his good motorcycle? But Horgan said in his experience the motorcycle was more durable than the rider and then brushed past her into the kitchen.

Hughie revved up the motorcycle and took off, jerking and skidding, skiting up pebbles and startling a hen that flapped away without much grace and dived into the ditch. But once he had control of the motorcycle he appeared to know what he was doing and handled it more smoothly as he sped away.

The doctor was a big, gruff, bearded man, but he was surprisingly gentle as he examined Susan's leg. Then he opened his medical bag, which was like a portable cupboard with shelves and little drawers, and poured salt-like powders into pokes of paper and secured them with a twist at each end. Then he wrote down instructions as to how and when they were to be used.

When Catherine asked him would he take a drop of tay, he sighed heavily and cast his eyes heavenwards and said no, he would not take tay. He was sick of tay. That useless man in the house he'd come from was lamenting about what would happen to him and the children if his wife died and never seemed to have heard of whiskey. He had warned him that if his wife was expecting again the same thing would happen and not to send for him as he was liable to arrive with a gun.

As Catherine stepped back from the onslaught, Bryan deftly diverted the doctor out to the barn where he kept the poteen hidden. The IRA did not approve of poteen or poteen stills and the Specials would confiscate it. They sat out on the wall exchanging stories about hunting and fishing until Hughie came roaring up with a windswept, laughing Sarah Cullen sitting side-saddle on the back of the motorcycle. She got off, adjusted her headscarf, waved to the men and then walked on down the road.

Hughie discussed all aspects of the motorcycle with the doctor before going into the house. He seemed to have a more than casual interest in the motorcycle, but Bryan decided that maybe that was normal in a young fella. He paid the doctor with poteen and made arrangements to take him and some friends hunting up the mountain.

"What oxter-cogging are you at with that Sarah Cullen one after what she done on you?" Catherine hissed angrily when Hughie came in. "Don't you know well the kind of trouble she could get you into?"

But Hughie shrugged. He was only giving her a lift, he said.

For a couple of days Susan's condition remained the same and then gradually she began to perk up. When the doctor and his friends arrived a week later for their hunting trip, he was pleased with her progress. He had also brought them good news and money, because Bryan would be paid for the hunting trip. It all seemed to guarantee good luck for the coming year.

On 6 January, when Catherine threw the holly on the fire, the crackling woke Ellen, but there was luck in holly that burnt well. Susan recovered, but was reluctant to walk and didn't go back to school with the other girls. Mary didn't like her being at home all day, but she had her own places to go and soon got used to it.

In the Dáil, in Dublin, the terms of the treaty were fiercely debated, and on 7 January it was accepted by sixty-four votes to fifty-seven. Ireland would not get the republic that the IRA had fought many years to achieve. They would remain within the British Empire as a self-governing free state, swear an oath of allegiance to the king and contribute to the upkeep of the Empire. The North was included in the new Free State, but with the choice of opting out. The British prime minister, Lloyd George, threatened the Irish people with "immediate and terrible war" if the treaty was rejected. The Irish president, Éamon de Valera, did not accept the terms of the treaty and the cabinet was split as a result. The king granted an amnesty, and over one thousand political prisoners were released from various jails and camps in the British Isles. These included twenty-five prisoners from Newry and the locality. Michael Collins, as head of the provisional government, met James Craig to discuss various matters, including the future boundaries between North and South. The British army was moving out of the South, and the IRA was taking over their bases. The Yorkshire Light Infantry based in Dundalk was one of the first British regiments to leave Ireland. Military lorries and cars were being stolen by armed groups all over Ireland. Specials who had been court-martialled on criminal charges also benefited from the amnesty.

Towards the end of January, as Bryan and Catherine were cutting seed potatoes in the barn, Hughie called and Bryan questioned him about the split over the treaty. Collins had said that home rule was the best he could get for the time being, and Bryan wondered why de Valera hadn't gone over and done the negotiating with the British himself. Hughie said that de Valera thought Collins should have brought the treaty home for him to read it and that the whole government should have agreed on it before it was signed. At the beginning he wouldn't look at the treaty, and then he said he couldn't recommend it. All the head IRA men from the North were going mad above in Dublin wanting to know what was going to happen to the nationalists north of the Boyne, and all de Valera would say was they wouldn't be forgotten. Collins's men and Dev's men were talking to see if they could sort something out that would suit everyone, but it was a hard task. The Specials were in charge in the North and Hughie didn't know if the military would be let out against the people again.

The girls were in the Spelig, getting rushes for St Brigid's crosses, and Bryan went with Hughie to help them. He told Bryan they were pulling out of the North because it was too dangerous now the truce was over. If the military left, the Specials would get their weapons and they would be very well armed. The 4th Northern would be no match for them. They were waiting on word from Frank Aiken and were moving into County Louth, near Dungooley Crossroads on the border, a mile directly south of Forkhill village.

It was a few miles from Cashel but was accessible by the back roads. The camp was set up in an unoccupied house below the Crossroads, but when numbers increased it was moved to the larger premises next door. Hughie would send messages with Annie McGuinness and the Cumann na mBan, and Bryan could do the same if necessary.

When Bryan wondered was that dangerous for the women, Hughie sharply reminded him that the women were trained fighters too. They weren't children and had taken the oath the same as the men. They knew well what could happen to them if they were caught gathering intelligence.

"Be cripes!" Bryan muttered softly. There was a quare difference in Hughie the laughing, playful joker and Hughie the committed soldier. Hughie was involved in attacks on the Specials and in other IRA actions in the locality and further afield and was always living on the edge of danger, but he wouldn't have it any other way. The Specials in the North would soon be fully armed and conflict in the South was inevitable if they couldn't come to an agreement about the treaty. Bryan shrank from the unwelcome images and patted Hughie on the back. "Look after yourself, son," he cautioned. "I'd better go back and help your mother with the pratas."

Hughie swung over the ditch and strode down the field, calling to the girls.

Back at the shed Bryan told Catherine about the impending move across the border and them waiting on orders from Aiken.

"Sure Aiken's only a lad himself, the same as the rest of them," she said sadly.

"War soon makes men out of them," Bryan said, "I can see that now in Hughie. Aiken was fighting from when he was about sixteen. He wouldn't be leading them if he didn't know what he was doing. You take your time and I'll go in and get the tea on."

Catherine shook off a feeling of foreboding and threw the potato buds into the yard for the hens, then followed him in. As he buttered bread and exchanged banter with Hughie, she could tell that his bonhomie was an act and that his eyes were troubled.

Then Hughie asked Ellen about the old ruined cottage in the Spelig. She told him that the people who had lived there, also called Grant, had cut down a stand of beech trees where a large flock of crows roosted and sold it for timber. The crows had nowhere to roost and died out and it was well known that where the crows die out the family will die out too. There was no luck in that place, but Hughie was unfazed by the story. It was a dry wee place, in there out of the way, and it might do to hide wounded men. The adults exchanged troubled glances. It would be difficult to keep wounded men a secret. He promised the girls a penny for the best St Brigid's cross then lifted his knapsack and left, with Bryan escorting him part of the way. Catherine folded her arms under her bosom and watched as they passed by the window.

"Lads are always a worry," Ellen said. "When they're young, they can see no danger and they think they can hop their arses off the moon. You can see danger everywhere, and I can see it too, but I'm an aul woman with the Divil pulling at me from one side and the Lord at the other and death holds no fear for me. Say your Rosary morning and night and I'll say mine, and if the lad's going to be all right, he'll be all right, and if he isn't, that's God's will and there isn't a damn thing we can do about it. What's for you won't go past you, good or bad."

"I know, Ellen, I know." Catherine sighed. "You're right, there's nothing I can do to save him. He's in God's hands."

"That's what I thought when George and Bryan went to work in the mines," Ellen said. "One was took, but thank God one was left. They're not ours to keep. We only get the lend of them."

Chapter 8

In the months following the truce, the officers in the IRA watched nervously as the men were treated like celebrities and drink was bought for them in pubs. They feared loose talk and a lack of discipline would leave the men unready to return to the fight. Thousands of young men joined up for the anticipated resumption of the war. They were known as the Trucileers. In the spring of 1922 there were complaints of indiscipline within the IRA, with goods being requisitioned and demands for money being made from businesses and citizens. The Specials were active, raiding the homes of known IRA Volunteers in an effort to drive all IRA supporters out of the North. Michael Collins made a complaint to Churchill, who referred the matter to James Craig. Craig replied that the charges against his constabulary were vague and not supported by any evidence.

At the shop at Redmond's Crossroads they took pride in being up to date with all that was happening at home and abroad. Old news impressed no one. You had to get your spake in first.

Jem told Bryan the most recent news from around the locality and the rest of the country, then paused. "Well, there's other news too," he said importantly. "The Pope, Benedict XV, the head buck cat of the Roman Catholic Church, is as dead as a dure nail beyant in Rome."

"What did he die of?" Bryan enquired.

"He died of a Sunday, I think," Jem replied. "Shusie, did the Pope die of a Sunday or a Tuesday?"

"I don't know," Shusie said. "It just said he died of a sudden."

"He died of a sudden." Jem sighed. "His heart must have give out. What else would make him die of a sudden?"

"Shortness of breath," Shusie suggested.

The men looked at each other and shrugged; it was as good a reason as any for dying.

"They'll have to get another one, an Italian, I suppose," Bryan surmised.

"Sure he'd have to be able to talk Italian or they wouldn't know what he was saying. If Rome was in Ireland it would be a different story," Shusie snorted. "They'll get another one surely and little change will it make to us where they get him. Now did your wee Susan's leg ever get better?"

When Bryan had given a full account of the healing process, she graciously dismissed him, leaving him feeling as if he had been squeezed dry. Susan's leg had healed, but she was reluctant to stand up, walk or put any weight on it. Then Bryan found Ellen's cat in the loft and it had a kitten. Ellen said that yon cat couldn't have a kitten because it was too auld and it was a buck unless mebbe it was a maphrodite. Bryan got Susan up on his back and off they went to see the kitten. Earlier Ellen had advised that a couple a skelps on the bare arse with a bunch of nettles would soon have her walking again, but Catherine countered that she might have bother sitting. This was a method said to have been used on babies that were slow to start walking. Susan was overcome with the wonder of the kitten and forgot about her sore leg as she ran back to show it to the women. Catherine laughed with delight to see her not only walking, but running.

"Clare to God, it's a miracle," Ellen cried. "And I thought yon aul cat was done! That's the loveliest wee kitten I ever seen. Now put it back where you got it, Susan. The mother mightn't take with it if you have it away too long."

Bryan told Susan that the kitten could be hers if she went to school every day. Then he spat on his hand and she spat on hers and they solemnly shook hands like cattle dealers agreeing a sale.

Later on, when she fell out with Mary, Susan smugly informed her that she had a secret in the loft and Mary wasn't getting it.

Next morning she was up like a lintie and Catherine knew that she would tell the others on the way to school. From time to time during the day, Catherine saw Mary looking intently at the door of the loft as if it might reveal the secret. The ladder was propped up against the outside wall, but she wouldn't climb it because she was afraid she would slip through the spaces between the steps.

The girls arrived home scared and subdued. They had narrowly missed an encounter with a Crossley tender full of Specials at Ballinasack Bridge, but the children heading on towards the Crossroads weren't so lucky. The Specials pulled their St Brigid's crosses to pieces and threw the rushes in the river. They shouted at the children and poked them with their guns then got back into the tender and drove away laughing. The girls had watched from behind a bush on their own road then ran for home. Catherine diverted them with food and reminded them that Hughie would pick the best cross when he came back, if he ever came back. She blessed herself at the unbidden thought and threw last year's cross in the fire and hung the new ones above the door. She silently swore God's curse on the Specials. Could they not even leave the children alone?

There were a thousand B Specials in Newry and their reputation was atrocious. Recently they'd gone into Newry Cathedral and sat down and smoked cigarettes then washed their faces in the holy water font. If the holy water had burnt the jaws off them it would have been too good for them. They cursed the Pope before they left the cathedral and then drove round the streets in Crossley tenders and "cage" lorries, singing "Dolly's Brae".

Catherine often felt helpless because she didn't know how to protect the girls except by prayer. But they'd seen what happened at the bridge and knew to give the Specials a wide berth if they could. Susan went to get the kitten, but a moment later she came hurtling back and ran at Mary pummelling her about the head and shoulders demanding to know what she had done with it. Mary cowered in fear until Catherine dragged Susan aside.

"You're lying up there not fit to fart this couple of weeks," Ellen scolded. "And no sooner do you get legs under you, but you're running ramstam through the house bateing people."

Between sobs Susan explained that the cat and kitten were missing, but Catherine was doubtful that Mary was to blame. A cat would take a kitten away if it sensed danger. Mary said that she had seen a weasel crossing the haggard out near the byre.

"Aye, a weasel would take a kitten," Ellen agreed. "It would take a cat too. Sure if it can take a big rabbit, it can take a cat. You watch yourself, Mary, and if it starts to dance forninst you, turn away quick, for it will be trying to mesmerise you. Then when it has you that you can't move, it will be at your throat sucking the life's blood out of you."

Mary stared at her wide-eyed and solemn, as if she was absorbing the words through her skin. Then she shook herself and stood up. "It won't touch me," she said matter-of-factly. "It knows me."

"I have no doubt that it does." Ellen nodded.

"Is that true, do you think?" Catherine asked. "That it can mesmerise rabbits and chickens into a state where they can't move and then it kills them?"

"I don't know about rabbits, but it wouldn't be too hard to mesmerise a chicken." Ellen smiled dryly. "I heard tell of it, but I never seen it happening. I met one on the road one time and even though I had the presence of mind to cover me throat, I thought I was a goner. But, when I moved, it leapt into the ditch and I never seen it again. People say they seen strings of them moving about the country, with one holding on to the other's tail, but I don't know if that could be right."

The girls found no trace of the cat and kitten and later, when Bryan came home, he said that a weasel might be hunting the mice and rats in the loft. When Susan asked would she still have to go to school if they didn't find the cat and kitten, he said a bargain was a bargain and she'd have to go to school every day till she was a big coortin' girl. Susan sighed wearily and said that seemed a long way away.

The next morning, Mary quietly led Bryan to the back of the loft and peered around the corner, gesturing for him to do the same. A small, sinuous animal with a reddish brown coat and white belly was making its way along the base of the loft. It was the weasel. Every few seconds it paused, black-tipped tail flicking as the sharp little face warily interpreted the smells and sounds, before it climbed through a ventilation hole and disappeared into the loft.

"Be cripes, Mary, you were right," Bryan muttered. "It could be looking for mice or mebbe after eggs. We'll wait till it comes out and get Jocko to hunt it away up the mountain."

The weasel re-emerged and shot off, followed by Jocko. It soon disappeared but they followed at a leisurely pace. On the mountain near the big rock where the arms were buried, they encountered two "lost" Englishmen, who explained that they were priests out on a cross-country ramble. They had come over from Forkhill Mountain but now couldn't get their bearings. They said that they were holidaying with friends in Newry, but Bryan was immediately suspicious. They were dressed in civilian clothing but looked like military. He tried to survey the area to see if there were more of them, without appearing too obvious. When they spread a map out on the rock and asked him to direct them to Redmond's Crossroads, he could tell by their hands that they weren't priests. There were no soft edges on these boys. They were sharp-eyed and watchful, and as Bryan pretended to study the map he could feel a sweat break out on him. The arms were buried not too far below their feet. They spoke politely about the weather and the beauty of the countryside then patted Jocko, and as they headed down the mountain in the direction Bryan advised, he felt his knees give way. Either they knew the arms were there and were waiting to see who would come for them or they had information that there was a dump but didn't know where it was. The arms would have to be shifted. He'd have to send word to the boys at the border as soon as possible.

"Sure who wouldn't help a couple of priests?" he asked Mary. "You'd wonder at them getting lost on this very spot."

Someone had informed and it was sickening to think it might be someone they knew. Sarah came into his mind, always coming and going, maybe hearing an unintentional throwaway remark, but there were others trading information too. It was hard to guard against everything. If he'd got the list of informers from Sergeant Ennis, the RIC man, he'd know who was informing now. But that had its own difficulties because if he had the list he'd have to act on it.

That night as a bad storm came in over the mountain, Bryan fretted about the safety of the arms dump and the girls worried about the cat and kitten. When Ellen struggled out of bed to use the commode chair, the window was rattling, the candle flickering and the curtains blowing towards the ceiling. In the gloom outside, she saw a shadow moving about and heard an eerie mournful cry.

"Och, suffering Jesus Christ," she said, looking heavenwards in exasperation and dismay. "Did you send the banshee to take me now, in a storm in the night-time, and me sitting on the pot?"

There was no direct answer from Heaven, but the shadow on the windowsill was too small for a banshee and then she heard a distinct "Miaow!" With a wry laugh she finished her toileting and hobbled over to open the window. On a gust of wind and a cold blast of rain, the cat, with the kitten in her mouth, jumped into the room, padded lightly across the floor, sprang into the armchair by the fire and began to lick the kitten dry. As Ellen fumbled to close the window, it dropped with a clatter that brought Bryan swiftly into the room. He thought the storm had put the window out, until Ellen showed him her visitors.

Next morning he made a nest for the cats in the wall outside with a door that could be closed at night. Ellen said that if she'd put the cat in through the window backwards when she'd brought her up from Umericam, there would have been no bother with her. The severity of the storm left the countryside flooded and farm work came to a standstill till it dried up again. Bryan was repairing the seed fiddle before planting when Annie and Lizzie McGuinness cycled down the hill and leaned their bicycles against the wall. Annie was twenty-three, two years older and taller than Lizzie. They were both blue-eyed with clear freckled skin. Clean-looking girls, people said. Their hats dangled from the handlebars of the bicycles and their dark hair, loosened by the breeze and frizzed by the mist, strayed down onto their shoulders.

"Play us an aul reel there, Bryan," Annie demanded, indicating the seed fiddle.

When she picked up her skirts to dance, her stockings and the hem of her skirt were splattered with large japs of muck.

"She's not in tune yet." Bryan grinned. "I'm having a job getting the bow working." The bow worked a wheel below the seed box and dispensed the seed across the ground in a wide arc.

When he invited them in for tea, they hesitated, but cycling in muck was thirsty work and they agreed to go in for a minute. When they apologised for the state of their shoes, Catherine assured them that they were well used to muck. She wondered what had them afoot in such weather. They said that they were coming from the IRA camp at Dungooley and that Hughie had asked them to call in to let them know he was all right. She could send up bread if she had any to spare, but the camp was well set up. They had a cook and there were about fifty local lads there at the minute.

When they had finished their tea, Bryan walked down the road with them. Annie told him that the lads weren't that surprised by his meeting with the priests. They knew there were spies going about and thought that Bryan had probably upset their plans. They would come for the arms soon, but it would be a last-minute decision as they didn't want to risk any information leaking out. Hopefully the Specials were unwilling to go out on the bad roads and the lads could use this to their advantage. Brian said the lads could get stuck as well and the Specials could be out on foot, but he'd keep a good watch and let her know if he heard anything. Annie assured him they'd have it well scouted and wouldn't come in blind.

Ellen thought these young women were getting like men, going about on bicycles, and if they kept going on the way they're going, no man would want them. In her young day women like that were known as camp followers and it wasn't a name that showed any respect for them.

As Bryan listened his face crinkled with laughter. "Be cripes, Mother, they're not camp followers. Them girls are risking their lives to help the lads, and you can't make little of them. They're fine and brave and as good as any man."

"They'll be wearing trousers next," Ellen huffed.

"They'd be better wearing trousers travelling on roads like yon."

He had just started the ploughing when Jem Redmond arrived to say that his aunt Rosie Redmond had died and would Catherine come over to help lay her out. As Catherine collected the requirements for the laying-out ritual and put them in a pillowcase, Jem carefully negotiated his way to where Bryan was working. His boots were highly polished to Shusie's specifications and he wanted to keep them that way.

"Rosie turned her toes for Drawda not more nor half an hour ago," he reported. "She sut straight up in the bed, looked at me and says, 'I'm away now!' and that was the last cheep out of her."

"And did the Headless Coachman come back for her in the end?" Bryan asked.

"Well, I seen him come for her many a time afore, but I didn't hear him about last night nor the day, but she must a knew it was time."

When Bryan mentioned the priests, Jem said he'd seen a pair of strange men juking round the Crossroads, but they hadn't come into the shop, and after the Specials passed by they were gone. He'd seen slithery-eyed boys like them before, but never the same pair twice. They were dropped near the Crossroads, mebbe dressed as tramps, and it might be a couple of days before they were picked up again. They must think the people were soft not to know what they were at.

A shout from Biddy Kane interrupted Jem. She'd spied him slipping up the road, surmised that Rosie had passed on and hurried down to meet him. As she waited for them to join her, she adjusted the fingers of her kid gloves and the jet beaded collar of her black American coat. The feathers on her high black hat were ruffled by the breeze.

"Be cripes," Bryan observed. "Biddy looks like the chief mourner. Shusie won't be pleased."

Jem looked at him and heaved a deep sigh.

They parted with Bryan, collected Catherine and set off quickly for the Crossroads.

"The Dead Coach was going up and down the road these three nights," Biddy informed them. "And I knew she'd go the night or in the morning. He won't come three nights in a row for nothing. Three nights is the charm, and if she didn't go with him now he wouldn't be back. I ris this morning and put on me Sunday go-to-meeting clothes and I knew when I seen Jem beetling up the road that he was coming for you, Catherine, so I came on down."

"Sound woman, Biddy," Jem said. "Isn't it lucky we have the likes of you in the country that always knows what's going on between the living and the dead?"

At the Crossroads, Shusie was fretting because the priest had been sent for, and it wouldn't do at all if he arrived and Rosie wasn't properly presented. The doors and windows were opened wide so that her soul could pass through unhindered. The curtains were knocking ornaments over and the breeze was slamming and creaking the inside doors. Catherine asked Jem to close the front door, but Shusie objected because she didn't want anything holding Rosie back.

They approached Rosie's corpse with caution, as on previous occasions they had encountered large white lice departing from the bodies. It may have been due to the chaff in the mattress becoming lice infested, but it was seen as a supernatural sign. The lice were caught in pads that were soaked in paraffin oil and then thrown into the fire. Rosie was washed and stretched out as best as possible. She had been bedridden for some time and her limbs had contracted. She was laid out in the blue satin shroud with white lace revers that she had ordered for the occasion from one of Shusie's magazines. Her hair was plaited and pinned in a bun the way she had always worn it, and her big toes were tied together. Her mouth was secured closed with a linen handkerchief that was passed under her chin and knotted at the top of her head, and pennies were placed on her eyelids to keep her eyes shut. They put clean white sheets under and over her and then folded a white counterpane down to waist level. This set of white bedclothes was owned by Shusie. It was only used for wakes and was loaned out all over the countryside as required. Rosie's gnarled hands were joined in prayer with Rosary beads entwined between her fingers. Two glass candlesticks with candles inserted were placed each side of the bed and the room was cleared of all clutter. The mirror was covered to prevent

Tam the Divil, or anyone like him, stepping in from the Other Side to claim Rosie's soul, and the clock was stopped at the time she died. She would go no further.

Shusie asked Jem had he sent for the keenogers to sing the dirges at the wake, but Jem hadn't bothered because Rosie said that she didn't want them crying like a bag a scalded cats at her wake. Shusie could send for them if she liked, but he didn't want Rosie glowering at the foot of his bed every night. No more was said about the keenogers. Arrangements were made with the undertaker and crates of stout, a couple of bottles of whiskey, a dozen clay pipes and wads of tobacco were brought in. Neighbouring women called to see if they could help. The priest was out on a sick call and would be delayed. By evening the mourners were gathering, and when Catherine suggested saying the Rosary, Biddy Kane shot in and took up a position by the head of the corpse, then piously closed her eyes and commenced praying.

"In the name of the Father and of the Son and of the Holy Ghost, Amen." Biddy blessed herself and ostentatiously kissed the Cross on the Rosary beads.

"The Sorraful Mysteries," she intoned. "First Mystery: Dragging Him into the Garden."

She said the first part of the Our Father and waited on the mourners to respond, then she went on to the Hail Marys: "Hail Mary, full of grace, the Lord is with thee ..." She took off like a fox in a hunt, her voice rising and falling as if she was clearing ditches, going faster and faster as the end came in sight. Then the mourners took off after her, in full cry, like hounds baying at her heels. "Holy Mary, mother of God ..."

"The Second Sorraful Mystery: The Scorching at the Pillar." Biddy continued each decade, getting faster and faster.

"The Third Sorraful mystery: The Hanging of the Three Thieves."

She continued praying with her eyes closed, blissfully unaware that the mourners were looking at each other, shoulders were beginning to shake and Shusie was glaring daggers into her back.

"The Fourth Sorraful Mystery: Trailing Him to the Cross."

There were splutters and hasty coughs, but the diehards continued praying, casting disapproving glares at the sniggerers as they strove to keep up with Biddy.

"The Fifth Sorraful Mystery …" Here Biddy paused and the mourners held their breath, wondering what this one would be, or could she not remember it?

"The Crucifixion!" Biddy announced triumphantly, as if she had personally arranged it.

The mourners breathed a sigh of relief as they sprinted for the finish. Then they stood, spent and panting, trying to catch their breath.

Fr Carron, who had arrived when Biddy was in full flight, looked stunned at her interpretation of the Sorrowful Mysteries and disbelieving as she launched into a litany of post-Rosary prayers. Catherine intervened to say the priest had arrived and would like a few private moments with the corpse. Biddy beamed at the priest as she relinquished her spot. She would probably get the opportunity to say a lot more Rosaries before the wake was over.

Shusie, knowing how much Biddy loved the limelight, resolved to block her if possible. At the wake, Catherine offered tea to everyone but also asked the more elderly women if they'd like a bottle of stout or a wee hot half one of punch. She knew there were professional wake-goers who only came for the free drink and they were welcome if they were good crack, but poorly tolerated and hard to get rid of if the drink made them obstreperous. When Catherine had done all she could, she went home. Bryan was waiting, dressed and ready to dander over. He would stay there until dawn broke. Someone had to sit with the corpse at all times until it was safely buried. The Divil was most active during the wee hours, and the soul was always in the most danger when it was between the two worlds.

On the second evening, when Catherine went back, she took Brigid with her. Brigid could negotiate through the people and round the furniture, dispensing tea and retrieving dirty delft without disturbing anyone too much. It was a quiet windless night, and a steady flow of mourners arrived to pay their respects, say a prayer for Rosie and offer condolences to Jem and Shusie. They were startled when the front door evaded the doorstopper and slammed shut, shattering the glass panel at the top.

"I knew she wasn't gone, Catherine," Shusie observed as she swept up the glass. "She's mebbe away now, thank God, but she didn't have to take door and door cheeks with her."

People looked at each other uneasily. They knew about Rosie and the Coachman, but the moment passed and when neither of them reappeared, they relaxed again.

Catherine and Brigid walked gingerly home, feeling with their feet for the grass verge. Stories were told of people coming from wakes in the dark and being hit suddenly and knocked over by something supernatural, either the spirit of the dead person departing or something evil and unformed lurking in wait for the soul. That it might be a wandering ass or goat was not considered, and when Catherine saw the light coming from their house, she blessed herself and thanked God for a safe journey. Inside Brigid climbed gratefully into the settle bed and closed her eyes. When Catherine told them about the glass shattering in the door at the Crossroads, Bryan and Ellen laughed and shook their heads.

"Sure they might a knowed that Rosie wouldn't go without some drama," Bryan said. "I'll be back a bit earlier the night. The lads will be here at daylight for the weapons. I went and took them down earlier and hid them under the straw in the haggard. There's too much stir at the Crossroads and I don't want the lads footering about from the yard to the dump and getting caught. I'm surprised the Specials aren't about."

When he returned from the wake, he kept watch, and when the lads arrived with the lorry, he helped to load it. It was a tense business, carried out as quickly as possible, with none of the repartee that was exchanged when the arms were put in the dump. The roads to the house were guarded by men with rifles, and up on the mountain, scouts scanned the countryside with field glasses. Catherine breathed a sigh of relief when the lorry moved off and was further relieved when the McGuinness girls called later to say that the lads had returned safely to the camp at Dungooley.

As Rosie Redmond was being transported to the chapel, a tender filled with Specials forced the cortège and mourners onto the grass verge and bulled their way past, but the mourners kept their eyes firmly fixed on the hearse and didn't acknowledge their presence or surly remarks. Rosie was buried without any further earthly or psychic interference, apart from Biddy Kane losing her footing in an ecstasy of grief and almost falling into the grave. Rosie wouldn't have been too happy about that, as she'd never liked any one stealing her thunder. Shusie warned the gravediggers to make sure that Rosie was well dibbled down and to put plenty of clay on her to keep her in there.

Chapter 9

The ploughing was resumed following the moving of the guns and Rosie's funeral. In the bigger fields the jinnet pulled the plough, but in the fields where they couldn't turn a jinnet, the digging was done with spades. Some men preferred the spade because the jinnet, bred from an ass, could be stubborn and hard to direct. Mickle and Oiney were helping out, and when Brigid and Mary arrived with tea and bread, they hunkered down to eat as the ground was too damp to sit on. Mickle wondered, as he did every year, how the seagulls knew they were ploughing. Oiney said it was a sign of rain when seagulls were so far from the shore, but if they looked at the almanac they would see that it rained at this time every year. When Bryan said that the Scots people thought seagulls were the souls of dead sailors that had been lost at sea, Oiney wondered what dead sailors would be doing out there looking for worms.

Lent was about to start. As penitence, the congregation was encouraged to give up luxuries such as sugar. To show the country the strength of their faith and that they were tough men who could take it or leave it, many hardened drinkers stayed off the drink during Lent. Mickle asked Bryan if he had ever heard of a custom called the pancake sieve, where if you were passing a house on Pancake Tuesday they would throw a bag of soot over you. Bryan thought that people might be cleaning their chimneys and maybe it was for luck, or maybe for sport, the soot would be thrown, but he knew of people that cleaned their teeth with soot, them that had teeth.

Oiney had heard that lorry loads of arms and ammunition were going to the camp at Dungooley Crossroads every night and that Hughie and the lads would be back in a lock a weeks to settle matters in the North once and for all. He wondered was there any truth in it. Bryan could see that the girls were engrossed by something near the sheugh at the edge of the field. He told the men that the arms were taken across the border to prevent the Specials from getting them, but the camp was very close to the boundary line and that was a worry. The Specials weren't supposed to cross the border now, but a line on the road that no one could see wasn't going to stop them. Their barracks and outposts along the border were well armed with guns that were brought there in funeral cars and furniture vans so that the IRA wouldn't know they were carrying them. Farmers out working in the fields were being shot at and the military was back in the barracks in Newry and Armagh. The Specials seemed to be in the better position, but Mickle was confident that the IRA would win, and Cashel would be part of the New Ireland. Nothing else would do. What good would the bloody treaty be if they were left on the wrong side of the border? And now there was a split in Dublin over the treaty, and that wasn't a good development.

Bryan was distracted by Brigid calling for him to come quick. Mary thought the young frogs in the sheugh were choking the old ones and she was trying to separate them and was getting very agitated. Oiney and Mickle looked a bit puzzled, but Bryan laughed. He told Brigid to collect up the mugs and tay bottle and he would see to Mary. He didn't think the young frog was choking the old one at this time of year. At the sheugh he found Mary trying to work her thumb between two entwined frogs to prise them apart. She was wet and perspiring and becoming very angry and frustrated. She detached a frog and plonked it on the edge of the sheugh. It looked momentarily confused before leaping back into the writhing mass of mating frogs. Jocko added to the chaos by barking and jumping in and out of the sheugh. Bryan sent the two girls home then rejoined his cousins and told them what had happened.

"God bless their holy innocence, the poor wee craters," Oiney murmured.

When he asked Bryan if he was going to Scotland when the crops were in, Bryan said no. He had a bad feeling about the way things were going. The Specials were never off the roads and he didn't want to leave the women on their own. Dungooley Crossroads was too near to be safe and there would be a settling of some sort; there would have to be. Oiney agreed with him. They would get the crops planted as quickly as possible for fear they would be needed. They would have to be ready for anything.

The situation in the country both North and South was very volatile with law and order at breaking point. Withdrawal of British troops from the South had been put on hold for the present. Michael Collins and de Valera were at odds over the treaty and each was trying to win the support of the people. Winston Churchill, as colonial secretary, was trying to get the treaty implemented in the South and mediating between Collins and James Craig about the North. Cardinal Logue sent out a pastoral letter expressing his concern at the divisions caused by the signing of the treaty. Old grievances were being settled by men using the name of the IRA. In Forkhill, a farmer was ordered at gunpoint to return land he had bought or he would be shot. In the pogrom against Catholics in Belfast, Frank McCoy, a twenty-five-year-old barman, was found injured in the street, but was dead on arrival at hospital. He had two bullet wounds in his back. His body was returned to his home place in Mullaghbane, where he was buried with full military honours. The countryside and beyond turned out for the funeral. Many people expressed great anger, but others felt powerless. Resistance only brought more bloodshed and heartache. The trouble in Belfast had seemed far away, but now it had been brought to their doorstep.

Bryan went to help Biddy Kane to sow hay and dig the garden to plant potatoes and cabbage. She had been out on her ceilidh in Silverbridge the night before and reported that a Special had been killed and one hurted the day before over on the border near Cullaville. When Bryan warned her to be careful as she could be mistaken for a Sinn Féiner and shot some night in retaliation, she casually informed him that she had encountered the Specials the night before when she'd gone behind the ditch to do her wet. She'd thought it was cattle moving about. Bryan said that she was taking a big risk both by rambling about after dark and letting the boys come to the house. Someone could inform on her. Biddy said the lads coming by shortened the nights for her, them sitting be the fire talking about the new Rising and her listening in the bed. General Aiken, or Frank as she called him, was there one night – an ordinary sort of a lad with no airs and graces for all that he was a general, but he was so young.

Bryan said aul fellas were seldom found dead on the battlefield and Biddy agreed. Michael Collins, the head of the new government above in Dublin, was only thirty if he was a day, and a fine, handsome-looking young man too. She had never met him, but she heard that he'd been in Crossmaglen and he'd stayed out be Whitecross. He reminded her a lot of her father. She handed Bryan the newspaper and an old sepia, leather-framed picture of her father, Padna, when he was younger. Michael Collins stood tall in his army uniform looking assured and confident in his triumph, while a young Padna gazed steadily from a photo that was more like a drawing, but there was a slight resemblance in the shape of the face and the cut of the jaw. Biddy watched Bryan expectantly and he didn't disappoint her. When he said they were the spit of each other and could be father and son, she clapped her hands in delight.

"Bryan, dear, you couldn't have put it better," she crowed. "And as long as Michael Collins is in charge we'll not be left on the wrong side of the border. Now what about Lent? The newspaper says that flesh meat is permitted every day except Wednesday and Friday and the first Wednesday and Saturday of Ember Week. I wouldn't be ating flesh meat except I kill an aul hen of a Saturday, but if they want me to ate it, I'll have to send to Newry for it. What should I do?"

Bryan felt as confused as Biddy sounded and advised her to ask Catherine or his mother; one of them was bound to know. As he led the jinnet homewards, he wondered did the lads know that Biddy was awake in the next room, listening to every word they said, and he hoped she had the wit not to repeat anything.

People often said that Biddy couldn't howl her water, but she gathered and delivered information on her ceilidhs round about and she had never spoken to him about that.

At 1.15 a.m. on 24 March armed men broke down the door of a house on the Antrim Road area in Belfast and shot five men dead and injured three others. The dead men, in their early twenties, were three of the McMahon brothers and a barman who lived with them called Ed McKinney. Owen McMahon, a publican, originally from Rathfriland, plus two more of his sons were critically injured. A six-year-old younger brother escaped death by hiding under a sofa. The women of the house were tied up and locked in a back room while the carnage was taking place. One woman was assaulted. Owen McMahon died at 7 a.m. that morning. He had no connection with the IRA. The killings were a reprisal for the shooting of two A Specials in Belfast the previous day. John McMahon, who survived, gave an account to Fr Hassan in St Mary's, Belfast. He said that the attackers had been dressed in RIC uniforms, but he knew they were B Specials. Michael Collins had informers in the RIC who reported on the sectarian murders in Belfast.

The murder gang or "counter terror gang" was set up by senior RIC members to avenge the killings of policemen and to terrorise Catholics into leaving the new Ulster state. In Armagh and South Down shootings and reprisals continued throughout the month of March. One Special was shot dead and another injured in an ambush in Newry. On 2 April six more Catholics, including a child, were murdered in the Arnon Street Massacre, in Belfast. One victim was an ex-soldier who was killed with a sledgehammer in front of his two children, who were then shot. One survived.

The Dublin to Belfast train was constantly held up at Adavoyle. Belfast goods were taken from it and copies of the *Belfast Telegraph* were burnt in Dundalk. Orior House in Upper Fathom was burnt to the ground by the IRA to prevent it being used as accommodation for the Specials. Adavoyle Orange Hall was also burnt down. Tenders continually patrolled the roads around Mullaghbane, forcing farm vehicles into the hedges and ditches and scattering sheep and cattle. Specials on foot appeared without warning in lonins and on farms. Men of all ages were questioned at gunpoint. It was hard for them to know how to behave in front of the Specials. If they kept their heads down, they looked like they'd something to hide, but if they looked straight at them it was seen as a challenge. If a man saw them coming and ran to hide he could be shot, but if he stood his ground he could also be shot. The people were at the mercy of the Specials. They'd shoot you as quick as look at you was the general belief. For women it was easier to ignore the obscene gestures and vulgar remarks if they were in groups. But Easter was approaching and maybe the new Rising would get them off the roads.

When Hughie called on Holy Saturday night, Catherine reminded him to make his Easter duty, to go to Confession and start the Holy Year with a clean slate. He said arrangements had been made for them to attend Mass. He went out to the byre, where Bryan was milking the cow. De Valera had been in Dundalk, surrounded by a big contingent of men, and he wondered had Hughie and the lads been part of the guard. Hughie said they had been there, but the guards had been Louth men.

De Valera told the people he wouldn't accept the treaty because it would be hard to get out of an Empire once they got in. There was only one government in Ireland and it wasn't Collins and Griffith, and if they accepted the king, they would not get an Irish Republic. He wouldn't accept the treaty or come to an agreement with Collins and Griffith. Civil War was looming.

Part of the 4th Northern Division was at the Dungooley camp, but Frank Aiken and three hundred men had taken over the recently vacated British military barracks in Dundalk. Aiken didn't want to see Irish men fighting and killing each other in a civil war. The North was the only thing that mattered to him, and if anything happened in the South, he wanted to stay neutral. Hughie said that the Rising Biddy had spoken about was coming soon and that Bryan needn't worry about her talking out of turn or giving away information, as she had taken the oath. They had sworn her in and she was now a member of the IRA. The 4th Northern was waiting for the word, and then they would come back in and free the North. He was marching the next day in Dundalk to commemorate those who had fallen during the Easter Rising and the War of Independence, then away he went to say goodbye to the women and girls.

Bryan wished him the best of luck and luck where he was going and luck when he was coming back. As he leaned his head against the cow's warm flank he could feel the hard round lumps of the warble fly larvae under her skin. "I'll have to give you a good dousing of louse powder," he murmured. "But sure the louse powder can no more stop the warble fly than I can stop yon boy that's out to get himself killed no matter what praying we do."

When Mary told Hughie they'd heard a cuckoo, he said that he and Gerard had heard a cuckoo on St Patrick's Day.

Ellen's head came up like a pointer dog. "Och, your arse and parsley, you never heard the cuckoo of a Patrick's Day!" she said, snorting. "You must have been mistaken."

"Mebbe I was," Hughie replied, winking at Catherine. "Right, Ma, I have everything in the bag. I'm away. Good luck."

"Have you your St Joseph's prayer?" she asked.

All the lads carried the St Joseph's prayer for protection.

"He's pulling your leg," she told Ellen as he disappeared through the door.

"Well, I would hope that he was," Ellen replied. "For you know what they say: them that hears the cuckoo before the month of April will be dead before the year is out."

Catherine nodded without replying and turned her attention back to bathing the children. She was using the water from boiled marshmallow leaves to keep their hair soft and shiny.

"Always look after your hair," she advised them. "It's your crowning glory." When they were all plaited and ringleted it was time for bed.

On Easter Sunday morning they wore new clothes and flowery Easter bonnets that would double as sun hats on hot summer days. On the way home from Mass, John Murphy stopped beside them on a bicycle and Eugene jumped off.

"That's our new bicycle, Brigid. It's a Royal Enfield, made like a gun. That's what the man in the shop said. I can ride it too," he boasted. "Well, I can stand on one pedal and if I put me leg under the bar I can work the other one. Can I show them, Da?"

Catherine and the girls watched as he awkwardly cycled up and down the road then returned the bicycle to his beaming father and fell in step with the girls. He strolled along with his hands in his pockets kicking at loose stones and ignoring the younger girls, who were trying to keep abreast. He asked Brigid what was she larning at school now? She said they were learning Hamlet, and when she explained that it was an English play, he was surprised at her. He wouldn't let them larn him a play that was wrote by an Englishman. Brigid sighed. He was very annoying. She walked on quickly, but he trotted up beside her, asking did they larn her how dogs kept their arses warm at the North Pole? She waited resignedly as he explained. He only met people at the chapel on a Sunday or Holiday of Obligation and all his information came from his father. If John didn't say it, Eugene didn't want to know. When Catherine asked him would he be rolling his egg he didn't know what she meant, and the girls were happy to explain to this know-all boy that on an Easter Sunday they boiled their eggs and rolled them down the hill. They asked Eugene to join them, but John wouldn't hear of it. The lad's insides were delicate; the look of an egg or rowlin' it would do him no good at all. Eugene seemed disappointed but climbed onto the bicycle without protest and waved to the girls as they pedalled off.

"Odd as be damned, them Murphys, the whole breed of them," Ellen said when Catherine told her about John. "The poor woman was lucky that she died when she did for she'd never have got out through the door again once that child was born, not with yon fella."

"He keeps the lad looking well, though," Catherine said in John's defence. "He had a clean white collar and a nice wee cap on him and a good warm coat and britches, and his boots were well polished."

"That's as may be," Ellen conceded, "but what sort of wee

necromancer is he going to turn the child into? Sure childer need to play with other childer."

The girls picked whin blossom to turn the egg shells yellow and then carried the eggs across the road in a pot of water to the circle of blackened stones where their fire was lit every year. Sarah Cullen came toiling up the road and lay on the ditch to watch them. She was visibly sweating, out of breath and very pale. The girls were a bit alarmed. This wasn't the lively Sarah they were used to meeting.

"Could you get me a drink of water, Brigid, please?" she requested hoarsely.

Brigid ran to the house and got the water and Sarah gulped it down. She declined the invitation to go inside, lifted her bag and trudged on up the road. When Catherine came out and shouted was she all right, she gave a backward wave of her hand, but kept going, almost bent over. Catherine went back to preparing the dinner.

Two hours later the girls came in dusty and dishevelled and reeking of smoke, but they were happy. When Ellen said the dinner was a poor bit of lamb that tasted more like mutton, Catherine didn't tell her that it was goat. When she asked was yon Sarah one above with Addy all the time now, Catherine replied that she was and with the way she was trailin' up the road the day maybe she wasn't well again. Then she rubbed her chin reflectively and felt her face flush as an unwanted thought crept into her head. The shape of Sarah today was like a woman that was expecting. She rose from the table to stave off further questions and began to noisily wash the dishes.

It was well after dark on Easter Tuesday when a rap came to the window. Ellen and the girls were asleep and Catherine was knitting, while Bryan relaxed in an armchair. It wasn't Hughie's rap, nor the harsh slam of a military rifle butt; it was a more hesitant and tentative rapping, almost as if the person didn't want to be heard. Bryan shot up out of the chair, stood for a moment to collect himself, then opened the door and peered out into the night. After a murmur of recognition, he stepped outside then returned and beckoned to Catherine. She threw her shawl round her shoulders and went out. It took her a moment to recognise Addy's hushed hoarse voice.

"You'll come over to the house with me straight away, Catherine," she stated. "And bring the bag with you. I don't want to go for Kate Nellie."

Kate Nellie was a well-known local midwife, and the bag Addy referred to was the midwife's lying-in bag. Catherine wasn't as skilled as Kate but had assisted her many times. She was neither surprised nor insulted by Addy's blunt approach, as Bryan was present and women's problems were never discussed in front of men. That was the way of it. She knew without asking that Sarah was in trouble.

"Bring a couple a clean sheets and a nightshirt as well and I'll pay you for them," Addy offered.

"I'll bring them and there'll be no need for paying," Catherine told her.

She gave Bryan instructions about what he should do in the morning, lifted the bag and followed the shadowy figure of Addy up the road. When her eyes adjusted to the dark, she was able to see where the ditches lay. They didn't speak because the road was treacherous at night with large potholes and deep culverts along the edges where the water ran down. Addy's house was in darkness apart from an odd flicker of light that may have been coming from the fire. As they were about to enter, Addy cast her body dramatically across the door barring the way.

"You're never to tell another sowl about this and I want your hand and word to God on that, Catherine," she demanded.

"You know that I'll not say anything, Addy."

"Swear to me now or you'll never cross this doorstep," Addy insisted forcefully. "If word gets out, Sarah Cullen will be finished in this part of the country. That is, God forbid, if she's not finished already."

"Me hand and word to God, Addy. I swear that I'll say nothing," Catherine promised, "except to Bryan, of course. He knows you came over for me and he knows it's not you that has trouble."

Addy agreed that Bryan could be told, then turned up the flame on the oil lamp, causing the shadows to leap back into the corners. The room was filled with steam from a large pot that was simmering over the fire. Addy waved her hands ineffectively to disperse it and then led Catherine into a bedroom. Sarah lay beneath a thin patchwork quilt on the bare mattress of a narrow bed. In the soft glow of the oil lamp she looked like death was about to claim her. Her hair was plastered wetly to her head and her skin was an unearthly shade of greyish white. Dark circles outlined her sunken eyes and stained her cheekbones and her full pale lips were parched and cracked. She felt extremely hot and would need to be cooled down as quickly as possible. Addy said that she had been sitting up with her for the last two nights, that she hadn't wanted to leave her alone, but when things got worse, she went for Catherine. She said that Sarah had been about five months gone, but avoided Catherine's searching look.

Women like Addy were said to use crochet hooks, knitting needles and herbal potions to induce a miscarriage. The dangers were haemorrhage and sepsis, with both causing death. There was no treatment. Many women died during childbirth even with a doctor present, but it didn't stop others availing of Addy's services. Poverty was one factor – another mouth to feed. An unmarried woman wanting to preserve her reputation was another, or maybe a woman likely to die in childbirth and leave a houseful of children. Addy was liable for prosecution if her activities were discovered or one of her clients died.

"I did nothing to her and gave her nothing. This came on her of a sudden," Addy stated flatly. "And take care what you're asking. There could be a trail leading to your own door!"

Catherine stood stock still as she absorbed what Addy was inferring.

"No, Granny, no," Sarah cried out weakly and then collapsed back, exhausted, on the bare pillow. Catherine gritted her teeth as a wave of surprise and anger washed over her, but she took a deep breath and quelled the urge to retaliate. She glared at Addy for a few long moments. Did she think that implicating Hughie would ensure her silence?

"You have me word, Addy. Don't bring me son into it," she said quietly. "Only this girl is in the state she's in, for two pins I'd lift me bag and go back down the road to me own house and let you go to Hell there."

"No, don't do that. I'm sorry, Catherine, I'm sorry. I don't know what made me say what I said," Addy bowed her head looking shamefaced. "What can I get you?"

They bathed Sarah with the tepid water then held the shift away from her body to let the skin dry naturally. The small window was kept firmly closed, for though it might cool her faster, it was well known that the night air did nobody any good. Wasn't that how the Spanish flu spread so fast a couple of years previously? When Sarah was cooler, they put clean linen on the bed and slipped a nightdress over her head. The crisis had passed for the moment and they were grateful for the break, as they didn't know what the night might bring. Over a cup of tea Addy said Sarah hadn't been feeling well but left for Newtownhamilton to see her mother on Easter Sunday. She wasn't long away when she took bad and had to come back. After a hard night of pain and suffering she had passed "a ball of stuff" the size of a turnip and Addy had buried it deep in the dung heap for fear a fox might get it. She often buried dead animals there under the manure and straw bedding that had been removed from the outhouses. If the cow calved in the byre she'd bury the afterbirth in the dung heap, but if it calved in the field she'd throw the afterbirth up on a bush because she believed that as long as it remained there, the cow would be fertile and the calf would thrive.

Addy revealed that she had given Sarah a powder to get rid of the afterbirth. It was one she had used before. She wouldn't harm Sarah. She was like her own child. But Catherine was wary of her methods and warned that if Sarah got worse, Dr Horgan would have to be sent for. Addy looked mutinous and threw up her hands in surrender. They would send for him if they had to.

"He said that if he ever caught me giving expecting women advice again he'd have the law on me," she explained.

Catherine smiled at Addy's notion of giving expecting women advice. But the doctor had treated Sarah for a lack of iron and that might be what was wrong with her now. Addy said that Tony, her boyfriend, was from a well-to-do family. His mother had married the son of the house where she was hired, though it wasn't often they married into Catholics. Sarah had told Addy that she was promised to Tony, but when Addy was in Newtown at Christmas she heard that Tony was matched to a girl that was from farming people the same as himself. Sarah was the kind of a crater that would believe anything, and he could be leading her on. She was staying in Cashel and meeting him at the Crossroads and the other girl knew nothing about it. If Tony married her, it would be the making of her, but men didn't often marry a woman that had a child out of wedlock, and who would know that better than Addy herself? She would have kept this child if it had lived and said it was her own.

When Catherine smiled, Addy said, "Aye that sounds a bit soft, but there's plenty would believe it even though I'm well past it. They think I'm fit for anything." A sudden yawn overcame her and she apologised.

Catherine told her to rest by the fire and she would sit with Sarah.

Just before morning Sarah awoke and dashed away the cup Catherine offered, then, with a piercing cry, she expelled the afterbirth. After that she looked much better. Addy helped settle her, but her head was soon drooping again, and Catherine slipped out, leaving them both sleeping and more peaceful.

She inhaled deeply as she gazed across the wakening fields. The bushes and trees were darkly outlined by the faint sunrise, and the birds were starting to sing. She felt as if the world belonged to her, but as she walked along, swinging her bag, she realised she wasn't alone. She looked behind her and saw the ominous shape of a Crossley tender on the road above Addy's lonin. Her knees went weak, but she forced herself forward and down the hill for home. Suddenly she heard a low rumbling sound and felt the road vibrating as the tender gathered speed. In the nick of time she hurled herself into the ditch then watched incredulously as it trundled past where she lay. Armed Specials swayed with the movement of the lorry as it rounded the bend and disappeared from sight. They gave no indication that they'd seen her.

"God's curse on yis, you crowd of bastards," she swore. "Were yis trying to kill me?" God's curse was the worst curse possible and Catherine didn't use it lightly.

She blessed herself then eased shakily upwards and shook out her skirts. After such a close call she was surprised to find that she wasn't as shook as she might have expected and that all her parts were working. She hadn't heard a motor and had the surreal feeling that the lorry had gone around the bend then lifted from the road and sailed away up into the sky. She wondered had Addy used the water in the black saucepan to make the tea. She knew about her coaxiorum and calming concoction. But she could see the tracks of the tender in the muck and only she'd leapt for her life they would have run her over as easily as a rat. There was no room for manoeuvre on this narrow road. She scrabbled for her bag and ran.

Home had never seemed more welcoming. After a lifetime Bryan opened the door and she was back safe on her own hearthstone, telling him what had happened. The only sound had been the swish of the wheels turning on the road and the Specials in the back were frozen there like a lorry full of dead, grey soldiers' ghosts, but Bryan assured her that it hadn't been a phantom lorry. The rattling of the window had wakened him. The Specials were on the prowl all the time now and would have seen the lights on in Addy's. Maybe they thought it was men playing cards and were waiting to see who would come out, but all they got was a woman with a lying-in bag. Their engine might have gone cold and they were probably cold too, and fed up. They ran it down the hill to start it and Catherine just happened to be in the way. They were showing the people who was in charge. It was still "croppy lie down" with them.

When she told him about Sarah, he was sympathetic. Rumour had it that Addy buried babies' bodies at the back of her house, but Bryan said Addy only had a potato pit at the back of her house and the doctor was the man to deal with the likes of that, not Catherine. The country was in a poor enough state without the authorities being brought down on Addy. Catherine didn't go back to her, but no bad news came either, and she decided that what had happened to Sarah was an unfortunate but natural occurrence.

Addy came over one day to return the bedclothes and nightdress that she had borrowed.

"She's on the mend now, the crater, blertin' and crying, but she'll come away from that," she said. "Now, Catherine, remember, if you ever need anything done, anything at all, give me a shout and if it's in me power, I'll help you out."

She pressed a penny into Mary's hand, patted her on the head then whirled out through the door and hurried back up the hill before Catherine could speak.

In a small community people had to rely on each other. It didn't do to fall out with anyone as no one knew when trouble would come to their door. She was glad that Ellen was still in bed, otherwise it would have been difficult to explain why Addy was there returning bedclothes. Mary picked up the kitten from the armchair and wrapped it in Catherine's shawl, then set it between her knees as if she was washing or baptising it.

"There now, child," she crooned. "There, now." When Mary carefully laid the kitten back in the armchair, Catherine asked whose child was she washing.

"It's not a child, Mammy," Mary informed her. "It's a kitten."

"Leave it, Catherine. You'll not get your answer from a simple-minded child," Bryan advised, laughing. "Let the hare sit."

Chapter 10

Towards the end of April the Catholic Bishops in Maynooth spoke out in favour of the treaty and against de Valera's anti-treaty stance. They were also concerned about partition in the north-east and compared the persecution of Catholics in Belfast to the atrocities committed by the Turks against the Armenians. They pointed out that the Northern government had tens of thousands of armed men paid for by the British and that Catholics weren't even allowed to have a shotgun to keep the crows from their crops. Every able-bodied Protestant was armed and nothing was being done to curtail their rampages. The Protestant churches responded, saying that Protestants were bending over backwards to accommodate an aggressive Catholic minority and that the bishops should rein these people in.

In County Cork, ten Protestant men aged from eighteen to eighty-three years were killed at their homes and farms between 26 and 30 April. Protestants fearing for their lives fled from their houses in their nightclothes and took refuge in the fields. The following weekend over one hundred men from these areas boarded the boat to England, leaving the women in charge of their households until it was safe for them to return home again. Some said that the men were killed for giving information to the British regiments during the War of Independence, while others thought it was in reprisal for the pogroms against Catholics in Belfast. The killings, said to have been carried out by the anti-treaty forces, were strongly condemned in Dáil Éireann by the president, Arthur Griffith, who said that where possible the government's powers would be used to protect the lives and property of all sections of the community. There would be no distinction of class or creed. In a joint statement with Michael Collins, representative for South Cork, he offered the relatives the profound sympathy of the Irish nation.

On Cashel Mountain they read about the killings; they were happening everywhere and no one was safe. One of the men murdered was originally from Cavan. It brought the atrocity nearer home and almost put a face on the victim.

On the last day of April the girls went to the Spelig and picked mayflowers to put on the May altar at school. Originally a pagan fertility ritual, May Day was now celebrated by Christians. The bright-yellow mayflowers were fragile when picked and soon became limp and droopy. The girls put them in a pint tin with water and went to the pond to bring the ducks home and check for frogspawn. Ellen had warned them to watch out for mankeepers, her name for newts, and to keep their mouths shut for fear the mankeepers would jump down their throats and live in their stomachs. They had encountered newts before and were very careful not to get close to them. The next morning the mayflowers looked poorly and Catherine went and got them more.

Bryan had been to Oiney and Mickle's and was hoping to juke past Biddy Kane's, but she was in her garden and saw him coming down the last stretch of road.

"Come in and rest yourself, Bryan," she said. "I have a question for you." Biddy was past the age when inviting a man into her house could harm her reputation. She had on a cream straw bonnet that was decorated with brightly coloured wax fruit and tied under her chin with a broad red ribbon. She removed the bonnet and set it on the dresser, then made a dive for the teapot and the big stone jug that held the cordial.

"No tay, Biddy, thanks, and no cordial," Bryan said quickly.

As the seasons dictated, she fermented the cordial from flowers, berries, crab apples, rhubarb, dandelions and anything else that grew and wasn't poisonous, although some said that she was flexible. It was very potent and of benefit to both man and baste. It could lift a cow that was lying, clear the tubes on a bad chest or help a man make his water if he was having problems in that department. It eased pains in old people and warmed their insides, and although some felt a bit fuzzy after a few glasses, it cheered people up that were feeling down. Bryan didn't feel the need to improve any of his functions and Biddy wasn't best pleased.

He was poking vigorously to clear a buzzing noise from his ears, until he realised it was coming from the stone jar on the table beside him. Then Biddy told him there was a bumblebee in the jar. It had flown in earlier and she followed it up and down the sideboard mirror till she caught it, but if she caught more bees would she get honey? Bryan had to be diplomatic.

"It's honey bees you want, Biddy," he explained, "not bumble bees. And you need a hive for them and a hat with a net on it so that they won't sting you. But mebbe you have a hat like that?"

"I have a wee hat with netting on it, but it's a Sunday go-to-meeting hat, not a beekeeping hat," said Biddy, deflated.

"Well," Bryan said kindly, "sometimes the bees take off looking for a new hive, so if they land in that ash tree out there, we'll catch them, and then you'll have your honey bees."

"It's as simple as that." Biddy sighed. "Watch the ash tree till the bees light in it and then run down and get you."

"And don't wear that hat with the fruit on it," Bryan advised her. "The swarm a bees might light on it."

"A swarm a bees on me bonnet, Bryan." Biddy laughed. "Did you hear the news about the Rising? It's coming soon. Frank Aiken will sweep in through the Gap of the North with thousands of men and take over the North and free us all. It's true, Bryan, it's true. We'll have to light bonfires on every hill."

"Keep it under your hat, Biddy," Bryan said. "Aiken will be looking to you to set an example."

"Me lips are sealed," cried Biddy.

When he told them at home about Biddy and the bees, Ellen

wondered why he bothered with her and her aul daft stories. They were only a ploy to draw him in. Hell slap it into him if a swarm of bees did land in her ash tree. What would smart Bryan do then? Bryan shrugged and laughed. He'd think of something, or so he hoped. He told them there was talk of a new Rising. Aiken was coming in with a thousand armed men to take back the North.

"Another Rising?" said Ellen scornfully. "The last Rising did nothing for us and I wouldn't like to be hanging while I'm waiting for the good of another one. Did that word come from Dungooley?"

"No," Bryan answered. "They're to let us know if anything happens."

He started for the field to look at the pratas but Ellen called him back. She looked out the window and saw Mary, the blessed child that hadn't a titter of wit no more than a sparra, going up the mountain with a gun. She told him to go after her before she killed herself or the Specials did it for her.

Bryan laughed and wondered if his mother was starting to dote. Where would Mary get a gun? Ellen replied that Hughie mebbe hid one in the loft or in one of the outhouses and she saw where he put it. Bryan hurried up the mountain praying that the gun wasn't loaded, and then, thank Jaysus, he saw her marching along with a wooden rifle slung over her shoulder. It was a replica that had been used for training purposes, but he was shocked at how realistic it looked. If the Specials saw her with a gun, they would shoot her. It wouldn't matter if it was a child with a replica. He steered her out of sight and range and waited as she checked old fox holes and fired a few pretend shots. Then, satisfied with her work, she started back down, stepping nimbly over the exposed roots, briars and stones that littered the path. She handed him the gun without argument and he put it behind the shed, to dispose of later. When the girls came home from school, they found the replica gun and Catherine let them play with it for a while, but then her nerves got the better of her and she broke it up for firewood.

At supper time, when Ellen asked about the May altar, Brigid said that when they got to school the mayflowers were nearly dead. Other children had brought lovely flowers from their own gardens and the teacher put them in a glass vase. Some wee children had brought daisies and dandelions and she just threw them in a heap with the mayflowers on the May altar, then squashed some of the dandelions with her foot.

"The world is ill divided," Ellen said and sighed loudly. "And sure we can't all afford to have flowers or gardens."

Very few country people had flower gardens as the ground could not be spared, but in the hedges beside their houses, women grew lilac, fuchsia, climbing roses and flowering currant. They also planted daffodils, crocuses, snowdrops and other seasonal bulbs where they could see them on the ditches across the road.

"If the teacher doesn't know that you only put mayflowers on a May altar, then I don't know what she's doing in that school," Ellen said fiercely.

"Say no more, Ellen," Catherine advised. "We don't want her hearing it and turning on the children."

Children were hit in the school, but the teachers were seldom challenged. They were appointed and supported by the Church and the parish and nobody dared question them. Because the children only went to school for a few years, it was felt by both teachers and parents that if the larning was battered into them they wouldn't forget it. The country people were mostly uneducated and thought that teachers and priests were a breed apart who possessed great wisdom and knowledge. Many were treated with respect, but others regarded with cynicism and amusement, looked on as educated eejits.

In the South towards the end of May, Éamon de Valera and Michael Collins agreed a pact to field a national coalition of pro-treaty and anti-treaty candidates for the upcoming elections. Burying their rivalries and differences, they put forward a full panel of names that would divide the seats between them. The population was caught unprepared and as they didn't have enough time to put forward their own independent candidates, the election was rendered farcical.

Winston Churchill said that he did not believe that the provisional government was working hand in glove with their republican opponents "to betray British confidence and Ireland's good name". However, an agreed election was against the terms of the treaty. The provisional government told him that the conditions in the country were so bad that a free election would be impossible. Churchill made no secret of the fact that he found the Irish situation one of extreme gravity. He indicated very clearly what would happen if the terms of the treaty were infringed. In Dublin it was feared that Ulster would be used as a corridor for the re-entry of British troops into Ireland. In the Mullaghbane area, lorry patrols of Specials had increased significantly since the lads had gone across to Dungooley. Joint patrols of Specials and military moved about between Urcher Camp, Crossmaglen, Newtownhamilton, Whitecross, Newry, Jonesborough, Dromintee and Captain Alexander's house at Carrickasticken, Forkhill. The Cumann na mBan reported that there were also plainclothes men operating in the area.

Forkhill Barracks was attacked in a battle that lasted several hours, but there were no reports of injuries. Hawthorn Hill at the foot of Slieve Gullion, the summer mansion of Charles Chambre, was burnt to the ground, as was the Foresters' Hall near Adavoyle Station. James Craig declared that the electoral pact in the South had put an end to the Boundary Commission and declared, "What we have, we hold." The IRA, the IRB, the Volunteers, the Cumann na mBan and the Fianna were all proclaimed illegal associations. The Unionists feared an attempted takeover by the South and urged all young men in the province to come forward and help.

Word began filtering in of attacks by the IRA on barracks and patrols of military and Specials in Fermanagh and Tyrone and other parts of the North, but no word came of a Rising by the 4th Northern Division. In the camp at Dungooley, fifty men were picked to form a flying column for service in the South Armagh area. Each man had a rifle, a revolver and a hand grenade.

They also had one Lewis and one Thompson sub-machine gun and landmines, but no armoured transport. Although Michael Collins had signed the treaty he covertly supplied the anti-treaty garrison in the Four Courts with arms that were then sent on to the 4th Northern Division along the Louth border and to the 3rd Northern Division in Antrim. These arms were to be used in the Rising. But then, for some unexplained reason, on the eve of 19 May the 4th Northern Division was stood down. No clear reason was ever given. Aiken was a seasoned guerrilla fighter and it was unlikely that he lost his nerve at the last minute, but Richard Mulcahy at headquarters in Dublin may have given the order because the political situation was very sensitive and a force crossing from the South into the North might look to the British like an invasion. It has also been speculated that Aiken ordered the stand-down because he didn't trust Mulcahy and Eoin O'Duffy. He had been occupying the military barracks in Dundalk since the British withdrawal but had taken a neutral stance in the split after the treaty. An order for the 4th Northern to take part in a Rising inside the North would effectively get rid of the Northern IRA for good.

On a rare trip to Newry, Bryan called into the ating house on Monaghan Street for his dinner. The restaurant was surprisingly empty for that time of day. Minnie O'Hare, the proprietor, took his order then enquired about all the people she knew around Cashel and Mullaghbane.

Bryan waited for his dinner, reading his shopping list, but leaned back surprised as a short, stocky, red-faced man hovered threateningly over him and glowered into his face.

"What the Hell happened to youse crowd of bastards out there?" the man demanded.

He sprayed a fine mist of saliva into Bryan's face, but Bryan didn't wipe it off for fear it might further incense the little man. He also knew that if he stood up he would be looking down on the top of the man's head, but decided to sit where he was until the onslaught ended.

"The South Down battalion was ready to go in, but the South Armagh crowd wasn't ready!" the little man ranted. "The military and the Specials were nearly all away, fighting over by Tyrone and Fermanagh, and the town was there for the taking, but youse weren't here, youse weren't ready. Look at the round-up that's going on now. Young lads lifted every day be the Specials, rotting in jails and on an aul prison ship. The ones in Dublin got what they wanted. Do you think they give one damn about us Catholics here in the North? They do in their arse! If we're to get anything from now on, we'll have to fight hard and sore for it ourselves. Go back out to Mullaghbane and tell them that. They'll be hanging up by the feet for another eight hundred years because they missed the only chance they're going to get."

Bryan felt disturbed and taken aback, and Minnie O'Hare rushed out of the kitchen to try and calm the irate little man.

"Bryan isn't the man you should be shouting at. Take it aisy. It's all right, Paddy," she said.

"Och, Jaysus Christ! Take it aisy? What are you talking about, woman? Take it aisy!" Paddy shouted in disgust.

He knocked over a chair then pushed past Minnie and stormed out onto the street, from where he continued to mutter and glare into the restaurant.

"I'm sorry, Bryan. When I asked about Mullaghbane and Cashel I didn't think I'd start that," she murmured. "God help Paddy, too. His two lads were shot dead by the Tans and it put him astray in the head. Och, he has a drop of drink on him the day, but he's not a bad crater. What happened with the Rising, Bryan? Did you hear any talk?"

"Aye, the dispatchers were going mad round our part of the country day and night and so was the Specials and military. We were waiting on word, but we didn't know when it was going to happen. And the town was getting ready for it too?"

"Och aye, Bryan, there was a lot of talk round Newry. We waited, too, but nothing happened. We heard that there would be fighting in the streets for days and that the town would be blown apart. People were warned to stock up on groceries and plenty did, but sure they won't go to loss. That's why the streets are so quiet. No one knows what's going on and people are afraid to come out."

When she brought his dinner, he ate quickly and without enjoyment, then paid up and warily made his way back to the pony and trap. He had been aware of an atmosphere coming into the town, but now he saw that the few pedestrians on the streets weren't loitering to chat or window-shop. The Specials patrolling on foot and in tenders had stopped him on the way in and searched the trap.

Jem had told him that people coming from the town were

complaining about delays, bad manners and rough treatment. On the way home the Specials who stopped him were edgy and abrupt. They poked their bayonets through his packages before ordering him to move quickly away. As the pony trotted briskly along, he mulled over what Minnie O'Hare had told him. They had expected to be under siege in Newry, and although the Rising hadn't happened yet, they were still waiting. In the countryside the opposing forces were camped almost on top of each other, and conflict was inevitable.

When he reached the Crossroads, he found Annie McGuinness at the side of the road, pumping up the back wheel of her bicycle.

"Well, Annie, the aul road is hard on bicycles. Do you want a hand there? Well, there's Specials everywhere in Newry and I was told that they were waiting for the Rising, but it never came. Is there any word of what happened?"

Annie said that she didn't know what happened either. The Cumann na mBan had been dispatched here, there and everywhere along the border with urgent, top-secret communications, and it looked like they were all set to go into the North. When the order came to stand down, they couldn't believe it. The explanation was that they weren't ready.

"But," said Annie, "in the Cumann mBan we were more than ready and we might never be as ready again. We were at confessions and Mass because we knew that when we went into the North, some of us wouldn't live to come out again. The lads in the camps were champing at the bit, armed and ready to go, and if we wait much longer, the Specials will be coming after us. The Captain's House in Carrickasticken is only a hen's race away from Dungooley, and Ravensdale is across the road from Jonesborough Barracks. It's very tempting when the enemy is that close."

"Aye, you're right about that. I seen the Specials in Newry and on the way out of it and they're fired up and ready for anything. And for God's sake, daughter, avoid them at all costs, for they have no respect for women and they'll wonder why you're on the road all the time."

She acknowledged the warning then got on her bicycle and pedalled off in a spurt of dust.

Bryan noted the dust in a detached fashion. If the weather kept up, they'd get the hay saved. When he told the women at home what was happening in Newry and about his meeting with Annie McGuinness, Catherine felt the nauseating rise of anxiety, but Ellen was more philosophical.

"There's too much talk about Risings," she declared. "Get the hay saved and in then we'll be ready to face whatever the Lord sends us."

As the good weather continued, Bryan honed the scythe to the point where it could split a hair and noted with satisfaction how cleanly it sliced through the thick docken stems. His confidence and work rate increased and soon he was cutting hay late into the evening. Then the hay was left to dry for a couple of days, and Catherine and the girls were called into action for the turning. If the hay was damp, the stack would go mouldy and the animals wouldn't eat it. The following day the dry hay was raked up and built into stacks that would be drawn into the haggard at the end of the summer. When the last twisted hay rope was secured to the last stack, they breathed a sigh of relief. The hay on the top of the stack was positioned in a way that repelled rain.

As they left the field, they heard the sound of an engine coming from Biddy Kane's direction, and down the hill sped a motorcycle. Both the driver and the pillion passenger wore goggles, but they knew from the large panniers at the sides that it was Dr Horgan's motorcycle, the Unapproachable Big 4 Norton. When the motorcycle stopped, the driver removed his goggles with a flourish, but it wasn't Dr Horgan at the controls; it was Hughie. The passenger sat immobile with his goggles still in place, neither speaking nor smiling. His wrists were tied together with a cord that was secured to the motorcycle.

Bryan motioned to the girls to stay back. He had a very bad feeling about the situation. "Who is that?" he demanded.

"That's a wee boy that talks too much to the wrong people," Hughie told him. "The lads at the camp want to have a word with him while we're waiting for the Rising."

Catherine took the girls inside, and when she brought water out, Hughie released one of the man's hands to let him drink. When he was finished, he threw the mug across the road where it landed with a clank, chipping the enamel. Hughie tied him up again, retrieved the mug then got back on the motorcycle and revved it up.

Mary ran up the field until she was parallel with him. Then she ducked down low behind the ditch. "What are you going to do with him?" she whispered.

"I'm going to take him far away," Hughie said. "And then I'll let him go."

"That's what you said about the rat I marked for God," she reminded him. "But I found him kilt behind the milk house."

"Well, you'll not find this boy kilt behind the milk house," he promised grimly. "Run on home, now."

As he started the motorcycle, the prisoner jumped awkwardly from the passenger seat, but the restraining cord didn't break and he landed on the ground. Hughie produced a pistol and ordered him back on the machine and they set off again. Mary ran alongside for a while as he drove round the road, but when she returned an hour later, she didn't mention him.

Bryan was very angry that Hughie had brought a prisoner to the house on a stolen motorcycle. Anyone that knew the doctor would know it wasn't him, but then they wouldn't know it was Hughie either. Catherine asked what would happen to the poor lad, and Bryan shrugged his shoulders. They both knew what happened to those who informed on the IRA. She said a prayer on his behalf. He was somebody's son, no matter about the circumstances.

Chapter 11

Biddy Kane had told Bryan that when the Rising came, thousands of men would sweep in through the Gap of the North to set the people free. At the end of May, while it was not quite as Biddy had predicted, a fierce gun battle lasting three days took place in that locality. On the Thursday night Gallagher's public house, once located on the main Newry to Dundalk road but now stranded in a no-man's land on a fluid borderline, was raided and ransacked by the Specials. Money, drink and cigarettes were stolen and the women working on the premises were abused and violated. A few of the large force of Specials stationed with the military at Jonesborough Barracks attempted a raid across the border to attack the 4th Northern Division at their camp nearby in Ravensdale Park, but the IRA immediately took up positions on the opposite side of the road and opened fire on them. Four Specials were wounded, withdrawn from the area and dispatched to the hospital in Newry.

The Specials and military in the barracks began shooting at anything that moved on the other side of the border, and heavy and insistent fire was exchanged well into the night. Throughout that night and the following day, the barracks came under heavy sustained fire from the IRA, who used a dry bog to get within two hundred yards of the military positions and cut the telegraph wire. Fire was returned from inside the barracks and the surrounding ditches, with rifles and two machine guns. A military sniper causing problems from the church bell tower was eventually shot by an IRA marksman. Due to the intensity of the battle, nobody went to his aid, and his body wasn't retrieved until the fighting was over.

Reinforcements dispatched from Forkhill Barracks came under such heavy sniper fire that they had to retreat. Other units coming from Crossmaglen were fired on as they drove through Mullaghbane. Specials abandoned their vehicles and, in their shirt sleeves, trying to look like local farmers, attempted to cross the fields to get to their beleaguered comrades, but they were forced to retreat. An armoured car eventually made it through, but the tender that followed it was beaten back and had to return to Newry. The situation became so desperate that carrier pigeons were sent from the barracks to request back-up. The fate of the birds is unknown. One Special is said to have dressed as a woman and cycled to Newry Barracks for help.

Reinforcements arrived for both sides and the area was congested with military. Some Crossley tenders were attacked and three soldiers killed. People crawling along the road saw their bodies covered in blankets. Those working in the fields were ordered to leave, but most of them didn't need an order. Initially it was reported that the bodies of local people were strewn along the roadside, but this wasn't true. A ram that had been grazing peacefully in Ravensdale Park was shot dead. Families living near the battle lines either went into Dundalk five miles away or to stay with neighbours or relatives. The road was blocked with refugees. Catholic families moved south and Protestant families moved north in the midst of the battle. Three lady cyclists from Rathfriland, who had been travelling between Newry and Dundalk, were trapped in Gallagher's public house for eight hours. A jarvey from Dundalk, who had been to Newry selling pigs, later reported that he had stopped at the halfway house for some refreshment, and while he was there the firing started. He was searched by the Specials and when they found a medal in his pocket from the war they didn't search him further or arrest him. As the battle raged back and forth, the customers and staff sheltered behind the bar counter. In the upstairs rooms, the chairs, tables and the roof were completely riddled with bullets.

A man who had cycled out from Dundalk was arrested as a spy. The Specials said that no innocent man would come there after hearing there was trouble. They put him up against a wall twice to shoot him, but a military officer took him to the barracks, where he was arrested by the inspector of police. They locked him up in the laundry room of a house where the Specials were billeted. Later when the firing eased and fifty of the Specials were boarding tenders to return to Newry he escaped through a window into a garden and then climbed a high wall and was out on the Dundalk Road again. He didn't go back for his bicycle.

Five Bessbrook Cumann na mBan wearing uniform and driving a trap on the southern side were arrested by the Specials and taken to the barracks in Newry. They were carrying arms, ammunition and field dressings. The forces in Jonesborough Barracks were so overwhelmed by the battle that they asked for a truce, which was negotiated through Frank Aiken in Dundalk. He agreed to a truce, but only if the five Cumann na mBan were freed immediately, and when that was done, the truce came into effect.

There were no reported casualties from the IRA side, but a man, unconnected to the battle, sustained a head wound when he fell from his horse near Thistle Cross on the southern side. He was taken to the Louth Infirmary by a motor car that was being used by the IRA to ferry arms and ammunition to the units at Ravensdale Park. He was later discharged and walked home.

A pedlar named McCabe, an ex-British soldier, who was passing through Jonesborough, was shot in the head by a stray bullet and his horse was shot dead beside him. He was taken to the hospital in Newry where it transpired that during the War of Independence he had been tried by the IRA in Monaghan and convicted as a spy. He was shot in the head, chest and back, but survived the botched execution by crawling into an outhouse and remaining there until he recovered enough to seek help.

During this period of unrest, a British gunboat dropped anchor in Dundalk Bay and remained there for several days, a reminder that the British army wasn't very far away and could invade again at short notice if the trouble on the border continued.

On Cashel Mountain they could hear the battle being fought at Jonesborough and knew that the Specials had been fired on going through Mullaghbane. They didn't know yet if the unit from Dungooley was involved, but if the battle was as fierce as was reported, it's likely they were in the thick of it. A strange mixture of anticipation and fear pervaded the countryside. Could this be the Rising at last? News was hard to come by and the local Cumann na mBan was nowhere to be seen. If the Bessbrook women arrested had been an active service and first aid unit, the local women had the same role and were with the men from the Dungooley camp.

Catherine and Ellen kept the children close by, and though the shock value of the oft-repeated warnings had long since worn off, the girls were always subconsciously on the alert for tenders. In the seclusion of the Spelig they paddled in the cool water of the duck pond and for a while were free from the anxiety that filled the house.

Five days after the battle at Jonesborough, simultaneous attacks by three IRA raiding parties took place at Crossmaglen Barracks and at a "big house" being used by the Specials at Drummuck. The IRA kept up a fusillade of rifle fire for over an hour, then withdrew. The Specials returned fire for some time after that, but no casualties were reported on either side.

Two days later Mickle was helping Bryan harvest his few acres of flax. He said the whole country was festering and nobody knew where the trouble would break out next. It was like a cockfight and it wouldn't be over till one side killed the other outright. There was no middle way.

The flax crop had turned the fields a cornflower blue. The seeds were sown close together so that the plants grew tall and the fibres long. The fibres were used in linen-making and the seeds for paint and cattle feed. It had to be pulled by hand and was a back-breaking chore. Recently the price of flax had fallen and they hadn't much heart for the work, but if they didn't save it they couldn't sell it, and that income would be lost. No rope, no skip.

At dinnertime Ellen was gloomy. The signs weren't good and she could feel it in her water – danger was all around them. The Divil was raging through the land and took the Rosary beads from under her pillow the night before, but she found them again on the hearthstone. He must have dropped them when he was warming his arse at the fire. A young magpie was pecking at the window every morning and the rest of them were cackling in the tree from early light. They knew when something was coming. She'd never seen as many of them and it wasn't lucky to have them about the place at all. There was nothing but hardship in the tea leaves in her cup, nothing but hardship if the whole country wasn't set free. People were jumping the ditches to avoid the two red-haired children. Red-haired women were unlucky and it was better to turn back than to meet one, but turning back was unlucky too. You changed your luck when you changed direction.

The men listened respectfully but ate their dinner quickly and went back to the flax pulling. By the mid-afternoon tea, they had cleared a good portion of the field and lay against the ditch as Catherine poured the tea and handed out the buttered bread. Suddenly they heard the sound of sporadic shooting, followed by the unmistakeable rat-a-tat-tat of a machine gun. They abandoned the tea and hurried up to higher ground to decipher the direction more accurately.

They looked southward, but all they could see was the distant blue horizon of Dundalk Bay. As the shooting continued unabated, they concluded that the battle was either at Forkhill or at the Dungooley camp. One way or the other Hughie was involved. Catherine gathered up the tea things and hurried home, but Ellen had called the girls in and had them unravelling old woollen jumpers on the settle bed. It was just by chance she'd heard the firing at all. She was lying over the half door getting air and thought she heard water dripping onto an aul bit of tin, but realised soon enough that it was gunfire and shouted for the girls. Then she told Katy that she was making a hames out of winding the wool up and took it from her; there was always something to annoy you.

The men came and stood indecisively in the kitchen. They would go as near to the camp as they could and try and find out what was going on. When Ellen reminded them about the people and animals hit by stray bullets in Jonesborough, they noted her concern but said they couldn't sit there and do nothing. She said she'd like to know herself what was going on and went to listen by the half door. She was only there two minutes when they heard a clatter and a muffled thud.

"There's no need to prostrate yourself forninst me," Ellen said impatiently. "Get up out a that. Anyone would think you were waiting to be ordained."

When Bryan saw Biddy Kane sprawled face down on the street he went outside and helped her up.

"Oh Bryan, dear, I thought the gate was closed when I leaned on it, and sure it wasn't, " Biddy said ruefully, brushing dirt from the front of her dress. "I ran down to tell you about the shooting, Bryan, and forgot about these aul high heel, curse-a-God American button boots. That's what I get for me consatyness and them doesn't fit me at all. Is it the Rising, Bryan? Is it the lads, beyant at Dungooley?"

When Bryan advised her to settle herself, she sat down in an armchair and tucked the offending American boots in under and out of sight.

Ellen cast her a glance that would kill quicks in a ditch. "Not a bit a wonder she fell, putting feet like grubbers into boots like yon," she muttered.

Catherine smiled to herself at the muttered words and the withering look. Poor Biddy had few places where she could show off her American style and could wear her high-heeled boots in her own house if she liked.

Mickle and Bryan headed for Dungooley by the back roads. The women, who weren't sure how far a bullet could travel, ventured cautiously out onto the road. Larry and his family walked down with Oiney. Addy came to the top of the road, shouted down for news and eventually joined them. The children crawled up the hill at the back of the house and reported that there was no let-up in the firing. They retired inside to fortify themselves with tea and Rosaries until the men returned around nine o'clock. At Carrivegrove, less than a mile from Dungooley, a man told them that the Specials were attacking the camp.

The firing was as plain as if they were in the middle of it, and no sign of it quitting. It seemed that the Specials had nearly got on the top of them, but the lads got the better of them at Jonesborough and they'd do the same again. They would clear them out no bother. They said a prayer for the lads and swore God's curse on the Specials, then the neighbours reluctantly drifted homewards. There was little they could do until the battle was over.

Bryan walked with Addy up the road then sat down on a rock. The setting sun was a faint line on the horizon as daylight faded into dusk. At one point there was shooting coming from behind him as well as in front of him. He thought it was an echo then realised that a second battle was taking place out towards Cullaville. That attack lasted for about an hour. Maybe it was to divert the Specials away from Dungooley. Night creatures rustled under the hedge and bats swooped in and away again. A grand night, he thought, then smiled ironically.

Around one o'clock in the morning, the battle at the camp began to peter out and then stopped completely. Larry and the others would be outside keeping a vigil too. They wouldn't go to bed and leave the lads to fight it out alone. Catherine was awake, waiting for him, when he got home, but they slept in spite of their worries.

Morning dawned too soon and dragged them heavy-eyed into the new day. They prayed for Hughie and the lads before they got out of bed and decided to keep the girls home from school. Bryan was anxious to get to Dungooley, but he needed more information and set off for McGuinness's. Annie opened the door and led him into the parlour then brought him tea. She said that Forkhill was sealed up tight and sandbagged off, and no one could get near the camp. They didn't know yet if there were casualties. The Carrickasticken Road was also closed and nobody could go anywhere in the area. She was apologetic and regretful. They should have been there. They had tried to get to the camp when the shooting started the previous afternoon, but couldn't get through and had few details of the battle, but she knew a tender had been shot at in Mullaghbane.

Later it emerged that about fifty of the Specials stationed at Captain Alexander's house came down across the fields and were within a hundred yards of the camp before they commenced firing. Captain

Alexander's, also known as the Captain's, was situated on high ground off the Carrickasticken Road, about a mile across the country from Dungooley Crossroads. The camp was in danger of being overrun, but the units there immediately returned fire. Other Specials, with rifles and machine guns brought there by reinforcements, fought their way across the border from the Northern side until they too were almost on top of the camp. Reinforcements coming through Mullaghbane in a Crossley tender were sniped at and some Specials were wounded. IRA units were rushed from Dundalk to help defend the camp, and the battle lines extended across a mile of countryside. By ten o'clock that night the Specials had been beaten back and hemmed in on three sides. Some had gone into Flynn's house, which was on the borderline, with the door and windows facing the IRA positions at the Crossroads, but the house became a death trap, and they couldn't get out of it. The IRA concentrated heavy fire on the front and both sides of the house, claiming the lives of four Specials and wounding four others. The house was riddled with bullets. Around one o'clock in the morning a British army officer who had come with the relief party asked for a truce to evacuate the wounded. When this was granted, the armoured cars and lorries that came to support the Specials during the battle helped to evacuate them as they withdrew to their quarters in Carrickasticken. During the retreat they were covered by an armoured car with a Lewis gun.

Many people had to leave their houses and look for accommodation in Kilcurry and the surrounding area. The next day people on their way to Newry were stopped and turned back, and part of Forkhill village was cordoned off. Three young local men were arrested and detained.

Bryan was mildly disappointed but not surprised that there was no news yet. He tried not to think about how the lads were faring inside the camp and was anxious to be on his way, but he didn't tell Annie in case she tried to dissuade him. He wondered who had shot at the tender in Mullaghbane, and she made an unwitting grimace. These young women were crack-shots and as far as he knew the lads were all in the camp. Hughie would be proud of them. As he got up onto the cart, Annie's parents and Lizzie came out to talk about the state of the country, and when he praised the girls for their courage, their father beamed proudly.

"Hearts like lions, Bryan," he said. "These girls have hearts like lions!"

Their mother seemed less certain, and as Bryan trundled away, he prayed nothing bad would happen to them. At Redmond's Crossroads he was surprised at the absence of the Specials, and Shusie said she had no news yet, but you would have to be living in a churn not to know the country was in a state of chaos or chassis, as Jem, the head of wit, would say. The Specials and military were out on the roads and at the Crossroads morning, noon and night, up and down, stopping and searching and annoying the people, but they were at home licking their wounds the day.

A Crossmaglen man passing by that morning said they went over the border at Cullaville the previous night and attacked an IRA post, but there was no word of anyone getting killed. Bryan said he'd heard that battle too. Shusie said that if the news was bad, time wouldn't change it, but that didn't help. When he got back home, Larry had called to tell him that a tender had gone into the river at Forkhill and Hell slap it into them that they might never get it out, the bastards! And to mind himself if he was going beyant because airaplanes were flying over the camp and Bryan could be shot if he was seen juking about.

They could hear the drone of the aeroplanes in the distance. Bryan went reluctantly back to the flax pulling and then set out after they were gone. At Carrivegrove a tender blocked the road, forcing him to backtrack and make a wide a detour into a farmyard. There a woman shushed a barking collie and showed him the narrow overgrown lonin that would take him to the camp. He hurried along till a voice whispered in his ear, "Stop or I'll shoot!"

He automatically raised his hands in surrender.

"Where in the name of Jaysus are you going?" the sentry whispered hoarsely and angrily. "And who the Hell let you out, you bloody lunatic?"

Bryan suddenly felt very foolish and reckless. He was in a battleground, where they were all primed to shoot on sight. They didn't need gobshites like him stumblin' about. When he said who he was and why he was there the sentry relented slightly and told him that a lock of the lads got shot, but nothing serious. Inside the camp chunks of masonry had been blown from the walls of thc old farmhouse, leaving areas of red brick exposed, bullet holes pock-marking the plaster. Machine-gun fire had flittered the trees and fuchsia hedges, scattering branches and leaves all over the ground.

Weary-eyed men watched him suspiciously, then Hughie recognised him and jumped up. He wasn't happy. He would have sent word when things settled and the Cumann na mBan got through. Bryan was going to say that if he hadn't come, Larry would have, and he was fitter than Larry, but here in the middle of the action it sounded lame and foolhardy. Hughie said it had been a very tight fight. At one stage they thought the Specials would get the better of them, but then help came from Dundalk and they forced the Specials back down to the hill to Flynn's house. They had them surrounded and could have wiped them out altogether, but then they asked for a ceasefire and were pulled out.

When Bryan asked how they had come so close without being spotted, Hughie shrugged. They simply hadn't expected them to attack by the back way. They came across the fields from the Captain's in shirtsleeves, using the same trick they'd tried at Jonesborough so that at first the guards at the camp thought they were farmers out saving the hay and didn't give them much heed. The camp had been fortified to withstand attacks from the Forkhill Road direction. Half walls with rifle holes had been put up to protect the riflemen guarding the perimeter facing Forkhill, and mines were placed at intervals on the road in case they arrived in armoured vehicles. The Specials had put up sandbags and stopped people from going through Forkhill, and the lads were preparing for an attack from there, but now they thought that had been done to divert attention from the sneak attack across the fields. The lads were exhausted and there was nothing left to say.

Gerard Molloy said to tell his ma and da he was still above the sod, then Bryan steeled himself for the return journey. A scout left him to the mouth of the narrow lonin, and he scurried along on his hands and knees, keeping his head well below the tops of the ditches. When he felt it was safe, he stood painfully upright. He was out of the Specials' sight and range and the lads were alive and unharmed, and for the present that was enough.

"Man was never meant to walk on four legs," he said aloud.

At the hill above the house, Larry Molloy hobbled up from his perch on the ditch and wiped tears from his eyes when Bryan told him the lads were alive. They had a jorum of ale in the house as he related what had happened at the camp and the journey there and back.

"Thank God they're not hurted. And you had to come back on your hands and knees, bejaysus," Larry said in wonderment. "Like a rabbit, Bryan, like a bloody rabbit!"

He repeated the details so that he would remember everything to tell his own people, then jumped up awkwardly and lifted his stick. Sally would surely kill him for not hurrying back, but it wasn't easy to get news that quick. He would shout in to the neighbours on the way home.

At Dungooley, the 4th Northern remained on high alert and the situation settled down again, uneasily. Barrett's house, not too far away in Plaster, County Louth, was well known to them as it had formerly been an RIC post. Relief patrols going to and from the house had been fired on many times. Following the truce the RIC vacated the place and the Barretts took up residence again. A few days after the skirmish at Dungooley, the IRA came in the early hours of the morning, ordered the occupants to leave and burnt the house to the ground. The place was gutted. The Barretts, a husband, wife and sister-in-law, took up residence in a shed beside the ruins.

In Dundalk, money was collected from the townspeople to set up a local police force to keep law and order until the arrival of the new Civic Guard. A number of Northern businessmen and others suspected of being Specials were arrested by the 4th Northern as they passed through the town. Some were later released and given a permit of safe passage to Newry. Others were arrested at their homes in South Armagh and in the border areas. Three men from the Dungooley camp went to within a mile and a half of Newtownhamilton and waited in a ditch at a bend in the road to see if they could find anyone of importance to abduct. Then two tenders full of uniformed police followed by a Model T Ford came from the Newtownhamilton direction. The men waited until the tenders had passed out of view before stopping the car. Inside was the captain of the Specials in the South Armagh area and his driver. They were disarmed and forced to drive by the back roads to Dungooley. Later they were taken to the military barracks in Dundalk and held as hostages to prevent reprisals by the Specials against Catholic people in their area, especially those related to IRA members.

Chapter 12

During the second week of June, the flying column from the camp placed landmines on the old road at Lislea near the Mountain House, not far from Whitecross. This was the main road between Forkhill and Markethill, and according to intelligence reports, heavy military traffic travelled along it daily. The column waited in this position for two days, but when no patrols came along, they dug up the landmines and withdrew. Their presence wouldn't go unnoticed and it was dangerous to stay in one place for too long.

On 14 June the bodies of two men, Thomas Crawley from Lisadian, Whitecross, and Patrick Cregan from Derramore, Bessbrook, were found on the road where the landmines had been buried. The previous evening, Patrick Cregan, a fifty-year-old unmarried farmer, was picked up in a lorry at the head of his own lonin by men wearing police uniforms and carrying rifles, who asked him his name. The lorry then drove off towards Camlough. Patrick Cregan was never seen alive again. Thomas Crawley, a farmer and auctioneer, was thirty years old and also unmarried. He had cycled to a farm in the Lislea area to buy sheep and was last seen around 9.30 p.m. that evening, when he was stopped and taken away in a lorry. His bicycle was thrown into the yard of a neighbouring house. The next morning a farmer from Lislea found their bodies. Thomas Crawley had a bullet wound and fracture to the base of his skull and Patrick Cregan had been shot in the centre of the forehead. Although neither man was involved with the IRA,

Patrick Cregan's brother, Mick, was a volunteer. They had been killed and their bodies dumped there as a warning over the placement of landmines on a military route. Witnesses said that the police involved were Specials from Bessbrook barracks. Following the discovery of the men's bodies, an armoured car and a tender came under fire in Mullaghbane.

Oiney told Bryan that the two poor fellas were took away be men dressed as polis. They were bate and shot then threw out on the road like two dogs. No, worse nor dogs, for you would bury an aul dog or throw it in a flax hole. The country was cowped and it could happen them here now in the field, for they'd just come along and shoot you. Questions were being asked in the parliament in England over the behaviour of the Specials, and that's what the people would have to face if the North of Ireland wasn't set free. They were the lawmen now and did whatever they liked.

The Specials had taken out in retaliation since the shooting of James Woulfe-Flanagan in Newry a couple of weeks previously. Woulfe-Flanagan, the resident magistrate of Newry, was leaving Sunday Mass in the Cathedral on 4 June when a Ford motor car with three gunmen pulled up. One of the gunmen asked him to come with them, and when he refused, the man pointed a revolver at him and shot him several times. Mr Woulfe-Flanagan, who was nearly sixty years old, was carried to a neighbouring house, but he died within ten minutes, and during this time he forgave his killers. His sister caught the gunman by the collar of his coat and held on, but he roughly threw her to one side then jumped into an already moving car as it sped away. A ricochet bullet also hit a young lad in the thigh. The congregation didn't know which way to run, and most went back into the Cathedral. People on their way to twelve o'clock Mass turned back and went home. Locals said that the magistrate's family were the relics of aul dacency from County Roscommon and that his brother was a colonel with the British army out in India.

But it didn't seem to matter who you were or what you were, because you could be shot by one side or the other if they took the notion. A Special had fired shots into a public house in Newry because they wouldn't serve him more drink. There was a curfew in the town and any person caught outside a minute after half past ten at night would be shot. People said you wouldn't see a mouse running through Newry after ten o'clock. It was an ongoing cycle of atrocity and reprisal, with the situation as bad if not worse than when the Tans were going about. Nobody was safe, not women or children, nobody. They were on patrol all the time, and Catherine worried that Mary would pop her head up over a ditch at the wrong time and it would be the finish of her.

In world news the Turks killed thousands of Greeks that were living in one part of Turkey and threw their bodies out in the hills and the woods for the birds and wild animals to devour them. According to this account, related by a refugee in Athens, the whole Greek population of the Caza of Batna in Anatolia, Turkey, numbering forty thousand people in one hundred and twenty-six villages, had been entirely exterminated by the Angora government during the past year, either by the knife or various other brutal and inhumane means. All the male inhabitants in the Caza were assembled in churches and schools and burnt to death. Five hundred young Greek women were collected, violated and brutalised. At Bafra the massacre went on for a fortnight. Thousands of corpses were left out for carrion birds to feed on. All the Greek professors of the American College of Melfizun were hanged. There were hardly any Greeks left alive along the Pontas Coast, and out of one hundred and thirty-two Armenian families, only thirty-two were left.

"The War turned the world on its head and all the blood-letting stirred up aul grudgeries again. Nothing settles down for a long time after that, and it doesn't look like it's going to settle down here for a while ayther," Bryan said.

The next day brought word of another attack by Specials and military in the locality. At Dromintee, a couple of miles away from Cashel on the road between Forkhill and Newry, a public house belonging to James McGuill, the Sinn Féin county councillor for the district, was raided by a number of armed men. The raid took place at three o'clock in the morning. On the premises were James McGuill's wife, who was pregnant and near her time of confinement, their two children, who were both under the age of three, and her mother. Mrs McKnight, who looked after the children, was also there, along with a servant girl and a shop girl. They woke to a loud knocking on the door, and when Mrs McGuill and Mrs McKnight looked down from the bedroom window, they counted seven armed and masked men who demanded that they open up. Using filthy and abusive language they then began smashing the glass panels in the door, and by the time the servant girl and the shop girl got to the foot of the stairs they had broken the door open and were in the hallway.

Although the men were all dressed in civilian clothes, their revolvers were attached to army lanyards. Two of the men, one with a Belfast accent and one with an English accent, came to Mrs McGuill's room and demanded to know were there any men in the house. On discovering that there weren't, they ordered her out of the room and began to search it. They pulled one of the girls into a room where two men were waiting with revolvers. They tore off the coat she wore over her nightdress, physically abused her and attempted to outrage her. When she began screaming one of them kicked her severely in the head and on the leg, but the other women came to her aid and fought them off. They then dragged Mrs McGuill into a bedroom where they physically assaulted her, tore off her nightclothes and tried to outrage her, but again the other women beat them off. Mrs McGuill was so terrified that she tried to jump out of the window, but the other women managed to drag her back.

The raiders demanded money, but Mrs McGuill told them that the money had been used that day to pay bills. They threatened to shoot her if she didn't give them the key for the safe, but she told them to open it with a hatchet and then they would see that there was nothing in it. When they couldn't get the safe open they stole everything of value that they could lay their hands on: rum, whiskey, cigarettes, tobacco, cakes, bicycle tyres, sugar, tea, hurricane lamps and all the loose change from the till. They even turned over the mattress on the bed where the two-year-old boy was sleeping, and when they found nothing there, they broke open his money box with a gun butt and stole the few shillings inside. The raiders were said to be both army and Specials from Forkhill.

The people of the countryside were shocked and horrified by the brutality and attempted desecration of the unprotected women. Nobody, only born savages, would do the likes of that. And how mane and low would a man have to be to take the few pence from a child's money box?

As time went on, other details of the raid on McGuills' were revealed; the premises had been ransacked for over an hour and a half by the raiders. They threatened the women that they would lock them all in a room and burn the place if they didn't tell them where the money was hidden. When the raid was over, they warned that if anyone left the premises or reported what had happened before two hours had passed they would come back and kill everyone there, including the children. Mrs McGuill was so shocked and distressed that a doctor was called to attend to her. James McGuill hadn't lived there for some time as it was no longer safe for him to do so. The pub had been raided more than a hundred times in the past couple of years under the pretence that they were looking for him because he was an IRA man, but robbery always seemed to be the principal motive.

A few days later the sound of gunfire echoed through the countryside again. A party of twelve Specials left Forkhill Barracks at midnight on Friday, 16 June and marched six each side of the road in stocking soles until they reached McGuills'. Then one party went right and one went left. Suddenly ten or more IRA men appeared from behind a wall and ordered them to halt before firing a volley of shots. One Special was killed instantly and one was wounded. They were loaded onto a lorry and returned to Forkhill for medical attention. After the ambush the IRA withdrew, leaving behind thirty rounds of revolver ammunition, mines and mine exploders. These items were found in McGuills' yard and on the Newry and Jonesborough roads close by.

The following day when Bryan got word of the ambush, he knew it was carried out by the 4th Northern and that Hughie would surely have been involved. The Dungooley camp was too near for the IRA not to have come from there. He hoped there would be no reprisals, then set his mind to clipping the sheep. In the afternoon the girls came out wearing their summer dresses and sunbonnets. The younger yoes were skittish and very hard to handle, and the girls watched with interest as he danced around the yard with one he was trying to subdue. Then the girls wandered off down the road.

Bryan was trimming dried dung from the back ends of the fleeces and wrapping them up, when Annie McGuinness stopped by. She had walked up the road with the girls who had been picking foxgloves and then putting them on their fingers. They went into the house to show their grandmother their "fox gloves" and Annie waited on Bryan to finish his task. When he asked about the ambush at McGuills', she said the lads were back at the camp and they were all right, but McGuills' public house had been burnt to the ground. She had cycled over to see it. It was still smouldering. The stench was awful and the local people were standing out on the road just looking at it.

She spoke to a woman who came from Dromintee but was married and lived in Belfast. The Troubles there were very bad, with Protestants killing Catholics night and day. As no one knew where the murder gangs would strike next, her husband and sons stayed in different safe houses in different streets every night. They decided that she should take their wee girl and go home to Dromintee where it would be safer. She had been back home a couple of months when her mother suggested that she should give Mrs McGuill a hand in the public house. But she hadn't been there a wet week when the place was raided, and then the Specials were ambushed. Mrs McGuill had been demented after the ambush. She knew they'd be back and that this time they would burn her out. The women who helped her in the pub loaded her and her mother and the children onto a cart and sent them away to stay with relatives. Then they threw blankets and mattresses and pots and pans and anything they thought that the family might need out into the yard at the back. No sooner had they done that than the Specials arrived and threw it all back into the public house again. Then they poured petrol all around the place, set it alight and burnt it to the ground. They didn't check to see if there was anyone inside. When the women tried to stop them, they turned their guns on them and ordered them to stand back.

The woman Annie spoke to said that she would sometimes stay over at night if Mrs McGuill was stuck. Luckily she hadn't been there the night of the raid, but she couldn't sleep thinking about it. She was going back to her man in Belfast because it was safer there than it was here. The countryside was in an awful state at the minute and it was terrible to look at McGuills', as fine a place as you would see anywhere in the country, there in ruins. She'd heard that Mrs McGuill was so terrified that the Specials would come back and kill her that she had gone into Dundalk with her mother and children, where they couldn't find her. She would never be back there again.

The women and the girls who had worked there were very brave women. They stayed there on their own in spite of all the times it was raided and robbed, but they would never recover either. Their lives were ruined too. The previous year James McGuill had been abducted and used as a hostage by the military. He was forced at gunpoint to stand in the front of the tender to prevent them from being ambushed when they were driving around the countryside. Following his release they came back several times to try and kill him, but he moved into Dundalk, leaving the women to look after the premises.

"I know I shouldn't be talking to a man about things like this, Bryan, but they kicked and battered that young girl and interfered with her and then did the same to a woman about to have a baby. My God, how could they do that?" Annie shuddered.

"They did it because they're getting away with it. It's a war, Annie, and war turns some men into savages. There's nayther law nor order in the country at the minnit. I've never seen it worse. Be careful on the roads and don't be on your own. Them bastards have no respect for women."

She got on her bicycle and pedalled off, leaving Bryan to absorb the news and the possible consequences. Annie knew that "outrage" and "violate" were euphemisms used by the newspapers when reporting rape and sexual assault. She also knew that the Cumann na mBan were targets. She had heard reports that women and girls suspected of being members had been taken to a house between Annalong and Kilkeel, where a notorious lady searcher ordered them at gunpoint to remove all their clothes, and if they didn't, the clothes were ripped off them. And it was said that armed Specials were on stand-by to assist if necessary. The thoughts of it had made her shiver when she heard about it, but it had seemed distant.

The abuse of the women during the raid at McGuills' and the raid on Gallagher's public house during the battle at Jonesborough had been shocking and very frightening and brought the threat much closer to home. It was a sinister and very worrying trend because women were no longer safe.

On Sunday morning at eight o'clock Mass, news of another atrocity was trickling in from Newry and it was thought to be very bad. Men spoke in low voices and out of the sides of their mouths as if what had happened was too horrific to be spoken aloud. They glanced over their shoulders to ensure they weren't overheard, for fear someone might report them and say they knew something about it. Bryan had a feeling of unnamed dread and a need to be away home.

At Ballinasack Bridge he met armoured cars and lorry loads of Specials and military heading in the direction of Mullaghbane. Patrols in the area had been stepped up dramatically, especially on a Sunday morning, but this was a show of military might, with Lewis machine guns prominently mounted on the vehicles. When Catherine and the girls left for second Mass at eleven, he worried that they might be walking into danger, but Ellen said that the military were likely going over to the border. Catherine knew that Mass was the only place she'd hear any news. When she saw the armoured cars and Crossley tenders lined up outside the chapel, she almost turned back. Some of the Specials and soldiers were jostling and harassing men of all ages and jabbing at them with bayonets. Others armed with rifles and revolvers barred the chapel gate, ready to open fire on the congregation at any minute. Nobody hung around outside to exchange news and gossip like they normally did, but instead edged very carefully past with their eyes lowered and hurried quickly into the dubious safety of the chapel. The Specials had been known to enter chapels and drag men out.

The turnout at Mass was high, with people seeking solace in religion and also trying to find out what was happening. The priest prayed for the victims of the Troubles and exhorted the people to stick to their religion and say the family Rosary and not give up the faith. Then he took a deep breath and announced that the presence of the military and Special Constabulary outside the chapel was not by chance. A terrible atrocity had been committed near Newry, with people of the other denomination being killed and their houses burned out. He advised them to leave the chapel in a quiet and orderly fashion after Mass and not to draw attention to themselves, as the men outside would not hesitate to shoot. Fear rippled through the chapel, and for a moment it seemed as if there would be a stampede for the doors, but the priest deftly wheeled them into a decade of the Rosary, and the familiar repetitive prayer calmed them down a little. He said the blessing and then left the altar quickly. Recently the Specials had been targeting the clergy and he was anxious to be away. Cardinal Logue and his deputy bishops had been stopped and searched by the Specials. Questions had been asked in parliament about the treatment of the Irish clergy, but Churchill, who was aware of what was going on, did not condemn it outright as the country was in such a state of turmoil.

In Mullaghbane the congregation had been depending on the priest for reassurance, but now they knew they were on their own. At the holy water fonts they blessed themselves then roundly doused the children, genuflected and reluctantly went outside to where the Specials waited menacingly, scrutinising each person who emerged. Catherine steered the girls through them, forcing her quivering legs to move at a steady pace away from the chapel. Her back felt tense and very exposed and she waited for a bullet to strike. Neighbouring women gripped their children tightly, dragging them along as they walked stoically beside her.

When they were at a safe distance, they collapsed gratefully onto the ditch, feeling as if they had run a hundred miles. They spoke in hushed tones about the outrages committed at Dromintee and what might have happened near Newry, and though they wondered who could have done it, they avoided making any suggestions. The reprisals that followed a raid on a Protestant community would be worse than the horrors perpetrated at McGuills'. They tried to conceal their dread about what might be coming, but the children knew that something terrifying was happening and anxiously watched their faces. Though the women were eager to get home, they knew their homes would not provide safety. Terror, in the dancing flames that silhouetted burning buildings against the night sky, in the harsh explosions of bombs, in the sharp whip of the rifle shot, the agonised cries of the dying and the anguished, lonely wailing of the survivors, could come to their doors too.

After dinner Bryan took Brigid and Katy with him to drive the sheared sheep back down to Umericam. It wasn't a good idea to be on the broad road at a time like that, but the sheep were starving and there wasn't enough grass close by to feed them. They met Jem near the Crossroads. He was very nervous and told Bryan that Protestant men, women and children were took out of their beds and shot and blew up and their houses burnt.

Around 2.30 a.m. on Saturday morning, an attack by IRA gunmen that lasted about an hour took place on a small community of Protestant families at Lisdrumliska and Altnaveigh, two miles outside Newry. The houses attacked were situated off the main road and would have been hard to find without local knowledge. Two landmines were laid out and exploded on the Dublin Road to obstruct the Specials on their way to the area. The IRA operated in three groups. Thomas Crozier struggled out of bed and was shot dead at his door, where he had been confronted by armed men, some of whom he is said to have recognised. His wife, who went to support him, was shot in the arm and bled to death within twenty minutes, as the family were unable to staunch the blood or find any assistance. Alice Crozier, their daughter, was injured in the leg by a bomb splinter. An incendiary bomb was thrown through the window, where it damaged furniture and ornaments but failed to ignite the building. The house was also fired on with rifles, but the bullets went straight through the back window, which was directly opposite the front window.

Joseph Little, whose house adjoined Crozier's, escaped with his four sons and two daughters through the back windows into the fields. They were pursued and a large number of shots were fired after them, but they got away. Mr Little sustained an injury to his heel.

Another group of IRA attacked the adjoining houses of Edward Little and William Lockhart at Drumliska. Edward Little had a wife and nine children; the oldest was fifteen and the youngest a baby. A bomb that was thrown into their house landed in the cradle, but fortunately the baby was in the bed with its mother. The family were ordered out and made to stand in their nightclothes at the side of the road. Then the IRA went in and set the house on fire, burning it to the ground. Next door the Lockhart family – William, his wife, their only son James and their three daughters – were also brought out and made to stand on the roadside as the attackers discussed whether to shoot Mr Lockhart or his son or both of them. Eventually they picked out one of Little's sons and James Lockhart. As they were led away, James turned to say something to his mother, which the IRA interpreted as disobeying an order and shot him dead in front of his parents, sisters and the Little family.

As bombs were thrown into the Heslips' house, John Heslip, his wife, his nineteen-year-old son, Robert, and sixteen-year-old son, William, fled out the back and hid in the stable. But they were brought out by one of the raiders, and John Heslip and his elder son were ordered to go along the road with the gang. They had only gone a couple of yards, with Mrs Heslip and William following, when the gang turned and shot the father and elder son dead. When Mrs Heslip pleaded for mercy, they came back and fired more shots into the bodies.

John Thomas Gray's household had thirteen members – four daughters, five sons and two cousins. They were brought out and the house set on fire. Then the male members of the family were lined up, and twenty-year-old Joseph was shot eight times in the chest and body. His father was shot in the leg. A couple of the younger boys collapsed in fright and another one, Abie, made a dash for freedom and got away.

Later Mr Gray and his son were removed to Newry General Hospital and a specialist surgeon was requisitioned to come from

Belfast to operate on Joseph. But his injuries were so critical that he died at 5.30 that evening. His remains and those of the other victims were removed to the mortuary at Newry Workhouse.

Following the assaults at Altnaveigh and Lisdrumliska the assailants went in the direction of Camlough and Bessbrook, where they proceeded to attack the Chancellor's House (where it is believed that the treaty of the Union was drafted over a century before), throwing in petrol bombs and an incendiary device that failed to ignite. Several bombs were thrown at Joseph McKnight's house in Cloughrea, and it was also subjected to considerable rifle fire. The bombs fell into the garden, damaging the windows and the roof of the house and the furniture inside, but no one was killed or injured. At The Woodhouse the windows of the morning room and drawing room were broken, and petrol poured inside caused damage estimated at one hundred pounds. At Mountcaulfield the windows were broken and petrol bombs thrown inside, but they failed to ignite. There was an attempt to burn a grocery and spirit shop in Monaghan Street in Newry, but it didn't succeed. The *Belfast News Letter* likened the attack to the massacre of the Armenians by Turkish Irregulars. Following the murders at Altnaveigh, many Catholics fearing reprisal moved to the Carlingford area for safety.

Although Jem didn't know all the details at that time, Bryan knew with sickening certainty that some kind of plateau had been reached. Where it would go after this he didn't know. He looked at the girls in their bright summer dresses, calmly waiting in the shade of a sycamore tree while the sheep grazed at the side of the road. The sky was blue and warm sunshine bathed his head and shoulders. Blossom from the chestnut trees lay like confetti on the grass; the birds were singing and he could hear bees humming. A tranquil scene shimmering in front of him, but it didn't seem real. It would disappear in an instant if a tender swung round the corner. Unless the countryside was being destroyed forninst you, it was hard to imagine that such terrible savagery was taking place.

Not very far away the sun was shining down on burnt-out houses and drying up the blood that had been spilt on their doorsteps. People who had expected to get up yesterday morning with no greater worries than saving the harvest would never get up again. Their families who loved them would forever more associate the month of June with death and carnage. Fear crept under Bryan's skin and crawled up his back and he found it hard to breathe. The bitter taste of bile, the aul dram of the Grants, burnt his mouth and the back of his throat. He wanted to scoop up the girls and run back as fast as he could and barricade the family inside the house using every board, plank and metal bar that he could find, but Jem was waiting for reassurance and he asked him for a sup of water.

When he returned, Bryan felt a little more settled, but as he took the mug, he found his hand was curled in a painful cramp from the fierce grip he'd had on the blackthorn stick. As he felt his courage return, he hawked and spat in the dust to make sure that his vocal chords were working at a normal level. He knew Jem was depending on him and he didn't want to show fear. Shusie said to tell him that the Specials knew all about Hughie and that Bryan shouldn't be sleeping at home from now on. Jem said that if Bryan was going to stay at the camp at Dungooley, he would go with him, but the camp wasn't a safe place either. Bryan felt that he couldn't leave the women and children unprotected with all that was happening. He wondered what Hughie and the lads would think if he and Jem straggled into the camp looking for protection and them on high alert. He put the sheep into the field and secured the gap. He told the girls they could run on ahead, but not to go out of his sight.

Back at the Crossroads he noticed that the grass verge had been churned into dust by the big wheels of the tenders. He knew that they would decide who and where to target for reprisal. Houses full of young men with family connections to the IRA in a quiet place that could be entered and left quickly would be the ideal target, with enough people to inflict maximum casualties and terror.

"I won't be moving out to Dungooley," he told Jem. "They can't burn us all out and I don't think that you and I are in any bigger danger than the next man, but you're welcome to sleep in our loft if you want to."

"If women are in danger, I'll stay with Shusie, but she knows everybody and I don't think they'll bother her," Jem said. "I might be better sleeping in your loft than here. The Specials from Ballymoyer House are at the Crossroads night and day. When I go out at night to pass water at the back of the garden wall there's one at each shoulder wanting to know what I'm doing, and the way it is now, I'm afraid go out at all."

Bryan left him to make up his mind.

At home he told the women about Jem's dilemma. Many men were now sleeping out in the fields, but Bryan thought it would be better if he stayed around the house at night. Catherine was torn between wanting him to be there and letting him go to where he might be safer.

"Look what your IRA has done for you now!" Ellen declared. "There'll be many a poor innocent crater will pay for their work the other night. We could all be burnt to death in our beds, if God hasn't said it. Is Ireland worth the blood that's spilt in her name? Was it Hughie and them lads that done that, Bryan?"

He was aware that Catherine was also waiting for his answer and assured them that Hughie and the lads would be guarding the camp. The women sighed with relief and Bryan sighed too. The 4th Northern Brigade were likely responsible, and Hughie was a soldier. He would do as he was ordered.

Tension rose in the countryside and the people waited in fear of what would happen next. Three more houses belonging to Protestants were attacked with bombs in the Newtownhamilton district. One man was injured and brought to the hospital. Two miles from Newry, a Catholic man was found dead in his house, riddled with bullets. Another house was raided and a man beaten up. A few days later a Dublin-born employee of the Great Northern Railway was taken from Edward Street station and shot through the head. His co-worker, who was also taken, escaped and spent the night hiding in a flax pond, up to his neck in water. Nine miles from Newry, two men out working with horses were shot dead in the field by Specials. Locally all of these actions were seen as reprisals.

Across the fields from Grant's on Cranny Road, the Specials

accosted young Jemmy Nellie and said he had the look of an IRA boy that was present at the ambush at McGuills'. They had him standing with his hands up and were about to shoot him when his brother Johnny came out to see what was going on. They were going to shoot him, too, but astonishingly, one of the Specials knew him because he had been hired on his family farm at Banbridge, where he was known as White Jack because he always wore a white cap. The Special vouched for both of the brothers and they were let go. They were said to be very lucky boys; only for the white cap, they would have been killed.

A few years previously, young Johnny Nellie had been taken outside by the Tans, put up against a wall and shots fired around him. Before that, as a child in England, he was near burnt to death in a fire in his mother's boarding house. Some people thought Johnny was an unfortunate sort of a hoor, but others said that a fella that had been almost burnt to death then nearly shot twice must have some sort of luck in him, but not the sort of luck they'd want. He needed it all for himself.

The Catholic population was on edge day and night waiting for a tender coming to burn them out, but there was no large-scale reprisal by the Specials, and the countryside settled down uneasily. Two weeks after McGuills' pub was burnt, the walls were blown up as a matter of military necessity, to prevent further ambushes. Two or three columns of fire-blackened stone remained standing – stark monuments to what had happened there.

Shortly after that a distraught Biddy Kane ran down to tell Bryan that she had a problem, but it wasn't bees this time, it was B Specials. The night before, they had come into her house when she was sleeping, wedged a chair against the room door then stirred up the fire and made tea. She'd heard four or five different ones talking about the blowing up of what was left of McGuills' and what they would do with the IRA and the Taigs. She explained that the door was always on the latch in case the lads were passing, and she'd often come back from her ceilidh and found the teapot still warm, but never thought it was the Specials. Bryan thought they must have been in the house before and knew it was open. Fortunately the lads hadn't stopped by. The plank that secured the back of her door at night was missing, and Biddy said she'd burned it when she sprained her ankle because she had no turf. She said that the Specials were talking about a young fella that was taken away from Newtownhamilton on the doctor's motorbicycle. When they got the boy that did it they would hang him up like a pig and slit his throat with a slash hook. And then one of them shouted, "And you along with him, you aul Fenian bitch." When Bryan said that she should stay with them and that Frank Aiken and the lads would want her to look after herself in case she'd be needed in the future, she straightened her shoulders, puffed out her chest and stood to attention. Bryan half expected her to salute. She told Bryan to get her another plank for the door. Her aul simple troubles and woes were nothing compared to what the lads were going through. Bryan advised her to take the heavy wooden beetle that she used for mashing the pratas to the room with her at night and keep it by the bed. Biddy nodded agreeably, knowing as well as he did that the beetle would be no good against armed men. She would be far better to just get under the bed with it, and with that, she decided she felt much happier.

When Ellen suggested sending Brigid to stay with Biddy, Catherine said that with several women being attacked and one killed in recent times, she didn't want Brigid staying in a house that was being used by the Specials. Bryan found Biddy another plank for her door, and though he wasn't convinced it would offer much protection she was well pleased with it.

When Jem, who had been sleeping in the loft, arrived later, he had a copy of *The Irish Times* and they laughed at the report that de Valera's wife had given birth to twins on 24 May, Empire Day, but the leading article soon sobered them up. Civil War had broken out in Dublin between Michael Collins's and de Valera's forces. Collins and the pro-treaty supporters wanted to get a government set up in the twenty-six counties, but de Valera and his supporters wanted to fight on for a republic. The anti-treaty forces had been occupying the Four Courts since the middle of April, and now at the end of June, in an effort to dislodge them, Collins's had shelled the building using artillery borrowed from the British and with help from the British army. The Four Courts executive, including Ernie O'Malley, Rory O'Connor, Liam Mellows, Joe McKelvey and Dick Barrett, surrendered the buildings unconditionally and the entire garrison were taken prisoner. Part of the building had been stormed in the early hours of the morning, and after daybreak the battle resumed against the main body of rebels. Sometime after noon the rebels exploded a mine that caused great destruction in the Four Courts, as well as injuring large numbers of Free State troops and civilians. The Probate Offices, the Law Library, the Bankruptcy Court and the Record Office, with its priceless manuscripts and documents, were all destroyed, as were the homes of nearby residents. Pockets of rebels still holding out in various hotels around Dublin, including the Gresham, were forced to surrender after being bombarded by eighteen-pounder shells. Four hundred republican insurgents were taken prisoner and it was thought that the back of the resistance had been broken.

Jem wondered why clever men couldn't come up with a treaty that they all agreed on rather than killing each other with British guns. This would leave the lads in the South fighting men they knew and had fought along with. What would happen now with the 4th Northern Brigade? Aiken said that he wouldn't fight his fellow Irishmen, but he had three or four hundred armed men in the barracks in Dundalk and along the border, and neither Collins nor de Valera would allow him sit on the fence with his own army. He couldn't move the men back North from the camps at Ravensdale and Dungooley because the military and the Specials were waiting on them. He was boxed in and would eventually have to make a choice to go with one side or the other. The combatants all knew too much about each other, so the Civil War might not last too long. The force with the most guns and ammunition would win it. Bryan likened it to hunting a fox: no matter how clever it was, when you knew its habits, you could wait it out and sure the fox couldn't better the gun.

Jem thought that the Civil War in the South would leave things quieter in the North and decided to go back home to the Crossroads.

And although he wasn't the bravest of men, Bryan knew he would miss him. It had been comforting to have another man on the premises at night.

Chapter 13

The following day Bryan found Jem's fob watch in the loft and decided to return it to him that evening. The girls were outside playing jacks, but Mary was swinging on a chair and Ellen was afraid that she would overbalance and cowp the dresser and break all the delft. When she ordered Bryan to take the child with him, he nodded amiably. His mother could see a whole chain of disaster in an ordinary event.

Mary ran ahead, barefoot, slowing briefly when she crigged her big toe on a stone. Jocko caught up with them just before the Crossroads. Bryan debated turning back when he saw a tender parked on the verge near the shop, but that might look suspicious, so he walked on. The Specials smoking by the ditch eyed him narrowly as he approached, and some nodded slightly in greeting. Sarah Cullen was sitting on the stone seat in front of the shop talking and laughing with Tony Hurst. His rifle was propped up at the back of the seat, ready to be lifted if needed. A short distance away sitting under a shady sycamore tree were Eugene Murphy and his father. John had his back to the Specials, with his bicycle resting against the ditch. Mary looked curiously at the armed men, then went to poke about under the hedge. Eugene Murphy asked if she wanted to see him riding the bicycle, but she ignored him. His father said it wasn't the place to be riding the bicycle, but Eugene was undeterred. When Sarah called hello to Mary, Tony asked was that the eejit child she had been telling him about. Sarah said Mary could imitate people and sounded exactly like them, but Tony lost interest and turned to watch Eugene Murphy showing off on the bicycle.

With one foot on the outside pedal and the other under the bar to reach the inside pedal he sailed down the curve of the road.

"Daddy, Daddy, look at me," he shouted in his boyish, high-pitched voice.

As he walked the bicycle back up, the Specials laughed and made comments. His father became uneasy and ordered him to bring the bicycle back, but Eugene was determined to have one last go. He was gathering speed when Jocko trotted across the road in front of him. The bicycle went out of control and they ended up in the ditch across from Sarah and Tony. Eugene angrily kicked the dog, and as it limped away in pain, Mary picked up a short stick and hurried over to where Eugene lay. She looked around briefly at the watching Specials.

"You'll not find this boy kilt behind the milk house," she said conversationally.

Then, holding the stick like a revolver, she adopted a military stance and pointed it into Eugene's face.

"Get up," she snarled. "Get back on that motorcycle you cowardly bastard or I'll shoot you!"

Eugene withdrew as far as he could into the ditch and began to scream for his father, but not before Tony had heard and seen all that had happened.

"Did she just say 'Get back on that motorcycle?'" he demanded. "We have a man missing and he was taken away on a motorcycle, so who was she imitating, Sarah?"

At first, when Sarah protested that she didn't know, he viciously nipped the soft inner flesh of her upper arm. Tears sprang into her eyes, but he persisted. If she knew everyone on that road then she should know the voice, so who was it? And where had she learnt to hold a gun? No child, especially an eejit child, would know how to hold a revolver unless she'd seen it done. He could question the child now in the tender or take Sarah and it back to Newtownhamilton Barracks for questioning. The men might enjoy that. It was up to her. Sarah capitulated. She would tell him if he promised not to hurt Mary.

Inside the shop a sixth sense made Shusie look out through the window. She knew that something had happened. She advised Bryan to go out in case Mary had got in a pickle of some sort with that smart lad of John Murphy's and to be careful of Tony Hurst because he had eyes in him like a ferret. He was a caldera that missed nothing. Them that were half and half were always trying to prove something to one side or the other and he was on the right side at the minnit. When she observed that Sarah Cullen had picked up again after not being so well, Bryan looked at her in amazement.

"I have eyes in me head," she said. "Och, she's a rattling sort of a girl, but she's keeping the wrong company and it'll come to a bad end. You go on out anyway, just in case."

Outside John Murphy was examining the bicycle. The Specials were waiting in the tender and drove off when Tony joined them. Sarah was rubbing at her arm and gazing at the ground and Mary was examining a snail shell. The scene seemed fairly normal. John Murphy explained to Bryan that the lad had cowped the bicycle in the ditch, but he was all right. Mary said that Eugene had kicked the dog and Eugene said that it was an accident, that his foot had slipped. The children glared at each other, with neither prepared to give way. John said he had been waiting for a parcel coming out from Newry, but he didn't like the way the Specials were watching Eugene or the bicycle. They didn't want people having bicycles, and he was afeared to be seen talking to Bryan ayther. Shusie had just told him that there was a new rule now called unlawful assembly. If them boys seen more than two people talking together they could arrest everyone and that would be the last was ever seen of them till they were found dead on the road like the men at Lislea. He was worried that they would come back and arrest him and the lad and the bicycle.

"Come on, me aul fellow-me-lad, up you get," he said to Eugene. "Thank God we have our health, Bryan."

And off they went. As Bryan neared Ballinasack Bridge, Sarah Cullen ran up beside him, panting and out of breath. She told him what had happened with Mary at the Crossroads and that Tony had seen and heard it all. When Bryan wondered why Tony would heed an afflicted child, Sarah said he didn't care how or where he got information. He knew that Mary could imitate people because she had told him, and the young fella that had been kidnapped was his neighbour. She had never told him about meeting Hughie with the motorcycle until he threatened to have the men question her and Mary. Then he said he would pay Hughie's house a visit to try and find the truth. What was she to do now? She wiped her fists against her nose and tear-stained cheeks like a small child as she waited, but he had only one answer.

"Get home as quick as you can," he advised her. "Pack a bag and go back to the Crossroads and take the first lift that's going in any direction, be it to Newry, Dundalk, Hell or Connacht, but get out of here for you'll never be safe again. When the IRA find out they'll tar and feather you or worse, and I don't know what the Specials will do when they find out what you told me. There's a few shillings, it's not much, but it might buy you a feed or get you on a bus somewhere if you were stuck. Run on now as quick as you can!"

She shook her head groggily like a boxer that was hit too often. It wasn't what she had expected to hear, but she took the money, thanked him and sprinted up the road. When Mary came up from the river with the tail of her skirt dripping wet, he wrung it out, and as she skipped ahead, it slapped wetly against the calves of her legs. An innocent crater, God knows, he thought, but look at the trouble she gets us into.

When he broached the possibility of a raid, Ellen sat up proud and fierce and commanded Catherine to do the same. It wasn't the first time they'd dealt with the likes of them boys and it wouldn't be the last. And they would come; there was nothing surer, bar dying. Everything of value was buried in the donkil because they'd steal anything that took their fancy. Although they knew that it was pointless, they filled barrels and buckets at the river then stood on the cart to douse the thatch, haystacks and outhouses. Then Addy Murray and Sarah came hurrying over the road. Addy knew that Sarah had to leave as quickly and quietly as possible. Bryan offered them a lift to the Crossroads, but Sarah was worried that Tony might be there, so Catherine gave them black wool shawls to put over their heads. Old women were covered up regardless of the weather and the Specials wouldn't look sideways at a pair of aul shawlies on a cart. Bryan advised Sarah not to write home or tell anyone where she'd gone, because the IRA read the letters they took from the mailcart. She could be followed and killed. People had been assassinated before in England, America and Australia.

At the Crossroads Shusie, who was used to strange goings-on, showed no surprise. She didn't approve of Addy and had her doubts about Sarah, but she loved a bit of intrigue and was willing to help. Nobody would be going to Newry at that time of the evening, but someone would surely be going in the morning. Sarah was welcome to stay, but she would have to stay out of sight. The Specials were outside every night, and neighbours often came in their ceilidh and someone might see her and talk.

Addy said goodbye to Sarah then waited outside by the cart. Shusie got Sarah settled and launched into a litany about Tony Hurst and the breed of him. They owed money and never paid it back. They were as mane as cat shite and would darn the dishcloth and live on the clippings of tin. Tight as a duck's arse, wouldn't part with tuppence, she concluded. The young one would be got away, all right, but she could only wish Bryan luck. Jem offered to go up and stay with him, but Bryan said they could be worrying about nothing.

At Bryan's house Addy jumped down quickly from the cart, refusing his offer to leave her on up. She could do with a bit of a walk. She never thought she'd be saying goodbye to her granddaughter that evening and might never see her again. She hoped Bryan would survive the raid, and if they wanted, she'd keep the girls overnight. Bryan accepted the offer, and when he left the girls over later on, she decided that they could all sleep in Sarah's bed. Mary was kept at home. After the Rosary, they asked God to spare them and went to bed before ten o'clock.

Catherine put her coat on over her clothes and lay down under the patchwork quilt. If they tried to violate her, she wouldn't make it easy. Ellen was fatalistic. If God ordained this was her time to go, there was little she could do about it.

The rattle of the window woke them as daylight was breaking: a heavy lorry with the engine switched off rolled down past the house. They heard a creaking noise as the tailboard was lowered, followed by silence. The dog's nails made a faint click as he padded across the stone floor to snuffle at the bottom of the door. Then, as the hammering and shouting began, he started barking and snarling. Catherine thought she might vomit from fear, but got up and fumbled to light a lamp. As demands from outside became more insistent, Bryan heaved the bar out of its restraints and the door burst open. Masked men poured into the kitchen shouting loudly and filling the small space. The lamp cast giant moving shadows as the breeze swayed the flame. Bryan was roughly seized by the ear and a pistol stuck into his neck and the dog clubbed to the floor by a rifle butt. A raider cast Mary aside like a rag doll. She hit her head against the leg of the table and lay still. Catherine rushed to her aid but was pinned against the wall with a rifle barrel across her throat. The Special demanded to know where Stephens was, but the gun barrel was choking her and she couldn't breathe.

"He isn't here," she croaked. "There's no Stephens here."

He pushed her aside then tipped over the upper part of the dresser, tumbling plates and mugs onto the floor. Mary's face was turning blue and bubbles of saliva frothed around her lips.

"Look to your child, missus," one raider advised. "She's foaming there like a bloody animal!"

Catherine cleared Mary's mouth with her cuff then cradled her head, trying to make herself as small as possible and not draw them on her. Ellen shouted that she was an aul woman trying to make her water, but they took her out and put her into an armchair. Mattresses and pillows were slashed with bayonets as they searched for valuables. The tick on the settle bed was ripped open, the chaff scattered on the floor and the chamber pots emptied on top. Several men hauled Bryan outside, his bare feet trailing painfully over the cobbles. They heard shouting and swearing, and the outhouse doors opening. Then, after shots were fired, came the hysterical cackling of hens. Catherine said an Act of Contrition on Bryan's behalf. The man left to guard them was young and became increasingly twitchy as Ellen's voice murmured monotonously in prayer. Catherine wished she would stop, but she continued, decade after decade. Finally the young fella could stand it no longer.

"Shut up, you aul bitch," he screamed. "Shut your bloody mouth or I'll kill you!"

As he pointed the gun at Ellen, Catherine laid Mary's head gently on the floor and moved up beside him. "For God's sake, if you have any nature in you at all, don't do that," she begged. "Don't shoot her. She's doting, she doesn't know what she's saying."

He pushed her back and retreated to the door, nervously watching the women and listening to what was happening outside. When a shrill whistle was heard, he fired a shot into the side of the water crock and ran outside. The water flowed out and mingled with the debris in the middle of the floor. When the tender moved away, Catherine went outside to look for Bryan. Dead hens lay in the yard and the cows and pigs were munching on the hay and straw that was strewn about. Bryan lay half sprawled on the loft steps. He was battered and bruised, with his eyes beginning to swell and his mouth and nose bloodied. She hurried over to help him up.

He had crigged his toes on every stone in the yard and the toenails that hadn't been torn off were broken. Catherine ran in and told Ellen that he was alive and brought out a pair of thick stockings, which she eased onto his feet, and then she helped him inside. Ellen, released from whatever malaise had afflicted her since she moved from Umericam, stirred up the fire and made tea.

"She should a put you in the barra," she remarked. "You're a bit the worse for wear, avic."

"I am that, Mother," Bryan agreed as he tried not to grin at the understatement. Jocko was breathing noisily and with difficulty. Catherine put him over in the corner and threw one of her shawls over him. He looked to be done.

Then, with Ellen's help, she lifted the dresser from the floor and surveyed the damage underneath. Several of the big serving dishes and some mugs were beyond repair. She threw all the debris out onto the donkil with the dead hens, then enticed the animals back into their houses. The Crown Forces seemed to have a grudge agin hens. The Tans had shot all the fowl in the country too.

Bryan was puzzled by the raid because they had got off very lightly. Quite often a place and everyone in it was burnt. But it might be a trick to lure Hughie down, or mebbe they thought the family knew more than they did.

Sarah Cullen had said that she only told Tony the day before about seeing Hughie and Stephens on the doctor's motorcycle, but these Specials knew he'd been brought round the mountain road the day he was kidnapped. It was hard to know if Sarah had been lying or if someone else had also informed. He wondered if he hadn't been there would they have bothered the women, but Ellen reminded him that James McGuill hadn't been there when they raided the public house and it hadn't saved the women. It used to be that a woman could walk the length and breadth of Ireland and no one would harm her, but sure them days is long gone. Women now had to take their chances the same as the men.

Catherine had been very scared when they came through the door, and suddenly the memory of it made her feel weak and she had to sit down and swallow a good dram of poteen. When she felt more settled, she repaired the mattresses and pillows with the packing needle and cord that were used for closing the woolsacks, then she swilled the kitchen floor with undiluted Jeyes Fluid, but even after that she thought she could still smell urine.

"Pish is healthy and at least it's your own," Ellen said dismissively. "I can't smell anything. It would be a different story if it was the Specials that pished on the middle of your floor. You'd have bother getting rid of the smell then. Thank God the pots were enamel or you wouldn't have a pot to pish in, nor me ayther."

Bryan groaned as he tried not to laugh. Ellen was taking charge and glorying in it. She had lived through many a crisis and her spirit was undiminished. She washed dishes, peeled potatoes and helped to put the sewn-up mattresses back on the beds, but she eventually ran out of steam, and when she retired to her room, Bryan went and lay down beside Mary in their bedroom.

Addy could barely read, but she had told the girls the story of the willow-pattern plate, the star-crossed Chinese lovers trying to escape across the little bridge. She gave Brigid a perfume bottle that Sarah had left behind. When she brought the girls back, she stood with her hands on her hips, surveying the scene. Catherine told them what happened and they listened very quietly. Mary emerged from the bedroom with a dark-blue bruise on her forehead. She picked Jocko up, carried him to an armchair and arranged him comfortably across her knees. The women didn't interfere. The girls peered in on Bryan, but the curtains in the bedroom were drawn and they didn't see the extent of his injuries.

Catherine walked Addy back up the road and told her about the raid. Addy said she knew Sarah was walking a fine line and that she should have sent her away long ago. What would become of her in a world where young women were seldom safe? She would miss her sorely. She said she would bring a powder over later on for Bryan, and when Catherine thanked her for keeping the girls, she said that it cost her nothing. She'd enjoyed their wee innocent crack and it had kept her mind off Sarah. Then each headed back to her own house.

Bryan found that he was better sitting upright, and when the girls offered to bathe his feet, he assured them he was almost cured. As Mary quietly crooned to the dog, the adults listened in silence. The raid had sapped all their energy, and the will to continue was temporarily drained out of them.

It was the same all over the North. Ordinary people were suffering and both sides were guilty. In Monaghan a Protestant woman said to be an informer had been shot by the IRA. Ellen said the Specials had probably shot her and put the blame on the IRA. They saw the Catholic people as being lower than rats, and that's what would be ruling them if the IRA didn't do something quick.

Bryan suppressed a rueful grin, thinking angry women were better than fearful women. They lined a box with hay and persuaded Mary to put the dog into it. Bryan would be sleeping in the chair by the fire and would mind him. They'd send for Annie McGuinness in the morning and she could tell Hughie that they were all right. Hopefully that would stop him from coming down into a trap.

Catherine made up Addy's powder and gave it to Bryan.

"You'd want to mind what Addy gives you," Ellen warned. "Take care it's not something for scouring a horse."

"If it is, we'll all know about it before morning," Bryan told her as he prepared to drink the milky fluid. "For I know I'll not be able to move too speedy."

They laughed as they went to settle in their separate quarters; laughter kept the terror at bay.

The powder was strong, and Bryan slept until it was almost daylight. He struggled awake, adjusting to the aches in his body, surprised that he was sleeping in a chair. A tender rattled past the house and he held his breath as it slowed down, but it passed on by. Relief gave way to worry as he wondered if they had thrown a lighted torch onto the thatch. As he got out of the chair, trying not to cry out in pain, he felt a warm, dry nose in his palm.

"Be cripes, Jocko, a warm nose isn't a good sign in a dog, but you're still here." He ran his hand over Jocko's head, feeling the swelling and ridges left by the gun butt. "If you can get up and not a squawk out of you after the blow you got, then I can do the same," he murmured.

He edged his way across the floor and opened the door. Jocko wandered outside, staggering sideways as he raised his leg to piddle against a stone. Dawn was breaking and the orange glow streaking the sky was the sunrise, not flames. He didn't see any smoke rising, nor smell the acrid stench of burning thatch. Ignoring the pain in his ribs, he inhaled the cool, misty mountain air deep into his lungs. The early-morning sky promised good weather.

We live to fight another day, he thought. Thank God to see it.

Chapter 14

Annie McGuinness arrived before they could send for her. A man out calving a cow had heard the shooting and seen the tender leave but had been afraid to investigate for fear everyone had been killed. He was timid and odd and had only found the courage to tell Annie that morning. Bryan knew the man and understood that he wouldn't want to bring trouble on himself, but it left Annie puzzled.

"What if you'd all been injured and needed help?" she said. "People are afraid of their shadows these days, and could you blame them?"

She would talk to Hughie later. Brian said to tell him that they weren't too bad and not to be coming down, for they would be watching and waiting for him.

"Will I tell him how you look?" Annie asked.

His forehead was swollen and his eyes mere slits. The bridge of his nose and his cheeks were scored with cuts, and the skin that was visible was shiny and mask-like. Bryan said to say nothing, the less he knew the better, and Annie agreed. She'd call with them on the way back from the camp.

They were almost tired of waiting when two girls arrived on bicycles. Annie was dressed in her ordinary clothes, but the other girl wore the Cumann na mBan uniform. When Bryan came out to talk to Annie, the other girl waited further up the hill as if not wanting to intrude.

Annie said she'd delivered his message, but Hughie was Hughie.

When the other girl bent to adjust the chain on her bicycle Bryan had a feeling he knew her. "She's taking an awful risk wearing the uniform," he said. "Didn't the Unionist government bar the Cumann na mBan?"

"Yes, they did," said Annie. "We were proscribed at the end of last May, us and the Fianna and the IRA, but she insisted on wearing the uniform."

When Bryan said she had the look of someone he knew, she strode down to where he was leaning on the wall.

"It's a poor father that doesn't know his own daughter," she said.

"Och, Jaysus, Hughie!" Bryan cried as he recoiled in shock. "What are you doing dressed like that?"

Hughie said he'd put it on for a bit of divarsion and thought the hat suited him well enough. He came down to see how things were. He said Bryan looked like the jinnet had kicked him in the face, far worse than what he imagined.

Bryan preferred that Catherine or the girls didn't know he was there and walked him back up the hill. He told Hughie about the raid and the incident at the Crossroads before the raid.

"Och, that Mary one is like a will-o'-the-wisp – you never know where she is," said Hughie. "And Sarah, we don't know what other information she was giving to them. She was always a security risk for us. Is she gone?"

When Bryan said that she was, Hughie said he was glad and he hoped she'd never come back because there would be no mercy. He said that Frank Aiken had been ordered to Dublin for talks with General Mulcahy, the deputy chief of the Free State army. Mulcahy and Michael Collins were very good friends. At the camp they had been waiting to go back in and free the North, but now they were boxed in and would have to choose a side. He said they were puzzled now as to how Michael Collins saw the six counties. He pulled a clip from the *Dundalk Democrat* out of his breast pocket and showed Bryan a speech that Collins had made in the Mansion House in Dublin prior to the recent elections:

> We see facing us at the present moment a very definite endeavour to restore the old ascendancy. Certain classes of

> action are playing into the hands of that ascendancy and if we go on playing into the hands of the enemy, the enemy will win. This is not the time to take on a war with the North-East of Ireland and with the British Empire as well. We have seen an artificial situation created on the Fermanagh–Donegal border, and British troops have been called to the aid of the Northern government. British troops have come into the Donegal area a certain distance, and it only needs that kind of advance to bring the war into the rest of Ireland. The policy of certain powerful elements in England who have agents in the North-East is not merely one of destroying the Irish Republic or the Irish Free State, but simply a policy of restoring the ascendancy all over Ireland and restoring the Act of Union. We can face this prospect. A certain amount of local government is of no more harm in the North-East than in the West of Ireland, provided there is no real severance. I can put it to our friends in the North in this way: a body may continue to live without a particular limb, but the amputated limb simply decays and withers. That is the attitude of Ireland to its limb on the North-East, and I don't think the sensible elements in the North-East will fail to grasp that.

The men at the camp didn't think the speech offered much consolation to the Catholics of the north-east, but it did offer a glimmer of hope. Collins feared that the British would invade again through the North if provoked, and wanted to have the insurance of an established government, complete with law and order, behind him, before he brought up the question of the North.

Hughie thought that Collins would help the North if he could, but it was on the long finger now with the Civil War. The Free State had already taken preliminary action. Cumann na mBan, who voted against the treaty, were put in jail to stop them helping de Valera's side. It didn't matter now that they had been comrades who risked life and liberty in the fight against the British. The Free Staters had got arms and ammunition from the British and were likely to come out of it best. The 4th Northern was waiting for the outcome of Aiken's meeting with Mulcahy. They didn't know how it would go.

Annie came up beside them and said it was time to go. She sped on ahead to scout the road, then signalled that it was clear. Bryan waited awhile then went home. He told them what Annie had said but didn't mention that Hughie was along with her.

Catherine sprayed the potatoes for blight using a copper container that held the bluestone, but as she wasn't fit to cut corn, Bryan cautiously began to practise with the scythe.

"Take care that you're not swinging that scythe too soon," Ellen warned. "Your rib could go into your lung and kill you, and mind you don't cut yourself – it's the worm month or you could get lockjaw."

Bryan assured her that he'd take all precautions. There was no cure for lockjaw.

Jocko wouldn't eat unless Mary placed the food into his mouth, and they wondered had he lost his sense of smell. Bryan singed a feather under his nose and he ignored it, but everyone else's eyes watered.

"Burning feathers always reminds me of the time I fainted when me corsets were too tight," Ellen remarked. "And sure that must be more nor sixty years ago."

"Why were your corsets too tight, Granny?" Katy asked.

"It was the fashion. Girls wore tight corsets to show off their figures. Me father was the only one that was strong enough to lace me into mine, and I had to hold on to the bedpost while he was doing it," Ellen told her. "And sure where's the man born that would know the first thing about that? He laced me too tight and I passed out. Burning feathers would take you round, but I never seen a corset that would fit a dog."

The girls looked at her to see if she was joking, but she kept a straight face. She said a dog with no smell wasn't much of a dog and to make sure he got enough to ate.

Everything was quiet until Sunday, 23 July, when twelve-year-old Margaret Moore and eighteen-year-old Mary Connolly were shot dead in Edenappa, Jonesborough, by soldiers from the Royal Sussex Regiment stationed at Jonesborough Barracks. Mary Moore,

Margaret's sister, also aged eighteen, was seriously wounded in the side and leg, while Kate Moore, aged fifteen, escaped injury. At first it was stated that the girls were fired on from the barracks, but it was later revealed that they were killed as the Moores' house, just inside the border, was being raided by the army. The house had been raided several times by soldiers and Specials who were looking for the Moores' sons. The Moore girls and Mary Connolly, their neighbour, had gone to meet another sister, Brigid, who was coming from Newry, where she worked, but they missed her. They came back home through the field that adjoined their house, crossed the stile down by the well and started up the path to the house.

The small group of soldiers that arrived around 9.30 that night had been joined by a further party around 10.30. Some of the soldiers entered the dwelling, while others went up to a shed at the corner of the cornfield, leaving one soldier on guard outside the house. As Mrs Moore was being questioned about the whereabouts of her sons, she looked out through the back window and saw the girls approaching the stile, and when she looked out again they were coming up the path. She was very worried because she had been down at the well the night before, and shots had been fired at her and around her and she had been forced to crawl back to the house on her hands and knees. The girls were twenty yards from the house when the first shots were fired. She heard them call out several times, "Don't shoot, we're girls!" She saw them drop down and she thought it was because they were frightened by the shooting. She heard a volley of shots and she and her daughter Brigid, who had arrived home earlier, shouted to the soldiers not to shoot at the children coming up the path. Then she heard one of her daughters call out, "I'm shot, I'm shot!" She ran out the back of the house and up the path to where her daughters and Mary Connolly had fallen. She found Margaret lying on her back and felt for her pulse, but thought that she had just fainted. She ran over to where Mary Connolly was lying in the ditch in a crouching position and she knew she was dead. She didn't go back to Margaret as she knew now that she was also dead. Her other daughter, Mary, was shouting that her leg was shot off, and when Mrs Moore reached her she could see a large wound in her leg that was bleeding very badly. The soldiers carried Mary and the dead bodies of Margaret and Mary Connolly to the house, and Mrs Moore sent for the doctor and the priest.

Mary, who had been shot six times, four times in the leg and twice in the side, was taken by ambulance to the hospital in Newry. Her leg was amputated and she remained critically ill for some time, but she survived.

On examining the body of Margaret Moore, the medical officer in charge of the troops at Newry found a wound in her left side, a rib and a portion of her left shoulder blade fractured and a wound at the back of her right chest near the bottom of the shoulder blade. The cause of death was shock and haemorrhage due to these wounds. Margaret Moore would have been thirteen on 13 August.

Mary Connolly, an only daughter, was shot twice in the head and died immediately. The soldiers reported that as they were conducting the raid, figures were observed approaching and were ordered to halt. When they didn't, they were shot. They said that it was after curfew, but curfew in the area was from dusk to dawn, and as that Sunday had been a particularly bright evening, it was still light at 10.40 p.m.

The following Tuesday an enormous crowd of people turned out for the funerals of the dead girls, who were buried on the southern side of the border in Faughart graveyard. The countryside was stunned by the casual brutality of the shooting. What kind of brutes would shoot young girls on a Sunday evening, curfew or no curfew? Although soldiers had been involved in the raid at McGuills', it was thought that they were still confined to barracks, but it seemed once the treaty was signed, they were on active service again.

"They don't care what you are or who you are," Ellen declared. "And they would shoot you of a Christmas Day if they took the notion."

A week or so later Annie McGuinness came to tell them that Frank Aiken's talks with General Mulcahy hadn't gone well, and after he returned to Dundalk, the barracks was attacked by the pro-treaty 3rd Northern Brigade from Monaghan. Two of Aiken's men had been killed and he'd been arrested along with his unit. Hughie and the other lads were still at the camp at Dungooley, waiting for orders. This meant that the 4th Northern was now on the anti-treaty side, and that wasn't what Aiken had wanted at all.

"Mulcahy didn't footer about. He put Aiken and his men out of action quare and quick. It's a wonder Aiken didn't see that coming after what they did to the Cumann na mBan," Bryan said. "The camps on the border will be next. They'll need to have their wits about them at Dungooley."

"They're on full alert. They call the new Irish army the 'Staters' because they accepted a free state. The Staters call the IRA the 'Irregulars' and the *Dundalk Democrat* calls the Northerners the 'Outlanders'," Annie said bitterly.

"The Outlanders." Bryan smiled. "That's a good one. That's an aul Scottish word for someone who doesn't belong to a place, like a blow-in. Aren't they quick to put a name on us? I don't mind hearing that they ever called the British, Outlanders."

"It's hard to believe that we're all fighting and killing each other now. But our women are still supporting the 4th Northern," Annie assured them.

They all knew that the fiercest, cruellest and most vicious battles occurred when one countryman turned against another. The Cumann na mBan were being hunted by the Specials in the North, and now the Staters would be watching and waiting for them in the South.

When Bryan walked over to the Crossroads to get a newspaper, Shusie had the *Frontier Sentinel* opened out on the counter.

"Well, if it isn't bandy Bryan Grant," she said. "Do you use that Shuk for your hens? I'm thinking of getting it for meself. I heard that snigger, Dan. Take care what you're mumbling under your tooth or there'll be no egg with your tay the night."

Bryan knew that the newspaper wouldn't be handed over until all the advertisements had been gone through and discussed. She didn't have too much heed on the news items.

"Do you think Rodine is any good for killing rats?" Shusie asked. "A woman told me she put it down and it was more rats she got.

'Rodine, the Piper O' Perth'! That's him in the kilt playing the bagpipes and the rats running behind him. A brave man, too, that went in amongst a crowd of rats with only a kilt on him."

When there was nothing more to absorb or discuss she folded up the paper and gave it to Bryan. "I'm sure you know about Frank Aiken and them getting arrested above in Dundalk," she remarked. "He'll never get out again. That crowd in Dublin have no heed on the North and they don't want any annoyance from him. They got what they wanted above and they'll all be feathering their own nests. It looks like it's 'Fare thee well, Killeavy' for us. I heard Sarah Cullen got on a boat at Warrenpoint and got off at Liverpool. Jem took her to Newry and got a chest of tay out of Quinn's the Milestone when he was in there, killing two birds with the one stone, so to spake. The Specials stopped him when he was coming back, but they didn't ask you nothing, did they, Jem?"

"They said nothing, but they stuck their bayonets into the tay and rummaged them about. God knows who or what them bayonets was stuck into before that," Jem said.

"You tell nobody about that," Shusie warned. "If people knew about it, they'd want it cheaper. Boil your water well, Bryan Grant, and you'll not have to worry about what's in the tay."

"All the bridges on the canal were lifted up and you couldn't get in that way, and they're guarding all the other roads in and out of Newry, too," Jem told them.

They wondered what might happen in Dundalk. There were still several hundred men at the camps along the border. Would they filter back north or try and hold their ground? They had no answers, and Shusie packed Bryan off home with the newspaper.

When everyone was ready, Catherine read them the official account of the capture. General headquarters in Beggar's Bush, Dublin, stated: "Dundalk is now completely in the hands of our troops. The military barracks in Anne Street, Bridge St. Barracks and the Gaol have been taken by the troops and 300 Irregulars made prisoners with their arms, Lewis guns, Thompson guns and large quantities of ammunition and bombs."

"So there you are," she said. "And here's a bit about Cardinal Logue being stopped again."

Cardinal Logue had been stopped in the Dromintee area as he was going to the funeral of another priest. The Specials made him get out of his car, used foul language to him and made him and the priests travelling with him remove their hats to see if they had hidden revolvers or ammunition on the tops of their heads. A priest who was slow in putting his hands up was told to put them up damned quick or there would be another priest's funeral in the district.

"Bad luck to them," Ellen cried angrily. "Can they not leave the clergy alone atself? Hell nor the cardinal would put horns on the whole lot of them."

But neither prayers nor curses seemed to work on the Specials. Recently they had by-passed the army at Jonesborough Barracks and made two lightning raids into the Free State, where they burnt and destroyed property. It didn't bode well for the people along the border that the Specials were able to roam freely on either side and do whatever they liked. They had the power now, and trying to change them was like a dog trying to turn a cow round by swinging on its tail.

In the Free State, as it dragged on, the Civil War became more bitter and vicious. Waterford had been captured by the Staters, and Limerick was expected to fall soon. West of the Shannon, the Republicans were still active, but in smaller numbers. They had been driven out of their North Donegal fortress at Inch and had evacuated Glenveagh. Galway and West Mayo were still fighting. Sligo was lost and it was expected that they would fight to the last in the hills of West Cork and Kerry. As they retreated, they blew up bridges and barracks, tore up railway lines and roads and demolished courthouses. They were becoming increasingly desperate, and people were being held to ransom for transport and provisions. Because of the damage to roads and bridges, food supplies could not get through, and in some areas the civilian population was said to be near to starvation.

It was a very dirty war, and Bryan knew that it would be no better in the Dundalk and North Louth area. He felt very restless and walked up and down the road in the evenings, looking anxiously in the direction of the border, but there was nothing to be seen or heard. The Cumann na mBan pedalled along the back roads to avoid being stopped by the Specials at Forkhill. Bryan knew by all the activity that there was something afoot.

The following Saturday, as Catherine and the girls waited outside the chapel for Biddy Kane, Annie McGuinness and her squad of women rode up beside them on their bicycles. They were full of excitement and high spirits, bubbling over with news.

"Come on, out with it," Catherine demanded. "What happened?"

"Frank and the men are free again. Our lads blew a hole in the jail wall and about a hundred men escaped and then they held off the Staters till most of the lads got away," Annie told her.

At a quarter to seven the previous Thursday morning, one hundred and five Republican prisoners had been liberated from the county jail in Dundalk. A bomb had been detonated against the jail wall, leaving a big gap through which the prisoners escaped. Before the explosion a crowd of men in uniform, thought to be Republicans from camps along the border coming to free their comrades, had entered the town on a Crossley tender. Most of the escapees had run quickly away into the countryside behind the railway station, and the Staters were busy trying to round them up.

"The Dungooley squad are all back at the camp," Annie said. "But the Staters have Dundalk all sealed off and nothing or nobody can get in or out. It was us that carried the messages and dispatches between the jail and the border camps. It was great to be able to be part of the action at last, but don't tell anyone we were involved."

Just as the Cumann na mBan cycled away, Biddy appeared. She stopped at the chapel gate and looked longingly after them. "Oh, to be young again, flying around the country on me bicycle, helping the lads to free Ireland!" She sighed and adjusted her sizeable bosoms with a deft twitch that made Mary jump back in alarm and hide behind Catherine. Biddy had given up wearing a corset and was surprised when her spine remained intact.

Catherine told her that Frank Aiken was free and Biddy regretted lighting candles for his escape, but it might do him good some other way.

Bryan's face was sombre as he listened to the news of the breakout at Dundalk Barracks. What seemed like a victory now might not be that in the long term. He hoped the country would stay quiet till after Crossmaglen Fair, otherwise it wouldn't be safe to be on the roads. He borrowed the pony and cart from Mickle and Oiney and took Brigid with him for company. They set off early, taking bread and milk to sustain them on their journey. They called with Biddy because she needed oilcloth for her table and a couple of yards of red flannel to make petticoats for the winter.

"And will a couple of yards be enough to go round you, Biddy?" Bryan asked with a straight face.

"Och, Bryan Grant, but you're a divil," Biddy cried. "A couple of yards will go round me surely."

The pony trotted on at a lively pace, and they were soon in sight of Crossmaglen. On a wide grass verge near the town, Brigid was delighted to see two gypsy caravans. Gypsies regularly came to the Mullaghbane area for the potato picking. One caravan was red with a green door and the other was green with a red door. Above each door was a horseshoe turned upwards to catch good luck. Mean-looking scrawny curs of dogs snapped and snarled at the passers-by. Tethered piebald horses with skittish, long-legged foals were eating the long grass by the roadside. A tethered goat leapt straight up in the air as if it was on springs. Fire-blackened pots and pans lay upside-down on the grass, and wisps of smoke rose from the charred logs of an almost-dead campfire. The pony slowed down to whicker at the piebald horses, but Bryan kept it going and they soon arrived at the side of the square. The ponies already there stepped back and forth, their harnesses jingling, and the smell of fresh horse manure rose from steaming piles.

The market was all movement and noise. Coats, blankets and lengths of material flapped in the breeze outside the shops. Milking cows rambled freely around the square, staring curiously at anything that caught their eye. Hawkers shouted out, advertising their wares. Women in shawls and large hats poked at the fish on a barrow as the fish man in a long apron exchanged repartee with them. Asses brayed, goats bleated, chickens squawked and geese honked. When a Crossley tender full of armed Specials suddenly backfired, it caused terror in the animals and panic in the people. Bryan pulled Brigid down behind a barrow of turnips, but the Fair soon settled down again.

Brigid pulled herself up and looked around. Dead rabbits hung upside-down on a nearby stall. The changing scene was reflected in their glassy eyes. Chickens and ducks, with their feet tied together, were sitting on the street. Lambs were squashed into small carts, and dealers with crooked sticks walked up and down, trying to decide which ones were the best. Bryan pointed out small yellow birds that cheeped and sang relentlessly in a cage that hung from a chain. He said they were canaries and they were used in the mines. If the miners took them underground and they died, they knew that the air was poisonous. Across the street a man had some doves in a cage that looked like a small castle. He said that the doves had been hand-reared at a big Protestant house that was burnt to the ground over by Monaghan. He didn't say how he had come by the doves and Bryan didn't ask.

"The same thing as happened below in Cork. The Protestants had the best land in the county and in the country, too, so they shot and driv them out," the man said. "That way of life is past and may all bad luck go with it. Collins and Arthur Griffith spoke out agin the killings, but that was only policy forninst the world."

"Aye," Bryan said, "but there was Protestants killed and burnt out nearer to us nor Cork."

"Aye, but that was retaliation," the man said.

Brigid tried not to listen. Talk about the Troubles made her feel anxious and scared. As they moved around the fair, she was embarrassed when Bryan haggled with a stall owner over the price of a spade, but then she realised that nobody paid the price the trader demanded. They haggled until the price suited both parties then parted, each convinced that he had got the better of the other.

The stall would keep the spade until they were ready for home. They ate their lunch with their backs to a wall. Brazen willy-wagtails and sparrows hopped right up beside them, but Brigid couldn't catch them. They bought the red flannel and oilcloth for Biddy Kane, some items for Catherine and Ellen and buns and clove rock sweets for the girls, then on to the Market House to check the time on the clock. A gypsy man was mending the buckets and tins that the country people had brought in. Beside him was a smiling, dark-haired gypsy woman.

"Ah, now, here's a fine gintleman that'll spare a few coppers for to help an aul woman," she said, with her gaze fixed firmly on Bryan's boots. "Ah, if it isn't yourself, Bryan Grant. I saw you coming."

"That's the story of me life, Maggie Joyce," Bryan said, grinning. "Someone always sees me coming. How the Hell are you?"

The Joyces were said to be an old Galway family that had been put to the road when Oliver Cromwell and the Roundheads invaded Ireland. They had nowhere to go and had become gypsies. Paraic Joyce, who was mending the tins and buckets, was the present patriarch of the clan. Although he wasn't very old, everyone referred to him as Aul Joyce. He tipped his hat to Bryan. The Joyces were a hard-working clan and the country people didn't begrudge them a field to stay in, fodder for their horses or milk for their children.

Maggie asked Bryan did he want his fortune told, but he declined, and when he suggested that Brigid might want her hand read, Maggie refused. There was too much in store for a child. She would grow up to be a grand handsome woman who would marry a rich man from across the sea and she'd have a wagonload of children. She pressed an object into Brigid's hand and closed her fingers over it. She said it was a lucky charm. She warned Bryan that they'd be coming by for the prata picking and to keep his chickens locked up.

"I'd sooner have a fox after me chickens than a Joyce," Bryan declared.

Aul Joyce spat a stream of tobacco juice then laughed and slapped his thigh. "Good man, Bryan," he wheezed.

The two men had known each other for many years and shared a love of hunting and fishing. When Bryan asked where they had been last year, Aul Joyce said it had been too dangerous to travel, as most of the roads were blown up and them that wasn't had landmines on them the whole way along the line. He couldn't take the horses or the family on them. It would take tears from a stone to see the animals that were killed in the firing across the border – cattle and sheep slaughtered and left dead and swelling up in the fields. What was wrong with the guns or the eyesight of the boys that's using them when they couldn't tell the difference between a man and a baste? Pettigo was near deserted. The people needed permits to go out, but they weren't allowed to go out to get the permits. They couldn't go to Mass if they didn't have the permit. Animals were dying of hunger because the farmers couldn't go to feed them. They didn't know if this Fair would go ahead the day, but it was quieter now with the Civil War in the Free State. If trouble broke out in the North again, it would be another hard winter for the Joyces, with no money got from the prata picking. Bryan told him never to be stuck for a bite to ate or a place to stay, and they saluted him as he walked away. Brigid opened her hand and looked at the charm that Maggie had given her. It was an Agnus Dei.

"Agnus Dei," Bryan read. "That's in the Latin. It means lamb of God. It's a holy thing like a medal. You wear it round your neck and it keeps you safe."

On their way to the cart, they passed a large woman with a fancy hat and shawl singing a song. The crowd clapped in appreciation and threw money into a hat. A man with a fiddle played some reels, and the crowd shuffled and danced along. Brigid saw a wee girl with long, wavy brown hair bouncing in time to the music as she danced in the dust in her little shoes. Throwing the heavy hair back from her face, the wee girl turned and glared straight at Brigid, who stepped quickly behind Bryan. Her face wasn't that of a child; it was the wrinkled face of an old woman. She turned away and joined in the dancing again, and Bryan and Brigid collected the spade then returned to the cart.

On the road for home Brigid asked what had happened to the wee woman. Bryan said she was the youngest child in a family of boys, and one time when the parents were in Newry, the boys buried her in a hole in the field, and with the fright of it she never grew an inch from that day to this. But mebbe that wasn't what happened to her at all; people would tell you many a thing.

When they reached home, Brigid was mobbed by her sisters asking all about her day at the Fair and she told them about the wee woman. "She was the funniest wee woman I ever saw," she said.

Mary said there was a funny woman with Annie, but it was Hughie. The girls looked anxious at this, so Catherine sent them to Biddy's to deliver her goods. Then Bryan told her that Hughie had been down wearing a Cumann na mBan uniform. He had tried to spare her worry, but he wondered was it a good thing. Hughie's life was constantly in danger now. Until recently he was a soldier in the South and an outlaw in the North, but now he was an outlaw in both places. The day of reckoning was coming, and cycling down from the camp wasn't the biggest risk he would have to overcome.

The girls walked up the hill and round the bend to Biddy's. She spread the new oilcloth over the old one then trimmed it until it hung to her satisfaction. It had blue and yellow squares on a white background. Biddy gave them rum and butter sweets and asked them where they were going on 15 August, the feast of the Consumption of Our Blessed Lady into Heaven. They'd be going to Mass if nothing else. Sure it was a big day out when all the sarvint boys and sarvint girls went down to the seashore at Warrenpoint to see the sea.

Biddy said she went one time with her father. "It was a long, long journey in a pony and cart, but he had to see what the seashore looked like before he died. It's a bit like Oiney Grant's meadow was the time of the flooding last winter."

"Is the sea wet?" Susan asked.

"Ah, child of grace, God bless your wee heart, the sea is wet, surely," Biddy said. "And you can take off your shoes and stockings and paddle into it, but you have to stay near to the shore or you'd be drownded. The water comes in waves and then it goes out again all the time, day and night. It was cowld that day and the seaweed got lapped round me ankle when I went for a walk in it and I give a gowl that would scar a banshee. Me father was in kinks laughing at me. And there was jelly fish too that had washed up on the beach, and I got shells too."

She found a variety of seashells and gave the girls one each. She told them they had eaten winkles, things like snails, and when the girls turned their noses up, she reminded them that the people of Ireland ate snails during the Famine and were glad to get them. She had seen in the paper that a sunfish twenty feet long was caught in Dundalk Bay be fishermen from Kilkeel, and they took it away home tied to the side of the boat. It was hard to imagine what twenty feet was like, but if she was laid down end to end four times, that's the size yon fish was. There'd be some ating in that, but you wouldn't bring it home in the basket on the front of the bicycle. A fish that size was hard for the girls to imagine, nor could they visualise how Biddy could be laid end to end four times, but the visit was over and they ran home, eager to show off the seashells.

Ellen said she could hear nothing from a shell that smelt of rotten fish and mildew. All she could hear morning noon or night was yon rooster crowing out there in the yard. It was a bad sign. Someone would be took and very soon.

Catherine told the girls she remembered Biddy and her father going to Warrenpoint. They might as well have gone to America. It was that far away.

On 12 August Arthur Griffith, founder of the Sinn Féin party and President of Ireland, died of natural causes. He had been the leader of the plenipotentiaries who negotiated the treaty with the British cabinet. Later he had tried to mediate between the pro- and anti-treatyites in the hope of preventing civil war, but his efforts were in vain. His death was a severe blow to the fledgling Free State at a time when it sorely needed a wise and experienced leader.

In the early hours of 14 August, Dundalk town was captured by the 4th Northern Division. The Free State troops, the former 5th Northern Division, comprised of Cavan and Monaghan men, were surprised, captured and imprisoned. The two hundred Republican prisoners who had been confined in the jail by the Free Staters were released.

Between three and four o'clock in the morning about four hundred 4th Northerners entered the town and captured a Lancia car from a Free State patrol along one of the main streets. They then captured the post office, surprising the troops that were guarding it. This gave them control of the telegraph wires, preventing the alarm from being raised in the barracks and the outside world. They then marched silently to the barracks and took up positions on the perimeter. Bombs or mines placed at the gates blew the main gate at Barrack Street and the north gate at the Point Road to smithereens. The attackers then ran through the ruins of the gates, hurling bombs at the barrack buildings, the officers' quarters in particular. There were twenty explosions in quick succession, followed by one massive explosion. It was later thought that Aiken's men might have wired up the barracks and placed mines when they had occupied it previously. There was a sustained exchange of fire, and after about an hour, the garrison, surprised and hopelessly outnumbered, surrendered. The 4th Northern captured all the rifles and ammunition and freed the prisoners. A Free State officer and 4th Northern officer were killed; eleven Free State soldiers and one 4th Northerner were wounded. The wounded were transferred by ambulance to the Louth Infirmary, where, due to lack of beds, some were placed on mattresses in the corridors. All the doctors in the town were called in to help deal with the casualties. One of the injured Free State soldiers died the next day. The captured garrison, about two hundred men, was imprisoned in the cells from which the Republican prisoners had just been liberated. Captured arms and ammunition were transported on lorries from the barracks to the border area.

At Mass on 15 August, Annie McGuinness told Catherine about the retaking of the barracks. Dundalk was under martial law and was closed to traffic, with no one being allowed in or out of the town and no trains running south. Aiken and his troops were ready and waiting on retaliation from the Free State army. They knew it would come, but they didn't know when. In the meantime they were well armed and patrolling the town night and day. Hughie, Gerard and all the lads from Dungooley were now in Dundalk.

"It's all in God's hands now," Biddy Kane murmured as she gave Catherine a bracing hug.

They lit candles and prayed that the lads would come through unscathed, while the congregation watched sympathetically. But moments later they sat in shocked disbelief as Fr Cullen, instead of a sermon, launched into a tirade from the pulpit.

"I strongly condemn Frank Aiken and the Irregulars of the 4th Northern Division. What they are doing is murder, murder before God!" he thundered. "On whose behalf do they challenge the legitimate government of Ireland, especially now, when we are mourning the death of our president, Arthur Griffith? On whose authority does the so-called General Frank Aiken cordon off the town of Dundalk on 15 August, one of our holiest days? I have petitioned the cardinal and the Holy Father in Rome for the mass excommunication of these ... these bandits and brigands who should be up in Dublin trying to rebuild the country instead of in Dundalk trying to destroy it!" He stomped down from the pulpit to finish the Mass, his face almost black with rage.

"Do you hear yon bastard, and God pardon me for saying it in the chapel? Do you know what's wrong with him?" Larry Molloy growled softly to Bryan. "He goes into Dundalk every 15 August to have a big feed in the Queen's Arms Hotel. He'll not be ating in the Queen's Arms Hotel the day!"

Fr Cullen swung round suspiciously as a subdued ripple of laughter ran through the back of the chapel, but all heads were piously bent.

On the way home Larry said that the 4th Northern had no real chance of holding Dundalk. The Free Staters were coming from Dublin with more guns, ammunition and men, and they would keep bringing men in till Dundalk was cleared out. They had taken back every town and city in the south of Ireland and it might take them a week to take Dundalk, but they would take it. Aiken took all the guns from the barracks and sent them out to the border, but sure what good was that? The lads would have to fight their way back to Dungooley, and then there was nowhere to go only north. He'd have the pony and cart ready to go to take them home before the Specials rounded them up. Annie and Lizzie said they'd commandeer a car to get the lads home and that they'd get word to Cashel as soon as possible, but that was all up in the air. What if they couldn't get a car and the lads were left sitting there? They would be better to keep one ear turned to Dungooley themselves and be ready to go for them when the time came.

Bryan said he would also ask Mickle and Oiney for help and when Larry took the turn for his own house, he paced the road unable to settle. The women prayed as they shelled peas and peeled potatoes. Ellen had heard a dog howling in the middle of the night. It wasn't their own dog and there were no other dogs near them. Death was waiting, and someone would be going with him. Catherine aired old bedspreads and blankets to make the cart more comfortable for the wounded, and sheets were set aside to use as bandages. She prepared for the walking wounded and closed her mind to all other possibilities. Oiney came running to say that heavy smoke was rising above Dundalk and he thought he heard shooting. He ran on to tell Larry, and they soon arrived back and lined the carts and animals up in Bryan's yard, but when no word came by dark, they went home.

Aiken hadn't wanted to fight the Staters in the first place, and Dundalk was his base, but he couldn't risk losing too many men if he intended to fight on for the North. It was hard to know what he would do.

On Thursday the Free Staters arrived in Dundalk. There had been shooting during the night and a large mine had gone off in the middle of the town. On Friday, when the sound of fierce artillery fire was heard from over by Dungooley, the men went there in a convoy. The noise of rifles and an eighteen-pounder gun that the Staters were using against the Dungooley camp was deafening, and they were relieved when two weary sentries barred their way. They said that the battle wasn't going their way. The lads were finished. The aul rifles had let them down a tarra. The barrels got red hot then curled up and they couldn't be fired. Several ruined guns lay on the grass where they had been discarded. The Staters had won. If they had got at them right in

Dundalk, there would be less fight in them now.

They had prepared an ambush for the Staters on Wednesday night. They had stripped the military barracks of guns and ammunition and taken them to the camps along the border. By six o'clock in the evening, they were finished and evacuated the barracks but didn't burn it down. The locals thought it had been mined. They thought that the incoming Staters would pass down through the town to retake the barracks, so they positioned snipers in the windows of the town hall and in upstairs windows and on rooftops all along the route, including the old monastery known as Seatown Castle. They cut the telegraph wires in the post office and ordered the residents of Barrack Street to leave their houses, and most did. In other streets the civilians were ordered to stay inside. Those who didn't comply, immediately had shots fired over their heads. Shops were closed and shuttered. A spirit lorry was commandeered, laden with petrol cans that contained bombs, and positioned on the crossing between Earl Street and Park Street. Bombs were also laid under the lorry and in a line to the footpath. A command wire for detonating the bombs was taken to the corner of the Queen's Arms Hotel, where it was guarded by a small party.

At 7.30 p.m. an advance party of Staters came into town by the Carrick Road as far as the jail. They stopped and fired a probing volley of shots, but there was no answering fire as the Northerners had withdrawn earlier, leaving the keys on the doorstep. Free Staters that had been captured and imprisoned there on Monday were freed to join their comrades. The troops were fired on by snipers and they replied with a burst of machine-gun fire. Around this time the bomb-laden lorry in Earl Street was detonated. The force of the explosion shattered not just the plate glass but also the wooden frames of the windows in the nearby buildings. In some of the houses interior doors were blown to pieces.

Following the blast there was a volley of prolonged shooting. Two passing civilians were seriously injured, one by a bullet and the other by flying shrapnel. It was a wild, wet and windy night and was all the more terrifying for the citizens because most of the street lighting was turned off. The only lights remaining were in Park Street, to show the snipers the advancing Staters. But they didn't advance very far and instead waited for the well-armed reinforcements, due to arrive later by road and rail. Earlier in the day an aeroplane had circled the town, and the Free Staters had spies who kept them informed about the movements of the 4th Northern. In spite of the bombing and shooting, there was wholesale looting of shops, especially those selling alcohol and tobacco, and even though the evacuated military barracks was rumoured to be mined, it too was looted and practically denuded of all its contents.

When dawn broke on Thursday, the storm had passed, the battle was over and the town was quiet except for sporadic sniper fire from an unknown location. The main body of the Free Staters arrived in force, but the 4th Northern Division had retreated to their camps along the border. On Friday a strong body of Free State troops left the town early for the Dungooley area, and at about twelve o'clock more went out. They were well equipped for fighting. At Dungooley the 4th Northern was pinned down under heavy fire, and the only way out was back to the border where the rescue party was waiting.

As Bryan and the others strained to see how the battle was progressing, stray bullets lifted spurts of dust from the road and tore at the branches all round them. The eighteen-pounder made their ears pop and their hearts jump painfully. Aware that a dead jinnet blocking the road would cause problems, they tethered the scared animals further down the hill, then crawled back up again. Battle orders were being roared out, with men swearing and shouting. Then an aeroplane droned high above, and the sentries said that an aeroplane had fired on some of the lads earlier, near Kilcurry. Shooting at their own countrymen from an aeroplane they got from the enemy – it was beyond belief.

As the battle continued, they crept down the hill for respite. People living nearby had come out of their houses. It wasn't the first battle they had experienced on the borderline and Wee Eddie Flynn, mindful of the recent battle with the Specials, got into the churn for safety. Women wept and prayed loudly on their Rosary beads. They knew many of the lads coming and going to the camp.

Then the nearest sentry threw down his rifle, cleared the ditch in one wild leap and went haring across the fields towards Carrive. Bryan stopped the second fella and demanded to know what had just happened. He said the order had been given to retreat, and they had to get away quick and lie low before the Specials came out. Then men started coming thick and fast, pounding down the hill, happy to see that people were there waiting for them. They all looked shocked and exhausted, with their uniforms dirty and torn. Some were swearing and wiping away angry tears, but they encountered no condemnation. The waiting men clapped them on the back, praised them for their courage and asked about their own sons. One lad with red-rimmed eyes and teeth sticking to cracked lips said that Hughie and Gerard were coming. Then he ran down the hill and shoved his rifle and bandolier into a cart that drove quickly away.

As the shooting became sporadic, they saw Hughie steadying himself with a rifle butt as he helped Gerard slowly along the road. Gerard was leaning heavily against him and didn't appear to be conscious. Hughie's face was badly scratched, with blood oozing from his cheek onto his collar. His right eye was swollen and almost closed over. Steam rose from his uniform, which was saturated with blood and sweat. Bryan ran forward to help, but didn't know where to touch. Hughie said that the blood was Gerard's. He had been shot in the leg and lost a lot of blood. He was in very bad shape.

They carried him to Larry's cart and carefully laid him down on a quilt. Larry said he would get him home right away. His mother would save him; she'd know what to do. He stood upright in the cart like a charioteer with his homemade crutch wedged between his armpit and the front of the cart. Hughie went along with him. Larry would be going as fast as he could, and if he hit a rut, Gerard could be flung out onto the road and that would finish him for sure. Maybe Bryan and Oiney could help the other lads who were coming. Then Larry whipped the pony up and sent the cart hurtling along the Carrive road.

"There'll be no Specials about yet," Oiney said. "They know well who the lads are and can go round the country now at their leisure and rake in these ones that come back from across the border."

Bryan and Oiney and the others gathered up as many lads as they could and the convoy started back the way it had come. The rescued lads swayed with the movement of Bryan's cart, but said little. Days of fighting, anxious waiting, no sleep and overwhelming defeat had left them shell-shocked. They asked Bryan to take them to a place near the Mountain House where they could get cleaned up and decide what to do. He left them there hoping they would meet again in better times. His knees buckled under him when he got down from the cart in his own yard and Catherine quickly fetched a milking stool. He took a few minutes to collect himself, then told her that Hughie was alive but he wasn't too sure about Gerard. He went out on the road and waited until Hughie came walking wearily towards him, with a bandolier across his chest and a rifle over his shoulder. When Bryan steered him into the barn and took the guns and ammunition from him, he shrugged and gave a short laugh.

"I should have threw them into Oiney's flax hole, but I couldn't do it," he said. "I was a sitting duck for the Specials, but I wanted to walk down this road one last time like a soldier. That's all I have to show for me fight to free Ireland. Hide them for me under the big rock, Da. Then I'll know where to get them when we rise again."

Bryan hid the weapons under the straw then fetched him clean clothes. He put the bloodied uniform into a meal bag for burning. Hughie said that Annie and Lizzie had come driving along in a big Maxwell touring car and stopped him and Larry. They took Gerard to the General Hospital in Newry, and Larry went with them. He then drove the pony and cart to Molloys' and told Sadie the bad news. She was very upset but made him go home as quickly as possible to get rid of the uniform. He called with Biddy Kane and she went up to Molloys' to offer what help she could.

When Gerard's condition worsened, Lizzie stayed with Larry at the hospital and Annie went and got Sadie. Gerard had lost a serious amount of blood and his shattered thighbone was protruding through the skin. The wound was dirty, and because the battlefield was on farmland there was a high risk of gangrene setting in. The surgeon said there was a slim chance that Gerard would survive, and Larry signed his X on a piece of paper giving the doctor permission to do whatever he had to do.

"Just save him if you can," he implored. "And if the leg has to come off, take it off, for he's better living with one leg than dead with two. If you can do nothing for him, tell me now and I'll take him home to die with his own people. It's in God's hands now."

Back in Cashel, Hughie told his mother, "I wouldn't give you tuppence for him, but we'll see what happens." He wiped tears from his face with the back of his hand, smearing blood across his cheeks. He said that a branch caught him across the face and a piece of it went into his eye. At first he thought it was sweat dripping onto his hand, but then realised it was blood. He was unable to open his eye and didn't know how badly it was injured. He was shaky and agitated and then snapped at Catherine and frightened the girls.

"I'm sorry, Ma," he said. "I have to get out of here. This house is too dangerous."

He was in no condition to go very far, and Catherine ran over to ask Addy would she keep him. When she explained their plight, Addy suddenly had the furtive look of an animal that was backed into a corner. The aul bitch, thought Catherine, after all I done for her, she's not going to keep him, but she pleaded her case. It was dangerous, but would only be for a short time; they had nowhere else to turn.

Addy looked at her for a long moment then shivered as if someone had walked on her grave. She straightened her shoulders and braced herself. "Bring the lad over," she ordered. "Sarah's bed is there, and if he's found here, it'll do none of us any good. There's people might tell on him, but that's a chance we'll have to take. What's for you is for you."

Catherine understood her reluctance, but was relieved.

As Bryan walked him over to Addy's, sweat beaded his forehead and he gasped for breath. Suddenly he gave a sharp cry. Bryan guided him down on the ditch, but he said he was all right; it was just an aul rupture that caught him now and again. He'd got it from carrying boxes of ammunition at the camp.

"There was times the day, Da, when I thought I'd never see the sun set on this mountain again," he said softly when he regained his composure. "I never thought the fighting would end like that. It wasn't a cat-and-mouse game anymore. We took over the barracks, then they took it over, then we took it back. We were fighting for our lives and I was shooting and trying stop the blood coming out of Gerard's leg, and I couldn't do both. Bloody horse flies were sticking to me face and I daren't move for fear a sniper would see me. I just kept firing and firing, and when one gun seized up, I picked up another. I don't even know if I hit any of them. I could only see out of one eye, and the pain in the other one was awful and it still is. I was afraid, Da. I'm not ashamed to tell you that. I thought both me and Gerard would die up there in the dirt, and he will die. He took a turn in the cart before we met Annie and Lizzie, a fit like the ones Mary takes. He was cold and shivering and grey-looking. I think he lost all his blood."

"Don't give up hope. God is good," Bryan said finally.

"I wish I had your faith, Da."

Addy was welcoming but cautious and agreed to keep Hughie for a short while. She assured them it was no bother. She made Hughie up a powder for the pain. He desperately needed pain relief and accepted gratefully.

Gangrene set in and Gerard's leg was scheduled to be amputated. Larry and Sadie were heartbroken, but clung on to a small shred of hope. Annie and Lizzie, travelling on by-roads no better than lonins to avoid the Specials, drove them to and from the hospital. When Bryan called, Larry told him that they didn't know what end of them was up. Gerard was lying there like a lump of boiled bacon. The poison was all through him now. He was likely to die if they operated and would surely die if they didn't. There was no redemption for him now. He was done, the death rattle was in him and there was no hope.

The following evening Addy rushed over to say that Hughie was in an awful state with the pain in his eye. It was all swollen up and pus was bealin' out from under the eyelid. No powder would fix that.

Catherine went to Addy's and applied padding and a bandage that made him feel more secure, but he'd have to go to Newtownhamilton in the morning to see the doctor. Addy said she'd give him her strongest powder to help him through the night.

Early next morning Bryan collected Hughie in the pony and trap and they set off for Newtown. Later on, when Mary went up by Addy's to wait for them coming back, a car with four Specials in it slid to a halt beside her.

"Come here, wee girl," Tony Hurst said as he opened the car door. "You know where Sarah is, don't you? Where did Sarah go?"

Mary backed away until she was on top of the hedge and couldn't go any further.

"She's away on the cart," she whispered.

"Away on the cart. And did your brother Hughie go with Sarah?" Tony asked. "No? And where is he now? Is he in your house?"

Mary looked around her in desperation, but there was nobody to come to her rescue.

"Och, leave the child alone, Tony, we'll get nothing out of her," one of the other Specials said. "Come on, start the motor."

"Where's Hughie?" Tony snarled, making as if to get out of the car.

"He's at Addy's," Mary whispered.

"He's at Addy's? Good girl. That's all we wanted to know."

When they drove off, Mary took off like a hare up across the fields. She ran into the kitchen and stood on the middle of the floor trying to catch her breath.

"Hughie, Mammy, Hughie, Sarah's Special boy at Addy's," she panted. She kept repeating the same words, but eventually they made sense out of it. The other girls had heard the car. It could only have been the Specials. Catherine sent Brigid to Mickle and Oiney's to stop Bryan taking Hughie back to Addy's. She waited for some time before hurrying up the road.

Addy opened the half door, dabbing her bloody nose with an incongruous white lace handkerchief. "I don't have much call for lace handkerchers round here, but Sarah got me them one Christmastime.

Little did she know I'd be cleaning up me blood with them after the skelp yon boy gave me." She laughed ruefully.

"I'm sorry," Catherine said. "They stopped Mary on the road and she told them that Hughie was over at your house. They scared the life out of her."

Addy said it wasn't the child's fault. There was a bad streak in him. He was reared on the hind tit of a weasel and two wicked wee eyes on him like piss holes in the snow. He came looking for Hughie, but he knew that Sarah was gone and he looked like an eejit forninst them boys he was running with. When she said that Sarah was better off wherever she was now, he lashed out and hit her. He had given Sarah the odd slap too. As he was leaving he laughed and said, "The Fenians are running like rabbits and we'll snare them and shoot them."

Addy would make it known that Hughie wasn't coming back there and that should keep Tony off her back. She knew the Specials, the IRA and the informers. It was both power and danger.

Bryan returned from Newtownhamilton alone. When Dr Horgan saw the state of Hughie's eye, he called a man in from the garden and he and Bryan held him down while the doctor gave him an injection of morphia, the strongest painkiller known to man. When he passed out, the doctor got his eye open. Bryan had never seen anything worse in his life. Horgan was on his way to the hospital in Belfast and took Hughie with him, as he would only be able to get treatment there. The family would know nothing about him till they let him out again. Belfast was the best place for him because nobody would be looking for him in the hospital and he hadn't been shot, so he wouldn't have to be reported to the authorities.

Chapter 15

Overwhelmed by shock, infection and blood loss, Gerard Molloy died with his parents by his bedside. His death left his family and friends reeling in sorrow and disbelief. The mountain community mourned the loss of their boy along with the loss of their country and identity. While the lads were camped at the border, there had been a certain sense of security, but now that was gone and they felt exposed and at the mercy of the military and Specials.

At first Sadie Molloy didn't want a military funeral, saying that if it hadn't been for Ireland, Gerard would still be with them, but Larry overruled her.

"Talking about freeing Ireland, reading about freeing Ireland and singing about freeing Ireland was all he ever done. He fought for Ireland and he will be buried as a soldier," Larry declared. "And if I have to fire the shots over his grave meself, I'll do it, Specials or no Specials, I'll do that for me son. It'll be the last thing I'll ever do for him!"

Sadie couldn't argue with that, and the Cumann na mBan assured them that Gerard would be buried with full military honours.

At the wake the men hunkered down for a smoke at the gable of Larry's house and wondered why the 4th Northern had cleared the weapons from Dundalk Barracks and left them in a house in Clontigora. Sure maybe if they'd had better weapons at Dungooley, it would be a different story. They applauded Frank Aiken's escape:

"Aiken is the boy. Too cliver a man for the Staters, and he'll come back here and put manners on the Specials too."

The old women who sat beside the corpse, smoking clay pipes and inhaling snuff, wondered why the goods taken from the trains hadn't been shared among the people instead of being left to rot in Ravensdale Forest. Big caches of fruit, food, linen and other goods had been discovered by the Free State troops searching for 4th Northern arms dumps in the Ravensdale area.

The second night of the wake brought the news that General Michael Collins, commander in chief of the Irish army and chairman of the provisional government, had been killed in an ambush near Macroom in Cork. The wake-goers were stunned. What would happen now in the North, and what would happen above in the Free State? Arthur Griffith not dead a week and now Collins was gone too. Opinions ebbed and flowed as people tried to absorb what had happened: "It was no ordinary man done that. Take care, but the British had a hand in it. They couldn't kill Collins when they were in Dublin and now they got an Irishman to do it. They must have used the silver bullet; that's the only one would kill him. The Staters are blaming it on the IRA, but the English are behind it, there's nothing surer."

Collins, in spite of the treaty, had been a hero to Gerard, and the people remarked that they would meet now in Heaven. Lads who had fought with him at Dungooley slipped into the wake to pay their respects. They were desolate and despairing. This was the final blow. Collins was the only man in the Irish government with any heed on the fate of the Northern Catholics. It was thought that he would have stepped into Griffith's shoes. He would have kept the fight going, but now he was dead and the North was lost.

"Character and adaptability and the place he held in the hearts of thousands of fellow-countrymen fitted him for the vacant leadership, but in the hour of his country's greatest need he has been struck down by the assassin bullet of an Irishman," was how one newspaper article described his killing.

People sensed a British conspiracy. They got rid of Collins before Collins could get rid of the border was the general belief. He had seemed invincible and immortal, surviving the War of Independence and the negotiations with the British with courage and audacity. It was incredible that he could be killed as easily as that when it was all over. The sinister, revengeful shadow of Britain hovered over the fledgling government. Could they hold on to a Free State without Collins to guide them?

Gerard's 4th Northern comrades promised Larry and Sadie that they would be at the funeral if at all possible and then hurried away into the darkness. They were fugitives now, both North and South. Their only hope was to try and blend in at home again and act as if they had never been away, or to emigrate. Gerard was buried with the tricolour draped over his coffin. His comrades and the Cumann na mBan fired a volley of shots over his grave as he was laid to rest.

"We can do no more for him now," Larry said sadly as he turned away from the grave.

He had aged considerably since he had rescued Gerard from the carnage at Dungooley. The flesh had fallen from his face and he looked gaunt and exhausted. He leaned heavily on his makeshift crutch, with his spine skewed sideways to accommodate his injured hinch. Sadie was like a woman made of marble, withdrawn and emotionless. Many of the mourners were afraid to approach her, some because of her appearance, others for fear that her bad luck might rub off on them. When Bryan said they would be up to get the harvest in, Larry squeezed his elbow and tears ran down his face as he gathered his children about him. His remaining son was only nine and seemed scared by the crowd; his five daughters were trying to be brave for their parents.

Hughie was still in hospital in Belfast, and when no news came, the McGuinness girls went to see what had happened to him. Had the authorities discovered that he was a rebel and put him on the prison ship? Many of the returning Volunteers had suffered that fate. But they learnt that after Hughie's badly damaged eye was removed, he was diagnosed with TB and transferred to a sanatorium in Antrim. They returned to Cashel Mountain without seeing him, and when they told the family about the TB, Catherine would have none of it.

"Our Hughie has no TB," she declared robustly. "What would they know about country people away below in Belfast? A couple a weeks' good feeding and a bed to sleep in and he'll be as right as rain in no time. That's all he needs."

Ellen pursed her lips and reached for her Rosary beads. "Antrim, a place where he has nayther kith nor kin nor knows nobody," she snorted. "What do them doctors be thinking at all at all?"

The McGuinness girls gave them an address where they could write to him. Bryan knew that they wouldn't have sent Hughie to a sanatorium unless he had TB. He hoped that good food and rest would cure him, but he knew it was unlikely.

Catherine agonised over how to tell Hughie that Gerard was dead, when he was so far away from home. The boys had been closer than brothers, inseparable since they were youngsters – hunting, fishing and rambling all over the countryside together, then away to fight for the Cause. But in the end she wrote that Gerard had passed away peacefully; the authorities would get no information from the short letter.

The following Sunday at the chapel gate, a carload of Specials drove slowly past the emerging congregation. In the back of the car was a hooded figure who was pointing out particular young men. The Specials, stationed at Ballymoyer House near Whitecross, closely observed those who were pointed out and took notes. Members of the 4th Northern Division quickly lowered their heads or turned their backs, but they knew it was too late, the informer, whoever he was, may already have betrayed them. They were now in a dilemma. They couldn't go on the run across the border because they would be picked up by the Staters and imprisoned or even shot, so it was either take a chance and stay at home or, ironically, go to England.

"Some people say it was Stephens that was with the Specials outside Mass," Bryan reported. "The lads had him prisoner over at the camp and then let him go during the battle with the Staters, a boy that seen them all and knows their names."

Ellen thought they should have finished him when they had him. Now that the Specials had a man that was well able to point out the rebels they would hunt them down now like dogs.

Bryan was wondering what would calm down his bloodthirsty mother, when Biddy Kane burst through the door in a flurry of skirts. She was bewailing the death of Michael Collins, which was confusing because he had been killed around the time Gerard had died.

"Och, I know that," Biddy admitted sadly. "But I didn't take it in till I looked at the newspaper Jem lapped round the candles I bought this morning. A fine, big, handsome young man shot dead in his own country, his own county, away down in Cork."

"He knew it was coming, Biddy." Bryan sighed heavily. "The minnit he signed the treaty, he knew he was a dead man. He didn't deserve that. He did the best he could. God rest him."

Ellen took the newspaper and peered at the photograph for a minute.

"Aye, he was a fine, big, handsome man, to be sure," she agreed. "But he wasn't long getting himself into the Black and Tan uniform."

"It isn't the Black and Tan uniform. That's the Irish army uniform," Catherine said tiredly.

Suddenly there seemed to be no point in arguing or explaining; the endless conflict had left her battle weary, and the uniform Michael Collins was wearing in the photograph did resemble the British uniform.

"How I'm going to thole it at all?" Biddy said. "Who's going to free us now?"

"We've tholed it now for hundreds of years," Ellen growled. "We're the fools that thought it would be over. It'll never be over, not in my day nor in them childer's day!"

"You're a hard woman, Ellen Grant," Biddy cried. "But you're not wrong. It'll not be over for us for a long, long time."

She went off to chase the rabbits out of the corn. Bryan cut it after Larry's was harvested. Larry spoke about getting his hinch seen to in Banbridge, and even though the neighbouring men knew it was just talk, they went along with it.

Annie and Lizzie went to the sanatorium in Antrim to see Hughie. He wasn't allowed out of the bed and he wasn't happy cooped up in there. They pushed him out onto the balcony, bed and all. He had been told that he would be there for another couple of months, if all went well. Catherine thought that if he had strained his chest, rest would cure it. Annie and Lizzie understood why she was in denial. Her son had been struck down with this terrible disease and if it became public knowledge the stigma of "wakeness" would be attached to the family name for ever. When they said that his eye wasn't as bad as they'd imagined, Catherine started to cry. They'd tried to talk to him about Gerard, but he held up his hand and shook his head. Bryan said he would go there with the girls when the threshing was over, and they discussed possible arrangements.

A month passed, the threshing in the countryside was almost done, the girls were back at school and Mary was out on the road picking late blackberries, when Hughie unexpectedly arrived home. He spied Mary on the road then crept up behind her and swung her around.

"Hughie," she gasped when she got over the fright. "You wee divil!"

He laughed and hugged her, then grimaced and made a face when she pointed at his eye socket. She led him up to the half door, then stood back and proudly ushered him in. Catherine dropped the heavy iron frying pan that she'd been drying and it landed on the floor with a loud clatter.

"Jesus, Mary and Joseph and all the saints," she exclaimed, blessing herself. "Where did you come out of?"

"I came from Antrim, Ma," he told her. "I came a long way."

He placed his hands on her shoulders and she looked at him carefully, shaking her head then gently touching his face. He looked drawn and tired and the clothes were hanging off him. He swayed where he stood.

"Sit down, sit down, for God's sake, and take the weight off your feet," she cried. "Give me them wellingtons and I'll get you some cold water for your feet."

Ellen came out of the bedroom and leaned against the doorjamb with her arms folded as if she was in a row of houses.

"Well, Johnny, I hardly knew you with your one good eye," she said, quoting an old song. "When did they let you out?"

Hughie told her to sit down, as it was a bit of a story. In the hospital where he got his eye done, they thought he was from Antrim, and they sent him to a sanatorium there instead of Armagh. He didn't want to draw attention to himself and said nothing. They couldn't send him back, so they kept him there in Purdysburn and it was an awful place. The windows were wide open all the time and that kept him awake at night. An aul grey crow of a nurse was always flapping about and she'd ate you if there was a wrinkle in the bed cover. The beds were tucked in that tight that if the place went on fire they wouldn't have got out. The patients were stretched out ready for the grave and all they had to do was wind the sheets round them. They were like ghosts of men dangling between Heaven and Hell. The women were down the stairs, but he never saw them. There was no cure for the disease. You were let out, but then you were back in as bad as ever again. He knew he'd have to get fitter before he broke out and started walking about at night after dark. Then he saw a suit of clothes hanging in the washroom and he took it as a sign. He climbed from the balcony to the drainpipe then onto the bank below. He found the wellingtons in the porters' lodge and walked out. He got a lift to Belfast in a cart and then got the train to Newry, and Jem Redmond gave him a lift as far as Ballinasack Bridge and he walked up the road. He'd got the money for the train from the man in the next bed. He gave Hughie a ten-shilling note he had hidden in the toe of his shoe. He said he wouldn't need money where he was going.

Catherine said she would light a candle for the poor man. She tried to persuade Hughie to lie down in their bed, but he was adamant that he was going to the loft. So she made a cosy bed for him on the hay and he gratefully lowered his weary body on to it.

When the girls came home, Catherine told them they had to be very quiet, and when Bryan came home, they dragged him to the loft where they found Hughie lying awake. Catherine had already told him about Hughie's escape from the sanatorium and his epic journey home. As the girls helped him up, he pretended to fall this way and that, and Bryan noticed the physical effort that even this mild horseplay caused him. It was hard to ignore the unhealthy red on his cheeks and the strange glitter in his good eye. When the urge to cough overcame him, he hurriedly left the kitchen and went down the street where he couldn't be seen or heard. When Ellen muttered that he'd kill the whole lot of them, Catherine said that Bryan would decide what was best for the family. Later, when Bryan joined him on the loft steps, he spoke about the sanatorium and what lay ahead of him.

They had all been dying in the ward he was in, and he was dying too. He asked Bryan to look at him and to listen to him because he had to be able to talk to someone. His mother didn't want to know and his grandmother knew all too well. He was hardly fit to go about. Did Bryan remember when he won the red glass bowls in the races at the sports? He was the fastest runner in the parish then and now he could hardly walk up the steps. When Bryan suggested that maybe the place in Armagh might be better, Hughie said that he'd rather die up on the mountain like an aul dog than die there in one of them places. He dreamt all the time about Gerard and the dreams were putting him mad and he didn't want to be closed in because he couldn't breathe.

Bryan laid a comforting hand on his shoulder and said, "Do whatever it is that you need to do, but be careful. The Specials are always at the chapel now at Mass time, with Stephens in the car, picking out the lads that were at the camp. They arrested men and sent them to the prison ship, but them that had no part at Dungooley were let go again."

"Well, it's not Stephens that's picking them out. He went down the well shortly after he got there," Hughie said grimly. "But another informer was sent out with the Cumann na mBan when we were fighting the Staters. Well, it was a bad move, I knew it at the time, but there's nothing can be done about it now. I'll just stay here in the loft for a while. I'll not give you any trouble."

"You know it won't be any trouble for us," Bryan said in exasperation. "But someone could inform on you, and if the Specials come, you'll not be fit to run up the mountain."

"There's little the Specials can do to me now," Hughie said quietly. "I'm a dead man anyway, and if they come after me, I'll take some of them with me."

Bryan was facing a dilemma because Hughie was putting them all in danger. But he couldn't put his dying son out on the road, and he couldn't ask anyone else to keep him.

"Jem says that the Free Staters are out patrolling on the border every day." Hughie smiled grimly. "And our lads are shooting at them from the Northern side. I'd like to have one more crack at them for Gerard's sake."

Bryan wondered had Gerard's death affected his mind and felt saddened and helpless. When he went out to the loft the next day, Hughie was gone. A slate was propped by the bed with "Gone to inspect the new border" written on it. When Bryan told the women, there was crying and wringing of hands, but as usual they found solace in prayer.

A couple of weeks later Annie McGuinness called to say that Hughie was ready to come home and would Bryan bring the cart. At a farmhouse near the border at Dromintee, they found him outside slumped on a chair. They helped him into the cart and propped him against the side so that he could breathe. Annie sat next to him, supporting his body. Moving him was like handling the carcass of a rabbit; his skin moved directly over bone with neither fat nor muscle in between. His smile held the rictus of death, and with cheeks so gaunt and eyes so hollow, his face resembled a skull. If he had died at Dungooley, he would be remembered as a hero, but now, if he was remembered at all, it would be as the young Grant lad that died of TB. Bryan thought of the fathers throughout the country and throughout the centuries loading their dead or injured warrior sons onto carts to bring them home. He pondered the futility of the conflict and shrank from the thoughts of the endless sorrow that now awaited them.

Once home, Hughie made a token plea to be put in the loft, but Catherine was having none of it and he settled gratefully into his parents' bed. Catherine would sleep in a chair by the fire and Bryan in the loft. When Hughie got worse, one of them would stay in the room with him. Biddy Kane sailed in with a carpet bag full of "knitting and things to be going on with" and plonked herself at the head of the bed. She would attend to her young man and Catherine could see to the callers and get on with her work. Catherine was initially taken aback, but knew that for all her frivolity, Biddy, the heart of corn, was a capable woman who had nursed her father, Padna, for several years before he died. Padna had got a bad founder from being out in a storm and it proved to be the finish of him. "He came into the house, and the water was running down the sheughs of his arse," Biddy said. "Then he got the brownkittlins and the nemonia. Heart failure took him in the end. He lay down in the bed and hadn't the heart to get up."

There were no back doors on Biddy, and Hughie was unperturbed by her presence. She was always in good form, clattering on, neither expecting nor needing answers. She bathed Hughie with cool water when his temperature rose so high that she thought he would go afire, and held him down when the rigours brought on by fever convulsed his body and rattled the brass bed against the wall. When his mind rambled, she answered him as if he was talking all the sense in the world and held his hand when he called her Sarah and spoke loving words to her. She read aloud from newspapers about Arthur Griffith's funeral and wept over Michael Collins lying in state, while Hughie dozed and Mary crept in unnoticed and sat under the bed with Jocko. Word at the Crossroads was that Hughie wasn't long for this world. He was going like snow off a ditch, away to scrapings and nothing left of him but a harrel of bones. It would be a God's charity if he was took soon. The customers passed it on, and the country prayed for a peaceful death.

When Bryan called in to chat about his day, he could see that Hughie was becoming weaker and was careful not to stay too long. Then one night Hughie caught his hand and pulled him back.

"Stay a wee while longer, Da. Tell me about the big pike in Cashel Lake that near took the leg off Oiney and Mickle's dog," he said. Then: "What about that time when you were out cutting the corn and Molloy's collie chased a hare and nearly caught it."

Bryan settled back into the chair again and stretched out his legs as he related these tales, adding embellishments that he knew would amuse Hughie. He spoke about working in the mines and about deliberately breaking his knee against a wall in front of the recruitment officer so that they couldn't send him to fight in the war. And so it went on; every time he finished a story, Hughie wanted another one. In his mind he walked the mountain and fished and hunted in the rivers and lakes, and Bryan walked with him, both knowing it was the last time they would traverse this ground together. Hughie told him he'd gone over along the border, but hadn't been fit for much. He'd lain out in a canvas hide provided by his old comrades, watching and waiting to see who would come along. He had blankets, but it hadn't been cold, and the lads brought him tea and food. One morning two armed Staters came out on patrol past where he was hiding. These were the men who were going to rule Ireland, patrolling on bicycles in one of the most dangerous places in the country. He fired at them surely. He couldn't help himself. Another time they came out in a Ferret car and a Lancia; motors they'd got from the British. The other lads joined him and they had a good go at them, but there was no satisfaction in it. They had lost the war, and when they rose again, he wouldn't be there. It was over for him. He was done.

Catherine put her head round the door a few times, but Bryan signalled that it was all right. Hughie said that they'd been returning one winter's night to a camp on the Killeavy side of Slieve Gullion and chanced on a group of Specials drinking around a fire. They didn't want to provoke a battle and hid in the bushes debating what they would do. Then a Special carrying a bottle of whiskey weaved over to relieve himself in the bushes near them, and when he set the bottle down and began to spray the vegetation, Gerard Molloy carefully reached over and grabbed the whiskey. As they circled quickly and quietly around the fire they could hear the other Specials shouting to their comrade to bring the whiskey back. They couldn't risk lighting a fire that night, but the whiskey warmed them up and provided them with a good laugh. Another night, Specials were patrolling on the road nearby, and they had to wade through a river to avoid them. They were carrying their guns above their heads and were making good progress until somebody sneezed. They remained frozen in that position for almost an hour as the Specials searched about above them and then decided it must have been a sheep.

They fell silent and Bryan realised Hughie was asleep with his hand tucked under his chin like a child. He covered him with a light sheet and quietly left the room.

The following afternoon Bryan had a premonition that he should stay close to the house, and before he went to pull stalks in the potato field, he called in to talk to Hughie. As he was leaving, he was surprised to hear himself say, "Goodbye now, Hughie."

Hughie quizzically raised his eyebrows, but only said, "Right, Da."

He was in unusually lively form, trying to confuse Biddy and joking with Ellen when she put her head round the door.

"It's not a good sign, I seen it before," Ellen pronounced. "He's in too good a form. I seen the girls following a frog that hopped into the kitchen the other day. Yon's not normal at this time of the year or any time of the year."

"We're having great fun down there, Catherine," Biddy said as she came up to the fire. "But he says that his feet are awful cold."

Ellen looked meaningfully at Catherine as she refilled the stone jar and wrapped it in a towel. Then Biddy returned to the room and placed the jar at Hughie's feet. She usually dozed off at this time of day, and as she began to snore gently, he let out a shout.

"Biddy, Biddy! The bed's on fire! The bed's on fire!"

Biddy jumped up all flustered and staggered round the room for a while before she got her bearings. "Oh, Jesus Christ," she cried. "Oh, God look after us and take care of us and save us from sudden and unprovided death from the kick of a galloping duck! Oh, Hughie Grant, but you're an imp of the Divil. The bed isn't on fire at all."

Hughie rolled in the bed laughing, but the laughter turned to coughing and blood spurted out in a torrent that threw him back on the pillows, drained and exhausted. Before that he had suffered several minor haemorrhages. Biddy shouted for help and Catherine came running in. They cleaned him up, conversing cheerfully but shocked and scared by the amount of blood. Hughie held Brigid's Agnus Dei like a talisman in the palm of his left hand. His eyes were closed and he was scarcely breathing. Catherine asked him did he want the priest sent for, but he declined. He would just like to rest alone for half an hour and would shout if he needed anything. She reluctantly agreed and left the room, and as she closed the door, Mary crawled out from under the bed and laid her cheek against the back of his hand. Still clutching the Agnus Dei, Hughie placed his other hand on the top of her head.

"Och, Mary, me wee pet," he murmured.

When Catherine found them, she knew immediately that he was dead. She closed his eyes and gently kissed his forehead. Mary pulled away from her and ran out of the house and down the field to the Spelig, from where they could hear her keening. Biddy ran to fetch Bryan and then got Addy to come and help with the laying out. Ellen swung the big iron kettle over onto the fire, stopped the clocks and covered the mirrors, while Catherine straightened Hughie's body out. In an hour's time he would be washed and prepared for burial.

"Ah leanbh mo grásta, mo chroí, mo chroí," she wept. "To be washing me son and him a man grown and laying him out for death." She noticed that he was very, very thin. He had always been hungry when he was growing up, you couldn't fill him. Someone said he could ate the arse off a bullock. Once she'd left soda farls cooling on the windowsill and he had stolen two of them. She went after him, but he jumped the wall and ran up the road and all she could do was throw the broom after him in frustration. He juggled the hot farls from hand to hand and such a clab of laughing came over him that he had to sit down on the ditch.

"Bad scran to you," she'd shouted. "Sure the Divil wouldn't fill you!"

Then he'd come back, swinging her round as she tried to scold him and dancing her across the kitchen. He could charm the birds off the bushes and he did that in the Sweep at Forkhill. Mesmerised them with a light, then lifted them from the branches and brought them home for the girls. He had been full of crack and joking with Biddy less an hour ago, and now he was gone. She could reach out forever more, but she could never bring him back.

Bryan hurried into the room to console and weep along with her. Ellen made a big pot of tea in preparation for the people coming in and out. She told Bryan that Mary had been in the room when Hughie passed beyond. She was over there at the Spelig lamenting since, but they thought it better to leave her there and Bryan agreed. He would go for the priest and to see about the funeral arrangements. When the girls came home, Catherine led them into the bedroom, weeping along with them as they gazed at Hughie's unnaturally still face. Fr Carron arrived and administered Extreme Unction. He was sympathetic and affable.

As Catherine was about to enter the bedroom where Hughie was laid out, she heard neighbouring women discussing his death. "It was TB took him in the end," one woman whispered loudly.

Her words rose up and hung in the air for a moment then crashed to the floor. The other women gasped and covered their mouths with their hands, then pulled their skirts in around their feet to avoid being contaminated. As they shrank back from the bed, Catherine came further into the room.

"Hughie got a rupture above at Dungooley," she said quietly and clearly. "A clot of blood went into his heart and killed him. Him and Gerard Molloy fought to free Ireland. They gave their life's blood for their country and that's more than any of you or your sons did."

When she left the room, the other women looked at each other in sympathy and thought God help her, her brain is addled with grief. The lad died of TB of the lung and the whole country knew it.

The military funeral planned for Hughie at the chapel was abandoned because the countryside was swarming with Specials and anyone caught with a gun could expect harsh penalties: imprisonment or even death. However, the Cumann na mBan smuggled guns into Cashel, and when the flag-draped coffin was carried out to be put in the hearse, Annie read the Proclamation, then with great dignity and solemnity they fired a volley of shots over Hughie's coffin.

"Thank you, Annie," Catherine said. "He would have liked that."

"It was an honour," Annie told her. "We've lost a brave soldier and a good comrade. We never thought last year that we'd be burying the two lads so soon. We were all so young and full of bravado. We would free Ireland and no one would die. I feel a hundred years older now."

Hughie was buried in sight of Gerard Molloy's grave.

"He didn't do a bit of good once Gerard was gone," Catherine told Sadie Molloy.

"Well, they're together now, God rest them," Sadie said. "I often think of them, laughing and wrastling and kicking the pig's bladder round the yard and doing the Mumming. 'Here comes I, Johnny Funny, I'm the man collects the money.'"

"Aye, the Mumming," Catherine smiled. "'Here comes I, Diddly Dout, the tail of me shirt hanging out.' They were innocent wee children then."

Gerard and Hughie would put on old shirts and blacken their faces with soot, then go around the houses at Halloween and before Christmas performing the Mumming rhymes and getting a few farthings or a bit of cake for their efforts.

Mary behaved like an angel at the funeral, and in the following days she seemed to be having a conversation with someone and holding out her hand as if waiting for someone to catch up.

"She's talking to Hughie," Susan told Catherine.

Ellen said that Hughie could be waiting for Mary to go with him and they should mebbe get the priest to bless the house. Catherine thought it was just Mary's imagination, and when the priest agreed to do a blessing, she was satisfied. Then one night Mary lifted Bryan's hand from his knee and placed it on the top of her head.

"Och Mary, me wee pet," she said.

Ellen's head came up like a dog scenting a rabbit.

"Say nothing, Ellen," Catherine advised her. "If he's still here, he's here to look after her and not to harm her, and isn't she better like that than breaking her heart over him. I wish I could get aise from the missing of him. God's curse on you, Ireland!"

Chapter 16

In Dundalk at the beginning of November, a tender was blown up at Greenore Road and a Free State soldier killed. At Rockmarshall another tender was ambushed and soldiers were injured. At Carrickmacross soldiers were ambushed and their weapons taken. The Free State was formed and James Craig opted out of the treaty. Along the border it became clear that fourteen hundred farms had been split, with land on both sides. At Lislea in South Armagh, James Crawley, a brother of Thomas, who had been shot dead earlier in the year, was also shot near his right eye and in the thigh and had to have his leg amputated.

Robert Dunbar, coming by before Christmas, found the mountain people battered, bruised, bowed-down and almost broken. He was surprised to find Larry Molloy sitting at the side of the road because he'd heard that Larry took to the bed after Gerard died. When he joined him on the ditch, Larry said that he prayed the Man Above might take him, but Heaven wouldn't have him and Hell wasn't ready for him. He got stuck in a deep hole and couldn't find a way out. He was thinking of hobbling down to the boghole to drown himself, when the wee lad came down to the bed and said, "Are you going to die too?" Larry knew then that he was doing the family no good at all and the neighbours were doin' all the work.

"No, me fine bucko, I'm not for dying yet," he answered. "I'll be out of this bed in the morning, and I was. I'll not get over Gerard dying, but I'll see him again, please God."

He hauled himself upright and invited Robert up to the house for tay, but Robert was tired and looking forward to resting that evening in Bryan's. The older he got the harder the roads got.

"I'm not the man you need to tell about that," Larry said wryly.

They parted at his gate, and Robert cut across the fields to Grants' house, where he was soon settled into an armchair. When Bryan asked how things were on the road, he inhaled deeply before he answered. "The border has destroyed the Northern people, and the Civil War has destroyed the southern people," he said finally. "Four brave men that were leaders in the War of Independence and should be leaders now in the new government have been executed by the Free State army. A man for every province: Rory O'Connor, Joe McKelvey, Liam Mellows and Dick Barrett. It's murder pure and simple, no matter how they try to dress it up, straightforward revenge and completely without justification. Those men had never been tried or convicted of any crime. How will that unite the country? Generations will curse them for their actions, and it looks as if John Bull is still pulling the strings. Forgive me for rambling on, ladies. I know the terrible trouble and sorrow that you have suffered yourselves."

"Aye, we had our share of trouble," Bryan agreed. "And we heard about the men being shot in Dublin. It's a sad day for Ireland. The first crowd of leaders shot by the British and the second shot by their own people. A heavy-handed way to show their authority. They'll soon have no leaders left. And it won't help to unite the country. Aye, there's many a change since the last time you came by. Little did we think that our boys wouldn't be with us this year."

Robert had been going to mention that the last time he was there the boys had just seen the Headless Coachman, but Catherine's sad eyes were fixed on him and he thought it wiser to change the subject. In many houses the wounds were still very raw.

"How is Biddy Kane?" he asked. "Of course, I will be calling with her tomorrow."

"Her house is a shrine for Michael Collins," Bryan told him. "If she finds an article about him in the newspaper she sticks it up on the walls. But he was a great leader and got a great turnout when he came to Armagh."

"He was well respected by the people and his men," Robert said. "He was negotiating with the men they've just executed when they were in the Four Courts. He was going to send them to the North with enough men and arms to finish the Struggle down here. He didn't trust the British and thought that they'd deliberately held onto the North and would use it as a gateway to come back in again. Many people wanted him dead."

"Aye, most people think that the British paid someone to do it. Mebbe when it all settles down we'll hear the right way of it, or mebbe we'll never know," Bryan said.

"The Free State is being set up without him," Robert said. "They've put customs' huts on the southern side of the border."

"That's the finish of us," Bryan said sadly. "The door is closed and no more needs to be said. The Staters have agreed to the border and we're left now with nayther side wanting us."

"They'll rue the day they split the country and put a border through it," Ellen declared. "It'll cause nothing but ructions from this on. We lost our two good boys for nothing. Ireland isn't worth one drop of your blood or one minute of your life."

"What about you, Catherine?" Robert asked.

"I'm still here, Robert, but Hughie is gone and all I have is the two red glass bowls that he won for running. What good is two glass bowls?"

"It's the memories they hold, Catherine. There is power in familiar objects," Robert said gently.

"Aye, you're right," she sighed. "I was going to throw them away, but then I remembered him running up to the finishing line and him laughing at having won. I'll just keep them there on the dresser, then I can look at them anytime I want."

Mary came along and stood outside for a while, laughing and talking to herself, but she behaved normally when she came in, and Robert thought he must have imagined it.

Catherine dropped the sock she was knitting and gazed dreamily into the distance.

"She's waiting for Hughie to come home," Bryan told Robert as they smoked their pipes outside in the evening gloom. "She listens for him whistling in the night. I miss him sorely meself. It's hard to know what to do. Lads from round here are still in jail and on the prison ship. That's very hard on families."

Robert agreed, but he'd heard that some women had gone to the authorities and said the IRA had led their sons astray with guns and money. These boys were needed on the farm and they were let go. The big Protestant landowners and businessmen would see no benefit in keeping men locked up when labourers were needed. They'd let them out when they'd learnt their lesson, then tabs would be kept on them and their families. Bryan agreed that he could be right, and they went inside to lie down for the night.

The next day after breakfast, Robert called with Biddy Kane. She fussed around, boiling the kettle and setting out the best china. Robert agreed that it was a sorraful house below, and as he waited for the tea, he studied her gallery of Michael Collins articles and photographs. Biddy said it was a poor end for the man that bate the English, and he agreed. They would never know how great a man he might have been. When he asked if she'd had more troubles with the fairies, she replied that the fairies were just like the rest of the people: they'd have to keep their heads well down from this on. No one knew what was in front of them. When Robert asked her was Mary getting worse, she smiled and explained about Hughie. Sometimes them that's took before their time can't go till they finish whatever it was they were doing. She'd prayed for him and Gerard at the sermons for the sufferin' souls, but they'd go in their own time. It wasn't the dead you need be worried about.

"Good woman, Biddy," Robert said. "I'm glad to see that you haven't lost your spirit."

"It's hard to keep your spirits up in these times, but when you get tired rambling and need an aul hearth to put your boots on, there's always one here for you," Biddy offered.

"That's the best offer I've had in years, Biddy," said Robert, touched and surprised. "I will certainly give it every consideration over the winter. It'll keep my heart warm."

Between the spirits of the lads still being about and her offer of sharing the hearth, he felt somewhat bemused as he left Biddy's.

At the Crossroads, Shusie was reading aloud from the newspaper, while Jem hovered uncertainly near the dresser.

"Oh, I see you got a new stove," Robert said. "Very handsome it is, too."

"Handsome or not, that man there bent over to put his trousers on and burnt his arse on it," Shusie said dryly. "Show him your arse, Jem."

"Well, I will not show him none of me arse!" Jem said as he carefully held his trousers away from his body.

"That man has been all over the world and I'm sure he's seen many a bare arse."

"Well, I wouldn't say that," Robert protested modestly.

"It's not the bare arse needs the opinion, Robert, it's the burn," said Shusie. "There's a new salve called Germolene and it looks like it'll cure nearly anything. I'll send for it to Newry the day if he needs it. Show him your arse, Jem."

Jem reluctantly showed him a blistered weal about three inches long that travelled across both his skinny buttocks.

"Send for the salve," Robert advised. "In the meantime it would be better if you kept it cool."

"You may go down and sit in the well till we get the salve," Shusie said to Jem. "You'll make a poor divil if you can't thole a bit of a burn. You were above at Bryan Grant's, Robert? They're grieving sore for Hughie and the Molloys for Gerard, too."

"Yes, different houses than last year. They'll never get back what they had."

"But please God they'll get some sort of comfort that'll carry them on for the sake of the other children," Shusie said.

"Please God, they will," Robert said.

Mary walked the mountain talking to Hughie, and Ellen shook her head and prayed for them all. For a time, school became an unlikely refuge for the girls. They dawdled about in the evenings until Susan, much to the dismay of Katy and Brigid, began taking parties of children to the graveyard.

"Our Hughie is buried here," she told them, "and Gerard Molloy is over there. Our Mary has the blessed sickness. She gets fits and that's why she doesn't go to school."

Eventually their lateness was noticed, and when Brigid told Catherine what had been happening, they were instructed to come straight home.

Sarah Cullen never came back, but one Christmas Addy got a newspaper from Manchester. She brought it over to Bryan, who read it from cover to cover. He carefully scrutinised the births and deaths and found nothing, but it was enough for Addy. She knew that Sarah had sent it.

The Civil War dragged on till the end of May 1923, when Frank Aiken, now the head of the Republicans, gave the order to dump arms.

Glossary

Afflicted – intellectually challenged
Afoot – out and about
Afore – before
Aul – old
Avic – son
Bandy – bow-legged
Bannock – cake of bread
Bawkies – head lice
Blade – young woman
Blerting – crying
Briaring – repairing hedges
Brownkittlins – bronchitis
Butter firkin – butter cooler
Cap – stop
Ceilidh – visit
Childer – children
Clart – slut, slattern
Claining – afterbirth
'Clare – declare
Consaty – conceited
Cowl – cold
Cowped – turned over
Crack – conversation
Crater – creature
Curk – feather
Divarsion – diversion
Droot – thirst
Fadge – slice
Fettle – form
Flure – floor
Forninst – before
Foundered – cold
Gowl – shout
Gra – notion
Graip – four-pronged fork
Griosach – hot ash
Haggard – hay yard
Hinch – hip
Hirplin – limping
Hoiked – hoisted
Hoult – hold
Huddered – crouched
Hunkers – crouch down
'Ithin – inside
Jinnet – jennet
Jist – core
Juking – ducking down
Ket – cat
Kip shop – doss house
Liberty – bodice-vest
Lintie – linnet
Lonin – lane
Man jack – man
Mankeepers – newts
Midden – dunghill
Oxter-cogging – courting
Pickle – situation

Po – chamber pot
Prata – potato
Sheughs – streams
Skelly-eyed – squinting
Skelp – slap
Scrake – first light
Slipe – sleigh-type conveyance
Smerry – berry
Sniping – nasty comments
Sodger – soldier
Sonsy – comely
Souple tailed – supple
Sprockling – bumbling about
Stays – corsets
Stir – action
Stirabout – porridge
Tarra – terror, wonder
Thole – endure
Tip – ram
Touched – intellectually challenged
Traipsing – rambling
Trinket – drain
Twig – broom
Weans – children
Wind – breath
Yoe – ewe
Yon – that

Acknowledgements

My thanks to: Brigid Murphy, Sheila McCartan, Bernice Murphy, Kevin Murphy, Sodilva Murphy, Lily Stuttard, Mary Ann McCreesh, Brigid Morgan, Kate O'Hanlon, Kathleen Murphy, Briege Murphy, Padraig McCoy, Aíne Ni Shuilleabhain, PJ McCartan, Marie Browne, Brian Murphy, Mary Murphy, James McCartan, Martin McAllister, Bernard O'Hanlon, Brian Tomany, Anita Bagnall, Ciarán MacMurchaidh, John Murphy, Majella Murphy, Erwan Acheson, Cado McCartan, Anthony Flynn, Josephine Flynn, Susan McCartan, Johnny McCartan, Seamus Murphy, Peter O'Hanlon, Paddy Crilly, Oliver Grant, the staff of Newry and Dundalk Libraries, Robert Doran, Chenile Keogh, Andrew Brown, Rebecca Brown and everyone who contributed to this book.

Printed in Great Britain
by Amazon

43036086R00147